ISBN: 979-8-218-64936-4 Cover design by John Bhenzon Printed in the United States of America First Edition

Published by Garratt Oubre

Table of Contents

Interlude: **The Pinnacles**

Act 2: **Granger Heights**

ACT 1: INEQUALITY

CHAPTER 1: WHAT A LIFE

Nathan Mercer laid relaxed on his bed, headphones in, letting the music blast at full volume. The bass pounded in his ears, drowning out the sounds of chaos erupting on the other side of his closed bedroom door. His stepfather's drunken shouts mixed with his mother's sharp, weary retorts, their voices rising and falling like a toxic symphony. It wasn't anything new, just the same argument replayed in different words.

By all appearances, Nate was an average 15 year old —black hair, unremarkable clothes, hazel green eyes, nothing that stood out. He blended seamlessly into the crowd, unnoticed in a sea of faces. But while Nate looked like everyone else on the outside, inside, he always felt... different. Separate. He felt like an observer in a world where everyone else seemed to belong.

It wasn't just the pressure of fitting in or the typical teenage angst, it was something deeper, a gnawing sense of otherness he couldn't shake. No matter how much he tried to laugh along with his classmates or engage in the same small talk, there was a wall between him and the world, a barrier no one else seemed to notice.

Nate carried this feeling like a weight on his chest—heavy, invisible, suffocating. He had friends, sure, but never the connection he craved. Nate wore a practiced smile and carefully timed his jokes. He did just enough to be part of the group without ever really being part of it. And no one seemed to notice. Or maybe they did and just didn't care.

He tried to lose himself in the music, but it wasn't working. His phone provided a temporary distraction. He scrolled through his feed, swiping past the

polished lives of influencers and memes that didn't make him laugh.

One headline caught his eye: **"An Elite Strike Team Was Found Catatonic in an Abandoned Warehouse."** Nate was dubious, tapping the article. The text described government operatives slumped and muttering incoherently about inescapable nightmares. "The perpetrator is unknown, but authorities suspect mutant involvement. The perpetrator is thought to be in league with a band of rogue mutants," it read. Nate closed the tab quickly, his stomach turning. Mutants had it bad enough without someone making them look worse.

Another headline caught his attention: **"Bio-Mutant Attack Devastates Downtown New Marlow."**

Nate hesitated, his thumb hovering before tapping it. The screen lit up with shaky footage captured by someone on the ground. A towering, grotesque fusion of mutated parts stomped through the city, its claws tearing through concrete and steel as though they were paper. Windows shattered with each guttural roar it let out, and people fled in terror. The monster was terrifying, raw, and unstoppable. Then the Pinnacles arrived.

Apollo streaked through the sky, a comet of blue and red, his heat vision scorching a precise line across a bio-mutant's torso. The creature bellowed in pain, its massive arm swinging in a futile attempt to swat Apollo out of the air. Aero swooped in next, the black and gold of his suit catching the sunlight as he inhaled deeply. A gale-force wind erupted from his lungs, slamming the mutant into a nearby building. The camera shook violently as the onlookers cheered.

Then came Reptile, whose massive clawed hands tore into the bio-mutant with vicious precision. Blood spattered onto the pavement as Reptile launched the monster high into the air with an almost casual throw. Apollo was waiting for it. With a focused blast of solar energy, he reduced the bio-mutant to ashes. The crowd erupted into a mixture of applause and stunned silence as the footage ended.

Nate stared at his phone for a moment before scrolling to the comments. They were the same as always divisive, passionate, and, sometimes, hateful.

"Apollo is a goddamn hero! We're so lucky to have him."

"Great, now who's going to pay for the millions in property damage?"

"Pinnacles are as bad as bio-mutants. Freaks fighting freaks."

The last comment made Nate's stomach churn. He tossed the phone onto his bed and leaned back against the headboard, staring at the cracked ceiling. His heart felt heavy, the weight of his secret pressing down on him. Those people did not know what it was like. They didn't know what it meant to live in fear, not of bio-mutants, but of themselves.

The yelling outside his room grew louder, his stepfather's voice breaking through the muffled barrier of the music. Nate couldn't stand it anymore. He grabbed his hoodie, yanked it over his head, and slipped out the front door before anyone could notice. The chill of the morning air hit him like a slap, but he welcomed it. Anything was better than staying in that house.

He remembered the day his stepfather and mother discovered his mutant abilities. His stepfather's reaction was violent. He beat Nate, calling him a monster, a mutt, and a freak. The pain and fear of that day never left him. The echo of his stepfather's harsh words and the sting of his fists still haunted Nate.

Frost crunched under his sneakers as he wandered. The world outside felt detached, like a movie playing out around him while he trudged forward in slow motion.

Nate exhaled, watching his breath swirl in the cold, feeling the weight of the house slip off his shoulders, if only for a moment. The distant hum of traffic and the occasional bark of a dog were the only sounds accompanying him. He shoved his hands into his hoodie pockets, pulling it tighter against the wind. Last night's argument still reverberated in his ears, but the familiar chaos of school seemed like a temporary escape.

He passed a billboard half-torn by weather, the words still visible beneath the peeling paint: "Register Today. Protect Your State." A faded image of Apollo stood tall behind the text, arms crossed, glowing with righteous light. Nate stared at it, jaw clenched. To the world, Apollo was a symbol of hope. But to kids like him, he was a warning. A reminder that the only good mutant was one in uniform, owned, documented, and leashed. Anything .else? That was a threat.

When he got to school, the morning bell was already ringing. The hallways were alive with the chatter of students, the slamming of lockers, and the sound of clambering footsteps all around. Nate moved through it all like a ghost, unnoticed and unbothered. He liked it that way.

Nate adjusted his hoodie, tugging the sleeve down over his wrist as he walked. The fabric brushed against the yellowing bruise on his forearm, making him wince. He kept his head down, dodging past a group of students in the hallway, shoulders tense out of habit.

The hallways buzzed with fluorescent lights that flickered inconsistently, casting everyone in a washed-out glow. Lockers lined the walls like rusted tin coffins, their chipped paint and bent vents telling stories of a hundred slammed doors and locker fights. The smell of bleach never fully masked the sour odor of teenage sweat and cafeteria grease. Chairs scraped against scuffed linoleum floors, echoing off walls papered with fading propaganda posters that no one looked at anymore.

By the time he reached the gym, the noise of sneakers squeaking on polished floors and the echo of Coach Williams' whistle filled the air. Nate slipped into the corner, trying to blend into the background as the gym came alive with activity.

Gym class was the worst part of his day. Normally, he could blend into the background, but not today. Today, Coach Williams had decided it was time for heart rate testing.

Nate stood at the edge of the gymnasium, his stomach in knots as the coach explained the assignment. "You'll partner up. One of you will run laps while the other takes their pulse before and after. Easy enough, right?"

The other students paired quickly, laughing and joking as they prepared. Nate froze, panic clawing at his chest. His pulse wasn't normal. Even at rest, it was stronger, faster than any human should be. Letting someone touch his wrist was out of the question. Nate quickly checked his own pulse. It was beating hundreds of times a minute, and his nervousness only accelerated it.

No one else's heart beats like this. No one else would have to hide something like this. If they find out…

"Mercer, you're with Matt," Coach Williams called, snapping Nate out of his spiraling thoughts.

Matt jogged with a lopsided grin. "Alright, man, let's get this over with. Wrist out."

Nate felt the walls closing in. "Uh, Coach?" he called, raising a hand. "I think I pulled something during warm-ups. Should probably sit this one out."

The coach gave him a hard look, his frown deepening. "Fine. Sit on the bench. But you're making this up later."

Relief washed over Nate as he slumped onto the bench. He watched the other students from afar, his fingers tapping anxiously against his thigh. They were so carefree, so oblivious to the weight of their normalcy. Nate envied them.

Nate sat on the bench near the edge of the gym, pretending to rub out a pulled muscle in his leg. His breathing had already slowed, but his heart was still beating harder than it should've been.

A few feet away, Coach Williams was talking to the biology teacher, casually scanning through a clipboard.

"We get more data from these fitness assessments every year," Coach said. "Muscle density, recovery rates, heart rate tracking. Had a kid last semester with numbers like a damn college sprinter."

The science teacher raised an eyebrow. "Were they a muttborn?"

"Wasn't confirmed," Coach said with a shrug. "But yeah. Some of them hit pro-level stats by fourteen. Faster oxygen processing, denser muscles. You can't always tell just by looking, but the numbers can weed the bastards out."

"Still though," the teacher added, "if the recovery rates outside the baseline, protocol says flag it. Doesn't always mean anything. Just good to have on file."

Nate looked down at his leg, pretending to wince as he shifted it slightly.

When it came time for the sprint races, he deliberately held back. He jogged at a leisurely pace, crossing the finish line dead last. A few of his classmates shot him curious glances, but he ignored them, plastering on a fake smile. Better to be seen as lazy than as... different.

The hours dragged by after gym class, each tick of the clock pulling Nate further into his own thoughts. His classmates chatted and joked around him, their carefree laughter a sharp contrast to the storm brewing in his chest. When the final bell rang, he couldn't wait to get out of there.

Nate took the long way home, his steps leading him toward the woods behind his house. The skeletal trees swayed gently in the breeze, their bare branches clawing at the sky. Here, amidst the quiet of nature, he finally felt like he could breathe and be free. Dropping his bag at the base of a familiar oak, he rolled up his sleeves and clenched his fists, ready to let the tension out the only way he knew how. Without hesitation, he started punching the tree. Each strike sent vibrations up his arms, the rough bark scraping against his knuckles.

Thud. Crack. Boom.

His hits grew harder, faster, until the tree shuddered under the force of his blows. The pain was a distant sensation, drowned out by the adrenaline coursing through his veins. Sweat dripped down his face, stinging his eyes, but he didn't stop.

Then it happened. Pain exploded in his chest, sharp and sudden. He staggered back, clutching at his heart as his knees buckled. The world tilted, the surrounding trees blurring into a mess of brown and gray.

"Not now," he gasped, his breaths shallow and rapid.

He collapsed onto the forest floor, the cold earth pressing against his cheek. His pulse hammered in his ears, erratic and uncontrolled. He forced himself to focus, to breathe slowly despite the panic clawing at his mind. Gradually, the pain subsided, leaving him trembling and drenched in sweat.

Nate lay there for a long time, staring up at the sky through the gaps in the branches. The adrenaline had faded, leaving an empty pain in its place.

"Freak," he muttered to himself, the word bitter on his tongue.

Nate's walk home from the woods was slow and deliberate. His chest still ached faintly, a sharp reminder of how fragile his situation was. Every step felt heavier than the last, his thoughts circling like vultures over the same grim truths. The forest was his sanctuary, but even here, his body betrayed him. He hated the lack of control.

The crunch of leaves under Nate's feet was the only sound as he trudged back toward home. His knuckles throbbed, the bark of the tree having left minor scrapes and bruises across his skin. The faint glow of the porch light came into view as the sun dipped below the horizon, painting the sky in deep oranges and purples.

He stood outside for a moment, staring at the chipped paint on the front door, the crooked mailbox leaning precariously to one side. Everything about the house screamed neglect and decay, but it was home, if only in name.

Inside, the tension hit him like a physical force. His mother and stepfather were already at it, their voices echoing through the small space. Nate slipped off his shoes and moved toward the kitchen, hoping to grab something to eat before retreating to his room.

At the dinner table, a milk carton with a missing child's picture sat front and center. Nate stared at it, his appetite disappearing. The face on the carton was young, maybe nine or ten, with wide, innocent blue eyes, bright blonde hair, and a birthmark on his temple. Another kid is gone. Another family left to wonder if they were alive or dead or worse.

His stepfather's booming voice shattered the fragile quiet of the house, yanking Nate from his thoughts like a slap to the face.

"What the hell is this?" Gary bellowed, his gravelly voice echoing through the small living room. He stood there, waving a crumpled piece of paper in his thick fist. Nate couldn't see what it was, but it didn't matter. The anger in Gary's voice was enough to make his heart race.

Wendy stood frozen in the kitchen doorway, her hands clutching the edges of her apron. Her eyes darted to Nate, silently pleading for him to stay put, to avoid provoking Gary any further. But Nate could already feel his blood boiling.

"You can't leave me!" Gary shouted, his face turning a dangerous shade of red. The veins in his neck bulged as he stomped toward Wendy, shaking the paper in her face. "You think you're better off without me? Huh? You think you can just run? I'll make sure your shitty son is locked up once they find out about the freak."

Nate's stepfather, Gary, was the epitome of unpleasantness. A grinch of a man with a gruff beard and unkempt hair that seemed to match the sour expression permanently etched on his face. He reeked of cigarettes and alcohol, a stench that clung to everything he touched. Gary towered over Nate by nearly a foot, his sheer size making him an imposing figure, and his age—thirty years Nate's senior—only added to the oppressive air he carried.

Nate's mom, Wendy, was a stark image of fragility. Small and delicate, she moved with a cautious hesitance, as though the world around her was too heavy to bear. Her dark hair, the same shade as Nate's, framed a face that always seemed tired, her eyes carrying the weight of countless sleepless nights. Her posture, already scrunched and slouched, seemed to collapse further in Gary's presence, as though she were trying to make herself invisible.

Wendy rarely smiled, and when she did, it was fleeting and strained, a ghost of the woman she might have been before Gary's looming shadow darkened her world. Nate hated seeing her like this—hated the way she seemed to shrink whenever Gary barked or slammed a fist on the table. But more than anything, he hated that there was nothing he could do to protect her from him.

"Don't start with me, Gary," his mother snapped, her voice sharp. "You've got all the time to yell, but none to find a job."

Nate slumped into his chair, keeping his head down. All he wanted was to eat in peace and survive another night.

"You think I'm going to sit here and let you talk to me like that?" Gary roared, slamming his fist onto the table. The impact sent the milk carton toppling over, the liquid spilling out in a slow, pale stream. Nate's mother flinched, her bravado cracking for just a moment.

Wendy didn't flinch when Gary raised his hand. She didn't plead or protest. She simply stood there, like she had accepted this was just another part of life—just another storm she had to endure. And that realization hit Nate harder than any punch ever could.

"Leave her alone," Nate said, his voice low and even. He hadn't meant to speak, but the words escaped before he could stop them. His fists tightened under the table, nails digging into his palms.

Gary turned his attention to Nate, a cruel smile spreading across his face. "Oh, look who's finally grown a spine. What are you going to do, huh? You don't want to end up in prison, do you? Because I'll make damn sure they lock you up the moment they find out what the fuck you are and I'd love to see it."

Nate's heart pounded. He wanted to fight, but Gary's threat wasn't empty. If the authorities found out what he was, it'd be over. The government didn't tolerate unregistered mutants. The government labeled them threats and dangers to society, no matter how harmless they tried to be.

Gary laughed, mistaking Nate's silence for fear. "That's what I thought. You're just a little freak. Go back to your room and stay the fuck out of my sight."

Nate didn't move. His eyes locked onto Gary's, a simmering rage bubbling beneath his calm facade. "Don't talk to her like that again." his fists clenching.

Gary's expression darkened. "What did you just say to me?"

Before Nate could respond, Gary's fist came down, catching him across the face. Pain exploded in his jaw as he stumbled backward, the taste of blood filling his mouth. He hit the floor hard, the world spinning as Gary advanced on him. Gary beat Nate senseless punch after punch, insult after insult.

"FREAK,"

"YOU DISGUSTING MUTT,"

"LITTLE SHIT,"

Nate's mother stood back as she had done before, but hit after hit, it became too much for her to bear any longer. She moved without thinking once she heard her son call for her.

"Mom…" Nate groaned as he was being beaten.

Nate's mother tried to intervene, pulling his stepfather off, but it only enraged him further. As she went to pull him off of Nate, he turned back, striking her with the back of his hand. That was the breaking point for Nate. A primal fury surged through him. He slowly stood up, fists clenched, his heart pounding furiously.

"You want more, freak?" his stepfather growled, the taunt echoing in Nate's ears.

A surge of adrenaline coursed through Nate's veins, his heart pounding dangerously fast. He caught Gary's wrist mid-swing, his grip like iron. For a moment, Gary looked surprised, his bravado faltering. A searing heat pulsed under his skin, his veins swelling, stretching. His heartbeat roared in his ears, his vision tinged with red.

Nate's vision blurred with rage. His stepfather's words faded into the background, replaced by the deafening roar of his own heartbeat. A sharp, searing heat surged through his veins as his fist swung forward. Then—impact. Bone crunched beneath his knuckles, blood and spit sprayed, Gary's jaw twisted with a sickening snap as his body hurtled backward. The impact sent Gary crashing through the drywall, a loud crack echoing through the room.

The silence that followed was deafening. He slumped to the ground, eyes wide, his breath ragged and uneven. His jaw hung at an unnatural angle, and when he tried to speak, only a garbled wheeze came out, thick with blood. Blood poured down his head. Nate's mother stood frozen, her hands covering her mouth as she stared at the scene in shock.

Nate looked down at his bloodied hand, his knuckles split and raw. The sight filled him with a strange mix of satisfaction and dread. He had done it. He had fought back. But at what cost? He had been terrified of this moment for years, of what he might do if he finally snapped. Of what he was capable of.

"I…" His voice faltered. His mother was trembling, tears streaking her face. Was she scared for him—or of him? Nate couldn't tell.

"Maybe I am a freak," he whispered, the words biting into him with both dread and an odd sense of liberation.

"Nate…" she whispered, her voice barely audible.

CHAPTER 2: ROUGH EDGES

A year had passed since that night, reshaping Nate's life in unexpected ways. His stepfather was in a coma, the result of their violent confrontation. The police didn't charge Nate. His mother had broken a chair in the melee, tearfully telling them she had hit Gary herself. If the police had suspicions, they didn't have the sophisticated resources to recognize Nate's mutation.

Without Gary, life had changed in ways Nate had never expected. His mother had found a job, and though money was tight, her spirit seemed lighter—like she could breathe for the first time in years. The house was quiet now. Not peaceful, not really, but something close.

But Nate hadn't changed much. He still kept his head down, still lived in the background, still carried the same restless energy in his bones.

The evening hummed to life as students flowed out of the gym, talking about homework and gossip and plans for the weekend. Nate trailed the crowd, his hood up and pulled low over his face. He was good at remaining invisible, but tonight something nipped at him, a vague feeling he couldn't let go of.

Life at school moved along with deceptive normalcy, though. Nate cruised through his classes, careful to avoid any sort of attention. The only one who ever got him to drop his armored shield was this new kid, Xavier. The first day he transferred, Nate expected him to fade into the background like anyone else—but he didn't. Xavier talked. A lot. Not in a way that was annoying, but in a way that made people listen. Before Nate even realized it, they were friends.

He was shorter, wiry, with these bright brown eyes that always seemed to read people too well, and a mop of dark brown hair he was constantly brushing out of his face.

They bonded on the outsider mentality. Soon, they began telling each other secrets, and spilled over lunchtime and late-night conversations in hushed tones. Nate was the first to confide his mutant powers in him, having watched Xavier closely for his reaction. Much to his relief, Xavier merely grinned and showed his own ability-to stretch his body like rubber.

"That's it?" Nate had joked, smirking. "I can stop a car, and you're basically a human balloon."

"Hey, don't knock it!" Xavier shot back. "It's practical. Besides, at least I don't have to deal with heart attacks just for running fast."

This kind of teasing became the rhythm in their friendship-a way of keeping things light when the world was so oppressively heavy.

He met Nate in the parking lot after school. The streetlights were yellow, lengthening the shadows. "You good, dude?" Xavier asked, his tone light but his eyes sharp.

"Yeah, I'm fine," Nate muttered, pulling his hoodie tighter. "Just didn't sleep much."

Xavier gave him a look, but shrugged. "Alright, but if you pass out, I'm not carrying you." Walking together, no sound but a gentle murmur, their stride perfectly attuned to the surroundings. Nate loved that about Xavier: no inquisitiveness in this area whatsoever. Not yet, at least.

Xavier leaned in conspiratorially. "Hey, you hear about that rogue mutant they're hunting?" he whispered.

"What mutant?" Nate asked, his interest piqued.

"Some guy out there taking down government teams like it's nothing. They think he is leading a group of mutants." Xavier said. "I read about it online. He doesn't just fight them—he messes them up. Leaves them screaming about their worst fears. Creepy, right?"

Nate shivered, but shrugged it off. "Probably just propaganda. You know how they love to make us look like monsters."

Xavier stretched his arms overhead, his movements unnaturally fluid. "You ever wonder what we could really do if we didn't have to hide?" he mused, his tone light, but something unreadable flickered behind his eyes. "Like, full potential, no holding back?"

Nate scoffed. "What, you gonna stretch yourself into a parachute or something?"

Xavier smirked, but the humor didn't quite reach his eyes. "Yeah, something like that."

On the ride home, they pulled into a convenience store. Inside, fluorescent lights buzzed loudly. Nate reached for a soda, while Xavier deliberated over which flavor of gum to get. At the counter, the cashier gave Nate a long look. Not casual—suspicious. Nate felt it immediately, a slow prickle down his spine. He kept his gaze down, his fingers tightening around the soda can.

"That it?" the cashier asked, voice flat.

"Yeah," Nate muttered.

The guy rang him up slow, too slow. Like he was watching Nate's hands. Like he'd seen something.

Nate forced himself to stay still, to breathe normal. He handed over the cash, snatched his change, and mumbled a quiet "thanks" before heading out.

As he turned away, he felt it—the weight of the cashier's stare. Heavy, assessing. Like he was waiting for something.

Don't react. Don't give him a reason.

He pushed through the door, the bell jangling behind him.

Outside, Xavier popped a piece of gum in his mouth and offered one to Nate. "You hear about that mutant sighting downtown?" he asked, his voice going a notch lower.

Nate tensed up and shrugged. "Yeah. What about it?"

"They're saying it was one of those bio-mutants," Xavier said, chewing thoughtfully. "Smashed up a few cars before the Pinnacles showed up."

Nate's hold on his soda can tightened. "So?"

Xavier faltered. "I don't know… I just think about it sometimes. What if we didn't have to hide? What if we could do something with this?"

Nate scoffed, taking a sip of his soda. "Like what, the Pinnacles?"

Xavier smirked. "Maybe. Or at least… be more than nobodies."

Nate shook his head. "They don't make heroes out of freaks like us."

Later that night, Nate sat alone in his room. The soft clinking of dishes in the kitchen told him his mom was still up, but the sound felt far away. He flexed his fingers, feeling the faint hum of his blood engine under his skin. No matter how hard he tried to ignore it, the same thought seemed to seep its way back in: It didn't matter how hard he tried to be good. To the world, he'd always be something to fear.

A knock at the door startled him. "Nate? You okay?" his mom called softly.

"Yeah, I'm fine," he said, trying to steady his voice. "Just tired."

"Alright," she said, lingering momentarily before walking away.

When finally the house went silent, Nate slipped out of his bedroom window, landing in silence on the grass below. The woods behind his house were always his sanctuary, a place he never had to fake it.

Veiled by the trees, Nate let loose, his fists pounding against a sturdy oak. With each punch, the vibration ran up his arms, the bark splintering under the force. Sharp sting shooting through his knuckles was grounding, reminding him he was alive, even if it hurt.

It let out a deep groan—loud in the stillness—as it finally gave way. The massive trunk crashed to the ground, the impact shaking the earth beneath his feet. The sound echoed through the trees, raw and final.

Nate stepped aside, watching the fallen giant with heavy breaths. His veins still pulsed with heat, but slowly, he let his heart settle.

He stared out across the small clearing he'd created over the years—a graveyard of felled trees and scarred trunks. Messy. Imperfect. But his.

Adrenaline was burning and fatigue set in. Nate rubbed his sore knuckles and headed back to the house. Whatever weight rested on his chest for tonight was just a fraction lighter. Tomorrow would be another day of hiding, of pretending, of keeping the world at arm's length. But in this quieted wood, Nate - for tonight - let the full weight of everything he carried fall.

For a while, that was enough. But he knew the feeling would fade. It always did.

CHAPTER 3: INDIVIDUALS

Nate wrestled with the silence, the weight of being different pressing down on him. He forced a smile at his reflection, but the glass only mirrored his unease. The reflection staring back at him was a life he fought to keep hidden: a mutant living in a world that feared and despised his kind.

This meant venting his ire on the poor punching bag in the local boxing dojo. The gym reeked of sweat, iron, and worn leather. Every bench, bag, and mat had the sheen of constant use, scuffed and stained from hours of punishment. The air was warm and humid, heavy with the sounds of grunts, slamming fists, and the rhythmic *thud* of gloves meeting pads. Posters of old fighters curled at the corners on the walls, their faces faded and eyes fierce.

Nate's fists pounded relentlessly into the worn leather, each strike echoing through the small gym. The raw power behind them made Mike-an ex-fighter of many years and owner of this little gym-sit up and take notice of Nate unloading his emotions into the bag. His face showed a mixture of admiration and curiosity.

"You've got talent, kid," Mike said in that gruff-but-nice voice of his. "Why don't you step into the ring? Sparring might do you some good." "I don't know, Mike, I don't enjoy getting hit..." Nate returned with a quip in his voice.

Nate screwed up his face, hands slowing as deliberation clouded his brain. He could not afford to risk it. The artificial, contained world of the gym was too great an inadequate cage for what he was capable of. But Mike's persistence wore him down, and Nate laced up gloves, stepping into the ring with another fighter.

Nate took hit after hit, dodging just enough to stay standing but never striking back—at least, not like he could. The guy threw another punch—Nate saw it coming before it even started. His body reacted on instinct, his muscles tensing to counter. Just one hit. That's all it would take.

He stopped himself at the last second, letting the blow land. He staggered back, pretending it hurt more than it did. The crowd cheered for the other guy.

Mike's words dug into him. "You're holding back, kid."

Nate knew that. He felt it in his bones. Every punch he threw in the ring was a shadow of what he was capable of. He could hear his opponent's breathing, track every twitch in their muscles. He could end this fight in a single hit.

His hands clenched involuntarily, his veins pulsing beneath the skin. He forced himself to let go, shaking it off. This wasn't a real fight. This was pretending. The fight ended with him on the canvas, his opponent raising his gloves in victory. Back in the locker room afterwards, mopping the sweat off his brow, Mike confronted Nate.

"You're holding back," Mike said frankly. His gaze nearly tore into Nate. "I've seen you on that bag. You're fast, strong, and you hold back like a scared kid," Mike said, arms crossed. "What gives?"

Nate shifted uncomfortably, avoiding his gaze. "I don't know… I just—choke, I guess. When it matters."

Mike's scowl twisted a little more. He laid a heavy hand on Nate's shoulder, firm but not unkind. "Whatever you're hiding, kid, you don't have to do it alone. If you ever want to talk, I'm here. And if you want to train after hours, just say the word."

Nate nodded and said a soft "thanks" on his way out of the gym as Mike's offer of personal lessons echoed in his mind all the way home, the weight of his secret weighing heavier upon him.

The next day, Nate's history teacher's monotone voice droned on in the background as Nate stared out the window, his mind far from the classroom.

"In State 3 vs. Vollen," the teacher recited, "the Supreme Council ruled that mutants accused of crimes could be detained indefinitely if deemed a national threat, even without formal charges. This landmark case paved the way for the Expansion of Mutant Oversight in 1993, ensuring public safety and reducing unnecessary trials."

Nate caught snippets of the lecture—but it all blurred together while he was lost in his thoughts.

When the bell finally rang, Nate gathered his things quickly, eager to escape the stuffy room. He hadn't made it three steps into the hallway before Xavier appeared at his side, a sly grin on his face.

"You're never gonna believe this," Xavier said, elbowing Nate. "Landry, she's been checking you out all week. You should go talk to her."

Nate followed Xavier's gaze to a girl leaning against the lockers. She smiled at him shyly as their eyes met, and to Nate's surprise, Xavier's teasing wasn't that off.

The girl was Landry Letters. She was about his age, had perfectly curly hair, freckles everywhere, brown eyes, and a prep in her step. Nate never really considered the fact that he would have any chance with her, but Nate considered that a quick conversation couldn't hurt.

"Go talk to her," Xavier urged, grinning. "What's the worst that could happen?"

Nate took a deep breath, approached her with jangling nerves, and tried to sound casual. "Hey Landry, what's up?" he asked, under his breath.

"Just waiting for my chem class. What about you? You seem more lively than usual. It's pretty cute," Landry teased with a glint in her voice.

"Oh, uh, thanks," Nate said, scratching the back of his neck. He wasn't used to compliments. "Yeah, just, you know... stuff. You look great too."

"Well, since we are both cute, don't you think we should go on a date, then?" Landry asked Nate. Before Nate could speak an actual word besides "uh," Landry asked, "We should go to the movies this weekend then?"

Nate replied excitedly, "Yeah yeah sounds great."

To his astonishment, the conversation was a success, and before he knew it, they had set a date. Pulling away, he caught Xavier's triumphant fist bump.

"See, told you she'd say yes," Xavier exclaimed

"That's not how it went down... but sure, let's go with that." Nate corrected.

Later that week, in a history lesson about mutant incidents, Nate sat at the back of the class, his mind elsewhere. The teacher was droning on with a long story of mutant registration laws and the dangers of unregistered mutants, oozing government propaganda with every word. Snickers and muttered insults about "freaks" fluttered through the class, stoking the anger Nate kept buried deep inside.

Nate clenched his fists under the desk, forcing himself to stay calm. He couldn't afford to react, no matter how much the words stung. Beside him, Xavier shot him a glance, his expression a mix of understanding and quiet rage. They both knew the truth: in this world, others would always see people like them as threats.

The day culminated in their long-awaited date: she drove them to the movies, and as they passed a mural celebrating mutant heroes, she murmured, "They're not all bad." Nate wondered if he would ever be considered a hero. They watched the movie and had a good time, shared popcorn, and laughed at the jokes in the film-a small moment of normality for Nate.

That was one of the few moments Nate felt happy. They went to the movies, laughed, and shared popcorn like any other teenagers. For some time, he forgot about his powers, his stepfather, and the ever-lingering danger of being discovered.

A peaceful evening unfolded as they strolled, the movie's gentle rhythm lingering in their minds. The warmth of her smile made Nate feel like he could be normal, at least for a little while.

A gentle evening breeze accompanied Nate and Landry as they left the cinema, their laughter a playful counterpoint to the quiet streets. For the first time in what felt like forever, Nate allowed himself to relax, to enjoy the simple pleasure of her company. For once, Nate wasn't overthinking everything.

Landry had just finished telling some dumb story about her older brother sneaking out and getting caught when she burst into laughter, and something about the sound—completely unguarded, genuine—made Nate smile.

"You should've seen his face," she said, wiping at her eyes. "It was like… I don't know, pure terror. Like he'd rather have faced an entire squad of mutant agents than my mom."

Nate shook his head. "I mean, your mom seems pretty intimidating."

The street they walked was narrow, boxed in by decaying brick walls whose faded graffiti told forgotten stories. Trash littered the cracked pavement—crushed cans, a torn backpack, and broken glass that glittered like stars beneath the dim orange glow of the flickering street lamp. The air stank of rot and something metallic.

As they turned a corner, Nate's senses peaked. The distant sound of heavy footsteps reached his ears, followed by a guttural growl that made the hairs on the back of his neck stand on end. He instinctively stepped in front of Landry, his body tensing as a figure emerged from the shadow.

Shadows came out of an alley. The gun flickered in the dim streetlight. "Wallets. Now," the mugger growled low.

Nate stepped forward, shielding the girl. "Just take it and go," he said calmly, his heart pounding.

The mugger's eyes narrowed. "No funny business, kid. I'm not afraid to use this."

Something snapped inside Nate as the gun pointed at the girl. In less time than it took for an eye to blink, he had disarmed the mugger; the weapon clattering to the ground. A punch landed before the man could even think, with Nate's blow sending him sprawling.

The others produced a crowbar and a knife, which Nate dodged with ease and some flair. That baffled them. Then he dispatched all of them into unconsciousness in rapid succession. His training was a blur with his natural strengths in skillful display.

Landry was initially in awe because Nate seemed not to know how to fight.

A gut punch knocked one of the bigger men unconscious, and the others fell flat onto the pavement. As Nate was catching his breath, Nate noticed one robber was convulsing in pain on the ground. Nate worried for a second that he had hit the man too hard, but it was much worse. The guy's body convulsed, his arms jerking at unnatural angles as veins bulged beneath his skin. His fingers stretched, splitting at the tips as claws pushed through.

His eyes rolled back, then snapped forward again—but they weren't human anymore.

Then came the sound—bones breaking, reshaping—a wet, sickening crunch that made Nate's stomach twist.

His skin started to stretch and tear, his bones jutting out, his muscles growing. He was turning into that creature of nightmares from the news, a partially mutated human, something nobody had ever seen. Grotesque, with bulging muscles, elongated limbs, and patches of rough scaly skin, its eyes were glowing with feral intensity, a low growl rumbling from its throat.

Nate stood baffled at the scene. "He's turning into a bio-mutant. How?" Nate's mind raced as the creature grew in size. Nobody had ever heard or seen such a sight. It was horrifying to watch.

Nate blocked a downward strike from the monster and, as passersby ran away from it and recorded it from a distance, he fought back. The monster wasn't as big as the one on the news and still seemed to keep lots more of the human-like features compared to most bio-mutants. When Nate saw it, his heart started racing fast. His fight or flight kicked in overdrive to protect Landry.

Nate barely dodged the next swipe. He was fast—but was he fast enough? This thing was bigger than him, stronger. His pulse pounded in his ears, and for a second, doubt clawed at his mind.

Then it lunged.

Nate's body moved before his brain could stop it. His fist collided with its gut— Boom.

The impact sent a shockwave up his arm, the force rippling through the creature's body. Its ribs cracked like dry wood, its body lifting off the ground before slamming into the pavement, skidding several feet before stopping.

Nate's veins started popping, and they covered his body, especially his arms. As his heart was racing, his skin turned red; Nate felt himself getting stronger and faster. Nate weaved a massive punch thrown at him from the creature and stepped strongly into a right-handed punch directly into the monster's gut. Many years of training had calloused Nate's fists and toughened his blows, even at his age. The monster stumbled back but caught itself, recovering fast. It lashed out wildly—Nate dodged, weaving through its attacks with practiced ease. It was powerful, but too slow. He was faster. Stronger. And for the first time, he knew it.

Nate cocked a hard punch into the creature's jaw. Each comboed one's momentum off the last. Blood filled his hands as they kept clashing. Down to the ground, the monster went when he tried tackling Nate. As it struggled to get back up, Nate was able to land an uppercut and flung the creature into a guardrail, where it impaled and bled out, its grotesque form twitching in its death throes. Nate had taken a life to save dozens. He stood out of breath, speechless at what he had just done.

Nate turned back "Landry—"

She flinched before he could even say the words. A step back, her hands clutching her bag like she needed something to hold on to. The warmth in her eyes was gone—just wide, darting fear now, like she was trying to decide if he'd come after her next.

Landry staggered back, her mouth opening and closing like she wanted to speak. Her eyes flicked from the mangled bio-mutant to Nate, to the blood dripping from his fists.

"Nate…" she started, voice barely above a whisper. Then her breath hitched, and she stepped back again.

"You—" She swallowed, eyes wide. "You're a freak."

Nate's face fell as the weight of his reality came crashing down again. Sweet only a moment before, his victory gave way to that all-too-familiar sense of isolation and despair: he had saved her, but at the cost of revealing the very thing he'd gone so hard to hide. He knew this world wasn't ready for him or any like him.

Nate stood frozen, the word freak hanging in the air like a brand seared into his skin. He had saved her, but all she saw was a monster.

CHAPTER 4: JUSTICE

Later that night, in the dead darkness of the boxing gym, Nate stood utterly alone, pounding the heavy bag. With every punch, a torrent of feelings raged within him-frustration, anger, and that gnawing sense of isolation. "You're a freak." Those words cut through his brain far more damaging than any real physical wound could ever do.

Nate replayed Landry's words in his mind. Freak. He'd heard it before—from his stepfather, from the whispers of classmates—but hearing it from her hit differently. He clenched his fists, staring at his reflection in the cracked mirror at the gym. His glowing veins and red-tinged skin stared back. "Maybe she's right," he muttered, his voice hollow.

Tears blurred his vision at the remembered reactions of the girl and the life he took: the fear, the rejection stark against gratitude he had hoped to evoke. His punches grew harder and harder, and that bag started swinging maniacally on every punch. With a final, rattling punch, the bag finally ripped its chain free, slamming into the wall with a loud thud. Nate froze, stood panting, chest heaving as he stared at what he'd just done.

"Damn, kid. You've got a hell of a punch," Mike said, leaning against the doorway with a raised brow.

Nate spun around, his breath hitching. Mike's expression was half-surprised, half-amused.

"Sorry," Nate mumbled, his mind racing to find an excuse. "The chain must've been rusty."

Mike stepped in closer, his head shaking. "Don't bullshit me. I've seen the way you hold back in the ring. I had my suspicions, but tonight? As clear as day. You're a mutant, aren't you?"

Nate tensed up, his body going rigid. "I…I don't know what you're talking about," he stammered, looking anywhere but into Mike's face.

Mike sighed, sitting on a nearby bench. "Relax, kid. I'm not gonna tell anyone. Hell, half the kids in this town probably don't even know what mutants really are. But you? You've got power—and I'm guessing a lot of pain to go with it."

Nate looked a little apprehensive until he sat down next to him. He pulled out his phone and flashed the news report of events from tonight. The headline read **"Bio-Mutant Attack Leaves Town Reeling; Unidentified Mutant Involved."**

"I probably won't be around for much longer," Nate said in a near whisper.

Mike glared a moment longer at the screen and then set the phone aside. "Kid, listen to me: If anybody comes after you, they'll have to go through me first, got it? And trust me, I still got a mean left hook."

A faint smile pulled at Nate's lips. "Thanks, Mike."

Mike clapped him on the back and rose. "Now, how about we use that strength of yours for a better purpose? Time to train."

For the first time that night, Nate smiled-a real, fleeting moment of relief.

Next morning, the school was full of rumors and speculation about some sort of bio-mutant attack. This sort of thing didn't happen in their small town, so it was something to be afraid of. Parents took kids out of school, while others who remained talked about the incident in nervous whispers down the halls. Nate moved like a ghost amongst the tide, his hoodie up, and pulled low over his face to avoid too much attention.

Everywhere he went, he heard snatches of conversations:

"Did you see the video? That mutant was a monster."

"Bet the guy who took it down is just as dangerous."

"They're all freaks. Bio-mutants, regular mutants-what's the difference? They're all mutts if you ask me."

Each word was a cut, each a reminder of the line between people like him and everyone else. He balled his fists, head down, as he pushed through the throng of students.

Nate turned the corner and saw her at her locker. Landry. She glanced up, eyes meeting his for half a second before darting away. He saw it—the hesitation. Like she wanted to say something but thought better of it. His stomach twisted. But he didn't stop. He just kept walking. Anger and sadness clamped around his chest because she might have kept his secret, yet the rejection lay still between them-an invisible barrier.

Nate leaned against the lockers, Xavier's voice a faint hum in the background. The murmurs of classmates discussing mutants rang louder in his ears. Freak. Dangerous. Mutt.

Nate's jaw tightened. If the world wanted to see him as a threat, so be it. He wouldn't cower.

"Xav, meet me in the woods after school tomorrow," he said suddenly.

Xavier raised an eyebrow. "What for?"

"To train." Nate's eyes burned with determination. "I need to be ready."

He sat that evening amidst ghostly silence during tall trees in the forest. For him, this was his sanctuary-the one place he allowed himself to drop his tight guard. In a clearing before a thick oak, Nate tightened his fists, prepared to train.

The first punch hit with a loud crack, the bark splintering beneath his knuckles. He started raining strikes, each harder than the last. The tree groaned under the onslaught until, with a final, earth-shaking blow, it snapped in half and toppled to the ground with a deafening crash.

Nate exhaled, sweat dripping down his brow as he stared at the fractured stump in front of him. His pulse still pounded, veins hot with adrenaline. But it wasn't enough. No matter how hard he hit, the weight in his chest wouldn't lift.

"I held back." The thought gnawed at him. He had been fast, strong—stronger than anything human. But against that thing, that bio-mutant… it had still been a fight. He should have crushed it.

What if there had been more of them? What if he hadn't been fast enough?

What if Landry had died? And would she still have called him a freak if he had let her die instead?

Nate exhaled sharply, shaking out his fists. His knuckles were raw, split in places from the force of his own blows. Still not enough. His hard breathing spoke to the small clearing he had made within weeks of training. Dozens of fallen trees lay strewn around, but in their place, small saplings were sprouting-a quiet reminder that within destruction always remained a space for renewal.

Now at the scene of the bio-mutant battle, scurrying around like ants searching piece by piece within the debris, the government agents were. A sleek black car brought in a high-ranked official. With the cold and unbending features-a mask of granite-his gaze stared back into the bio-mutant because its partially human constituent brought into his gaze the hard bite.

"Is it?.?" One of them fumbled.

The official cut him off. "No one can know. Spin the story. Focus on the mutant's destruction, not its origins. We can't afford mass panic."

The agent hesitated. "Sir, with all due respect… if people knew someone just transformed out of nowhere—"

"They'd start asking the wrong questions," the official snapped. His tone was bitter, final. "Questions we don't have answers for. If this wasn't an underground bio-mutant… if it was made right here… then we have a problem."

He turned back to the corpse, eyes narrowing. "Find out where this man came from. If there's another like him… make sure no one ever finds out."

The agent nodded, issuing quick orders to his team. The official tarried a moment, staring at the grotesque remains of the creature, before turning and walking away.

At Nate's house, he and Xavier lounged on the couch, controllers in hand. Xavier cursed loudly as Nate landed a combo, earning a smug grin. "You cheated," Xavier muttered, to which Nate only laughed, the tension from earlier easing in their familiar banter.

"So the dude just started transforming into one of those things?" Xavier pondered to Nate

"Well, yeah, just like I said earlier, it was disgusting. I always just thought they came from underground like everyone else," Nate said with a chill in his voice. "I just don't understand what made him mutate like that."

"I don't know, man.." Xavier said, as they drifted into a cold silence, their thoughts racing.

"How come I've never been to your place?" Nate asked, nudging Xavier with a grin.

Xavier froze for a second, then shrugged. "It's not worth the trip. Trust me. It's... Complicated."

Nate frowned but didn't push it. They went back to their game, the sounds of button mashing filling the room.

As the match ended, Nate leaned forward to grab a soda. Xavier's gaze lingered on the back of Nate's neck, his jaw shifting slightly, like he was weighing something in his mind. He exhaled quietly, a breath through his nose. Then, as soon as Nate turned, his expression smoothed over like nothing had happened.

"What?" Nate asked, catching the look.

Xavier blinked, shaking his head fast. "Nothing. Just zoning out."

In a sterile government facility, the Strike Force agent assigned to the bio-mutant case Captain Ironclad sat at a computer reviewing security footage. The video was grainy; the mutant's features obscured, but his sharp eyes caught every detail.

One agent leaned toward another, his voice low. "Do you think this mutant is connected to the nightmare guy?"

The other agent shook his head. "Doubt it. But the higher-ups are frightened. They think he's building some kind of mutant army. Said he's more dangerous than the bio-mutants."

"The girl," Iron muttered, interrupting them, pausing the footage on her terrified face. "She knows something."

His hand clenched into a fist. It slowly turned to metal glinting under the harsh fluorescent lights. "We'll find her—and whoever else was involved."

CHAPTER 5: RIPPLES

The world was quieter in the days following the fight between the two mutants, but in Nate's head, the silence was screaming. The school seemed to have a hundred theories on what had happened downtown. Students spoke in hushed tones of morbid fascination and fear. Nothing usually happened in the small town of Whisper Pointe State 6.

"I heard it wasn't even a Pinnacle who took him down," one boy said to his friend, low but excitedly. "Just some freak."

"Probably some other bio-mutant," his friend replied, belittling. "They should just lock them all up."

Nate gritted his teeth, his hands clenched into fists as he passed them. He knew better than to react, but their words seemed to linger in his mouth like an unpleasant taste. The fight replayed in his mind constantly: the chaos, the terror in people's eyes, and the moment he'd revealed his powers, even if only to save someone.

That afternoon, Nate and Xavier had abandoned their post-school ritual of snacks and nonsense-talking in favor of heading into the woods, where Xavier had promised to teach Nate some tricks about keeping a low profile.

"Man, you can't just rush in like you're invincible," Xavier said, stepping over a fallen branch. "I get it—you wanna help—but we don't have the luxury of making mistakes."

Nate shot him a look. "And what would you have done? Let them die?"

"No," Xavier admitted, "but I wouldn't have blown my cover, either. Look, you're strong, stronger than me, but strength doesn't mean shit if the government catches wind of you."

Nate sighed, running a hand through his hair. "I didn't choose this, Xavier. I'm just trying to survive."

Xavier sighed, his gaze dropping to the ground. "I know, man. That's why I'm here."

The next few hours had them sparring, Xavier showing him how to make Nate's attacks come across less-and more-controlled. He taught Nate to use everything to his advantage: trees or uneven grounds became shields and deterrents to diversion. For all his kooks, Xavier was sharp. Time had dulled none of that part, living in survival mode.

"See that? You're throwing too clean. You gotta look like you're struggling," Xavier said, jabbing a fist into Nate's shoulder. "Humans don't move like you. You gotta sell it—stumble, hesitate, miss on purpose."

Nate tried throwing a punch that looked less clean but to little avail

"That was terrible," Xavier said, sighing. "You still moved too clean—your stumble looked rehearsed."

Nate scowled. "How the hell am I supposed to make it look real?"

"Panic," Xavier said simply. "Think of something that actually scares you. When you fake a mistake, don't just act—feel it."

Nate tried again, deliberately stumbling as he swung. He overcompensated, making it too obvious. Xavier sighed.

"Better," he admitted. "Still needs work, but if you squint, you almost look human."

Nate and Xavier continued training until the sun began to set.

"Not bad, Nate," he said, patting him on the back. "Not bad at all."

By the time Nate got home, the sun was setting, casting a warm orange glow over the neighborhood. He slipped inside quietly, his mother greeting him with a tired smile from the kitchen.

"Oh, did you have a good day, sweetheart?" she asked in a soft tone.

"Yeah," Nate lied, grabbing a bottle of water from the fridge. "Just hung out with Xavier."

Her smile faltered slightly at the mention of his friend, but she didn't press further. "I'm glad you've got someone to talk to," she said, her voice light—but her eyes flicked to his bruised hands, lingering for just a second too long. Nate looked away, pretending not to notice.

Nate nodded, retreating to his room before she could catch the tension in his face. He sat on the edge of his bed, staring at the faint scars across his knuckles from training. His Heart Engine hummed faintly, reminding him of the power he carried with him-and the burden that came with it.

Lying back, his phone buzzed with an incoming news alert. The headline made his blood run cold: **"Government Expands Mutant Surveillance Following Recent Incident."**

The article detailed strike force patrols being increased and specialized agents deployed to areas with high mutant activity. It was inevitable: the bio-mutant fight had drawn some unwanted attention, and Nate knew it would only be a matter of time before the spotlight fell on him.

Nate's chest tightened, an icy wave of realization washing over him. This was no longer about the danger of being caught anymore; it was survival. He thought for a bit if he should go rogue and run, but he realized that if they knew who the mutant was, then he'd be in custody already and all running would do is tell them who to chase after. Nate was going to stay put and hope for this to all pass over, but he knew it'd only be a matter of time.

The next day, Nate sat at the back of the classroom, staring at the clock while seconds ticked by. His body still ached from the fight against the bio-mutant days ago, but all that pain seemed so insignificant compared to the gnawing feeling inside of him. Every whisper, every glance from his classmates felt like a spotlight turned on him. No one said anything outright, but he could feel their eyes lingering on him just a little too long.

He glanced at Xavier, who was sitting a few seats away, doodling idly in his notebook. Xavier caught his eye and gave him a small nod, as if to say, You're okay. Stay cool.

But Nate was not sure how long he could continue keeping his secret. The fight of the bio-mutant had left a crater in the street-and questions in everybody's mind. News coverage had been relentless, and even though nobody so far had identified him, Nate knew it was just a matter of time.

Over lunch, Nate and Xavier sat at their tree again, this time in the middle of the courtyard. The air was cool, fresh, but so were the hundred-odd murmurs going on around them. Xavier leaned back, reaching farther than he needed, just to get an apple from Nate's tray. "Seriously?" Nate said, raising his brow. "What?" Xavier smirked. "You weren't gonna eat it."

Nate shook his head, tugging a small smile onto his face. For a moment, it almost felt normal. Then he saw the principal of the school standing at the edge of the courtyard and talking with a man in a dark suit. The man in the suit was standing rigid, his eyes raking the crowd hawk-like.

"Xav," Nate said softly, nudging his friend. "Don't look now, but I think we've got company."

Xavier followed Nate's gaze and immediately stiffened. "Government," he muttered slowly. "I've seen those guys before."

Nate's stomach took a nosedive. He had hoped the government would not get involved-not yet, at any rate. His mind flashed to the fight with the bio-mutant, the unleashing of his strength despite the onlookers. There was no helping it then, but now it was coming back to haunt him.

"What do we do?" Nate asked, his voice tight.

Xavier glanced around, lowering his voice. "For now? Play it cool. Running is just gonna make them think you're guilty."

The rest of the day was a blur. Nate had worst-case scenarios running in his head, and he wasn't focusing on class. When the final bell rang, Nate was about to blow the roof up. He and Xavier met in lockers. They carefully controlled their movements, avoiding any suspicion.

Heading out to the exit toward school, Nate made another turn to spy the man in his suit-also now between two other agents, speaking to several students as they watched onto his tablet. Nate's heartbeat doubled up suddenly.

"They're asking questions," he told them quietly.

"Yeah," Xavier muttered in return. "Let's not hang on to these kinds of questions."

They went out the side door and took a turn right down towards the edge of the school grounds, with their heads bowed. Nate felt his heartbeat pounding and clench his hands into fists down the sides of his legs.

That night, Nate sparred in the woods behind his house, channeling frustration into every punch and kick. That tree that did duty as a punching bag was full of dents and splinters. Witness to the power he couldn't always govern.

"Dammit!" Nate shouted, punching into the bark with such power it cracked under his fist. He leaned against the tree, his breathing low and ragged.

"You're gonna wreck yourself," Xavier said, leaning casually against a tree.

Nate spun around, his frustration boiling over. "What else am I supposed to do? Just sit around and wait for them to find me?"

"I know," Xavier said, his tone softer. "But you're no good to anyone if you collapse from a heart attack."

Nate took a deep breath and ran a hand through his hair. "I don't know how to do this," he said. "I don't know how to keep hiding."

Xavier came closer and set a comforting hand on Nate's shoulder. "You're not the only one going through this, whatever happens, we'll face it head on."

"We?" Nate asked curiously, glancing up at Xavier

"Yea I mean, it's only a matter of time before they bring in the machinery to test for mutants and test everyone to cover their bases." Xavier said, while staring off and biting his nails.

The tension was thick the next day at school. Nate noticed the agents in the halls, and it was impossible not to. Kids whispered and looked at them warily, their curiosity and fear feeding into the atmosphere.

It all came to a head during gym class. The teacher divided the kids into relay race teams, and Nate tried to avoid attention. When it was time to run, however, his panic surfaced. The agents watched, their eyes on him like lasers.

"Don't overdo it," Xavier had whispered before the race started.

He kept his pace measured, deliberately letting others overtake him. But as he rounded the last corner, one of the other runners tripped and fell directly into his path. Instinct took over, and Nate leaped over the fallen student with ease, his movement unnaturally smooth and precise.

A murmur ran briefly around the crowd, the agents in emotionless glances at one another. Nate's stomach knotted up. He just made their jobs so much easier.

"Dude, what the hell was that?" one runner muttered, eyes wide.

"What?" Nate said, forcing a shrug.

"You just—" The kid shook his head. "Never mind."

Nate kept his head down as he walked past the group of agents. His heart nearly stopped when he caught a glimpse of one of their screens. A school file—his school file.

His stomach dropped. They weren't just asking questions anymore. They had names.

Later in the afternoon, Nate and Xavier sat in their tree groove area, nerves running rampant.

"They know," he whispered. "They may not have any evidence just yet, but they know."

Xavier nodded with an ashen grin. "Yes, and they will not have to wait anymore to pay us a visit."

"What do we do?" Nate asked, twiddling his fingers together nervously..

"We wait," Xavier said, but his tone had shifted. Calculating. "We figure out who they're talking to, and if it gets worse—" he nudged Nate's foot with his own voice low, "—we don't wait to run. We run first."

CHAPTER 6: POWER

Nate had been careful—too careful. Every step home felt like stepping on glass. He swore he saw the same unmarked van twice yesterday, parked across from the boxing gym. It could've been nothing. But it could've been something. The air felt heavier lately, like it was pressing down on him, waiting for him to crack.

The school day started off like any other, kids flowing into the halls, laughing and chattering on their way from class to class. The loud clanging of lockers and teachers calling across the hall brought about the expected chaos of any morning in a typical high school. Nate looked down at the floor as he walked through the throngs of students trying to melt into them. His hoodie was over his face, the music in his ears loud-the useless attempt at drowning out the world.

But somehow, something didn't feel right. There was an uncommon tension in the air, a quiet unease that prickled at Nate's senses. It wasn't until the lunch bell rang that the calm shattered.

The alarms wailed across the school, their shrill din slicing through the chatter to send ripples of confusion amongst the students. Teachers were going about, attempting to round up their classes and make for safety, when, before it would really sink in, the loudspeakers crackled. "All students and staff are to remain inside the building. Do not leave. Authorities are on location," a cold, unknown voice announced.

Nate's stomach bottomed out. He shared a nervous glance across the cafeteria table with Xavier. For once, the joking expression that always seemed to grace Xavier's face had turned into pure fear.

"We gotta get outta here," Xavier whispered, leaning in closer.

"What's going on?" Nate asked, though he didn't want to know.

"I don't know," Xavier whispered back, shaking. "But I can feel it-it's about us."

No sooner said than heavy footsteps echoed down the hallways, pounding louder as they drew closer. The doors to the cafeteria burst open, and the room fell silent as a squad of fully armed government agents flowed inside, black tactical gear and helmet masks over their faces, nothing like humans.

Now, behind them, he stepped forward, towering over the agents. Iron was impossible to ignore: his metallic plating gleamed under the fluorescent lights, and his every movement spoke volumes of power and command. His face partly obscured by his metal-coated jaw, he scanned the room with a cold, calculating gaze. When he spoke, it came in a boom that demanded absolute attention.

"Listen up!" he barked, his tone brooking no argument. "We know there's an unregistered mutant in this school. Step forward now, and no one else has to get hurt."

It made the round in the canteen with students turning toward friends and nudging each other in apprehension. A few were talking of bio-mutants; still others were speculating on which schoolmates were covering up. Nate's palms rubbed underneath his thighs as, heart pounding in his chest, he felt them check faces, their gazes heavy for an ounce of guilt.

"We haven't got all day," Iron growled, his patience obviously wearing thin. His eyes landed on a group of kids sitting near the front, and his gaze narrowed on one girl in particular-the same girl that Nate had gone on a date with just days before.

"You," Iron said, his finger pointed at her. "Come here."

Landry froze; her eyes were wide in terror. Head shaking, unable even to move. Iron's face darkened, and in an instant, he reached down and tore a hunk of concrete out of the floor. He hurled it at her with dizzying speed.

Before his brain could wake up, Nate was moving. He launched from his seat, traversing the length of the room in a blur of speed. No onlooker could register. The block of concrete was less than an inch away from her when Nate plucked it mid-air, with the force of it driving him backward one step. He stepped forward, protectively, in front of her, as the room exploded in a series of gasps and shocked murmurs.

Around the room, seets scraped against the floor as students recoiled. One girl clamped a hand over her mouth, her eyes wide and glassy with disbelief. A few others backed toward the door, expressions twisted in fear—some like they were about to run, others like they were watching something monstrous unfold. Even the class clown, usually too loud for his own good, sat stone still, his mouth hanging open but silent. Nate could feel it: the shift. Not just from Landry—but everyone. Every breath in the room now felt like it was being held hostage by his presence.

"Well, well," Iron said, a smug grin spreading across his face. "Looks like we've found our muttborn."

Nate pulled off his hoodie, revealing his determined expression. "Leave her out of this," he said, his voice steady despite the adrenaline coursing through him. "I'm the one you're looking for."

Iron's grin widened. "Brave. But you're going to regret that."

"So will you." Nate snarled, his hand clenching on the concrete until it burst into shards. His veins popped out; his red bulging muscles were clearly visible.

The agents raised their guns, but Iron lifted a hand to forestall them. "No need," he said. "This one's mine."

The fight began in a blur of motion. Iron charged forward, his massive frame shaking the ground beneath him, each step reverberating like a minor earthquake. Nate barely sidestepped the first swing, the sheer force of it sending a gust of air past his face. The moment Iron's fist struck the ground, it cratered the concrete, sending shards flying.

Iron through a haymaker towards Nate which was caught by Nate's hand, causing a small shockwave of wind throughout the room. Everyone looked on in awe of Nate. No one had expected Nate to be capable of such things. Nate moved back as Iron tried to retaliate with another strike.

Nate moved swiftly, darting to Iron's side and aiming a sharp hook at his ribs. His fist collided with what felt like solid steel, and pain shot up his arm. He grimaced but didn't let up. Observing closely, he noticed something unusual: the metallic sheen on Iron's ribs receded, sliding like liquid to his forearms. Nate watched this, noting how he can move the iron in his body around.

Iron's retaliation came fast. A metal-coated fist swept toward Nate, forcing him to drop to the ground and roll away. Around them, chaos reigned. Students screamed, some diving for cover under tables while others pressed themselves against walls. A few stood frozen, phones raised, recording every moment.

"Fast," Iron growled, his tone sharp with frustration. "Let's see how long that lasts."

Nate didn't respond. He focused on Iron's movements, watching the flow of metal crawl across his body. It shifted to his legs as he charged again, making them gleam like polished steel. Nate sidestepped the first kick but miscalculated the follow-up—a spinning backhand that sent him skidding across the courtyard.

Wincing, Nate pushed himself up. His ribs ached from the impact, but his mind worked furiously. If he can only cover certain areas with iron at a time, I can use that against him.

As Iron lunged, Nate ducked low and sprinted behind him. He planted a kick at the back of Iron's knee, hitting a spot not yet reinforced. Iron stumbled, his leg buckling momentarily before the iron surged downward, bracing his stance.

"You're smarter than you look," Iron admitted, frustration edging into his voice.

Nate didn't answer. He sprang forward, closing the distance in a flash. His fists flew in rapid succession, each strike targeting areas where the iron had vacated. Iron grunted as the blows landed, the metallic groans of stress fractures echoing with each hit.

Roaring, Iron swung wildly, his frustration mounting. Nate dodged and weaved, staying just out of reach. Then, in a calculated move, he allowed Iron's next punch to graze past him, using the momentum to maneuver into a grapple. Wrapping his arms around Iron's waist, Nate heaved with all his strength, lifting the giant man off his feet.

With a roar, Nate slammed Iron forward with a massive tackle. The ground cracked beneath the impact, a cloud of dust and debris billowing up around them. For a moment, silence hung over the courtyard.

Iron groaned, pushing himself up. His metal shifted to his arms as he steadied himself, the iron in his legs retreating. "That's all you got?" he spat, his tone venomous.

Nate didn't answer, charging in again. Iron swung, but Nate ducked under the blow and leapt onto his back. Wrapping his legs around Iron's torso, Nate locked in an arm hold, wrenching Iron's arm backward. The metallic coating screeched as it resisted the strain, but cracks began to spider web across the surface.

Iron roared in pain, slamming himself backward into the ground to break free. The impact knocked the wind out of Nate, but he scrambled to his feet just as Iron rose, his movements slower now.

Iron moved like a wrecking ball, tearing through the cafeteria with near inhuman speed. The moment Nate sidestepped, Iron adjusted mid-stride and caught him square in the chest with a metal-coated shoulder. The impact sent Nate flying backward, crashing through a table with a deafening crunch. His vision blurred. He barely had a second to breathe before Iron was on him again, grabbing him by the throat and lifting him off the ground.

"That all you got?" Iron sneered, his grip tightening.

Nate kicked at his chest, but it was like kicking a steel wall. Iron grinned and hurled Nate across the cafeteria. He smashed into a vending machine, glass shattering as his body collapsed against the debris. A dull ringing filled his ears. His limbs felt sluggish.

Heart Engine. He had to force it. He tried to move, but his body screamed in protest. Iron was already closing the distance, metal-fisted knuckles cracking. Nate barely got his arms up before the first punch drove into his guard. His forearms took the brunt of it, but the sheer force sent him skidding across the tile.

Black spots danced at the edges of his vision. If he took another hit like that, he was done.

His heart pounded, blood rushing through his veins. *Push it further.* The warmth in his chest ignited, surging outward like a furnace. The pain faded, his muscles tightening.

The two squared up again, their breaths heavy. Iron charged again, but this time, Nate met him head-on, creating a massive booming sound. Their hands interlocked in a brutal test of strength. Nate could feel the metal shifting to Iron's fingers, reinforcing them, but he pressed forward, his muscles burning with effort. Nate had to win, for himself and Xavier.

"Give up, kid," Iron snarled. "You can't—"

A loud crack interrupted him. Iron's eyes widened in shock as Nate bent his metal-coated fingers backward, the reinforced iron splitting under the pressure. Nate's burning determination filled his eyes. Pain twisted Iron's face, and he let out a guttural yell, stumbling back.

Nate seized the moment. He ducked low, wrapped his arms around Iron's waist, and with a surge of adrenaline, lifted him off the ground. Using every ounce of his strength, Nate executed a massive suplex, driving Iron into the concrete. This time, the ground shattered beneath them, leaving Iron partially buried in rubble, launching dust and debris everywhere.

The courtyard fell silent. Nate stood over Iron, his chest heaving, his body trembling with exhaustion. The once-imposing figure lay motionless, the metallic coating receding as Iron's consciousness faded. Fully armed guards stayed with their weapons locked onto Nate, but a giant plume of smoke covered the area, obscuring their view. Using this distraction and his speed, Nate sprinted as quickly as possible towards the exit.

At the edge of the chaos, Xavier waited, his expression unreadable. Nate knew what this meant. His secret was out, and he couldn't stay here anymore. With one last glance at the wreckage, Nate sprinted toward his friend, leaving his old life behind.

"Move!" Nate barked, grabbing Xavier's arm and dragging him forward.

Their footsteps echoed loudly as they sprinted down the school's empty halls, hearts pounding in unison.

Nate could hear Iron shouting behind them, his heavy footsteps getting louder as he gave chase. The two friends burst through the main doors and into the city streets, weaving in and out of the maze of alleyways to lose their pursuer.

It felt like it took forever until they finally reached the shelter of an abandoned rooftop complex. The building was decaying, full of overgrown weeds, but at least it was a place to catch one's breath. A low, moaning wind whipped between the broken AC units and half-toppled antennae, carrying the distant hum of traffic and the occasional bark of a dog. The city sprawled below like a restless beast, blinking with windows and headlights. Nate dropped onto the cold, cracked floor and hunched over, chest heaving as he worked to catch his breath.

Nate had nothing. His head ran over options and actions for them to do, each a little riskier than the last. They couldn't just go back to school. The government was probably looking for them. Too much risk for one city.

Above the city, the rooftop complex loomed ominously, abandoned and ghostly against the once-thriving building. Nate and Xavier ran up crumbling stairs, both their breathing ragged. Reaching the top, they collapsed on the cold cracked floor, distant sounds of sirens.

"What the hell do we do now?" Xavier's voice cracked under the weight of the question.

Nate raked his fingers through his hair, his eyes darting nervously. "I don't know, man. But staying here? That's not an option."

As they debated their next move, a sudden noise sliced through the silence of the night-air, faint creaking of metal and then the unmistakable sound of feet meeting with the ground. Nate and Xavier jumped to their feet, immediately tense, prepared to see another fight.

A figure dropped from the rafters and landed with silent precision. In an instant, two more had appeared, blocking every avenue of escape. Their movements were a study in practiced efficiency, low stances combative.

Nate did not wait for explanations. He launched himself forward in a punch at the nearest figure and hit-but the feel of impact wasn't just exactly right. This figure rolled with the punch and countered with a kick at the chest, which sent Nate flying backward.

Xavier would have risen to his aid, but another figure cut him off, his arm behind his back in a fluid motion. "Stay down," the figure growled, his voice firm yet not unkind.

Nate sprang up, his eyes darting between intruders. "Who the hell are you?" he demanded, his fists clenched and ready.

One of them stepped forward, their hands up in a gesture of peace. "We're not here to hurt you," they said in a steady voice. "We're here to help."

Nate hesitated, his breathing heavy. "Help? You sure have a funny way of showing it."

The figure chuckled, drawing back its hood to reveal a sharp-featured woman with piercing eyes. "We had to make sure you were worth the effort. And from what we've seen, you are."

The others followed her example and, thrown back hoods, came one after another to introduce themselves: Natalie, the leader-true master of command; Michael, tall and powerfully built, with quiet strength; Morgan, quiet-perhaps his nature could assure one of his calmness; Ryan, the genius with strategy, wearing a mischievous grin; Ava, whose fire blazed in each confident stride.

"And we're supposed to trust you? Just like that?" Xavier asked, his tone sharp.

Natalie crossed her arms, staring him down. "If we wanted you dead, you would be. Trust me on that." But you aren't alone anymore. We're the Rogues, and we've been keeping an eye out for mutants like you-people who need a little help to stay hidden.

Nate exchanged a glance with Xavier, the weight of their situation pressing down on them. Finally, he lowered his fists, his shoulders slumping. "Alright," he said, his voice tinged with exhaustion. "We're listening."

CHAPTER 7: THE ROAD AHEAD

Nate and Xavier stood amidst the aftermath of their impromptu brawl with the Rogues, their ragged breathing breaking the quiet on the rooftop. Natalie gestured in a 'follow us' manner-the scar-faced leader was still leading them somewhere, though Nate could not help the tension that simmered in his bones, nor was Xavier any less trusting of the strangers offering him sanctuary.

Introductions by the Rogues were swift, and their dark cloaks and hoods gave them an air of mystery. As imposing as they were, a camaraderie among them was in place, setting them apart from any government agents Nate and Xavier had encountered thus far.

The first, Morgan, had come forward, sort of young, short black hair framing her razor-sharp features and a stare that was, for sure as hell, older than she seemed. She didn't look any older than Nate or Xavier.

Next in line came Michael, the biggest guy who had thick shoulders and a tall frame, looking like a walking fortress. From his tanned skin to the low-cut hairstyle, it seemed like he had come from an islander generation, and though his size was threateningly big and perhaps the first thing anybody would notice, the warm, protecting smile showed him to be big-brotherly. He appeared to be in his 30s, the eldest of the Rogues.

Ava was behind him and far more retracted inside his aura, downcast eyes with a shy character, not speaking of the decisiveness of their peers. Her delicate, soft-featured brunette face and quiet demeanor suggested a frail character, though her posture and bearing contradicted this, showing she could hold herself and not buckle under pressure; this mid-twenties woman seemed a soothing presence amidst the tension.

Natalie was undeniably the pack leader, gleaming with a surety bordering on conceit. The dark skin glistened in faint moonlight of gray; from bright, curly, blonde hair spread a circle of light at the rear of her skull, almost a halo. Muscular legs beneath stood firm to speak volumes unto themselves. In Her late twenties probably, she shifted with calculating command.

At the back was Ryan. He hovered there, playing with his sunglasses against the dark background. Tall and gangly with a slight stutter, this relaxed slouch made him look like an indolent-man, though those bright, incisive eyes behind reflective shades gave away his astuteness. His dirty-blond hair tumbled messily upon his forehead, maybe about Xavier's age or probably one to two years older.

"This way," Natalie said, her tone brisk though not unkind. She jerked a hand toward a rusted fire escape that dropped down the side of the building.

Nate exchanged a look with Xavier. They were tired, battered, and out of options. Xavier gave a small shrug, his face resigned. Nate nodded, signaling his agreement. Together, they followed the Rogues into the shadows of the city.

It had been a tense journey through the city: the Rogues moved with real precision down alleys, dodging and weaving into abandoned buildings to avoid discovery. Natalie kept point in stealthy fashion, while her eyes constantly scanned the surroundings for threats. Bringing up the rear was Michael, his massive shoulders relaxed as quiet strength seemed to ooze from him with every step.

Every drone that zipped overhead made Nate flinch. Each flickering streetlamp cast shadows too dark, too long. They cut across alleys with their backs pressed to crumbling brick, the scent of rot and rust thick in the air. At one point, a few patrol vehicles cruised past, their engines purring like predators hunting for motion. The Rogues quickly made their way onto the rooftops to avoid detection.

"Where are we even going?" Nate finally asked, his voice no louder than a whisper, but with an edge of frustration laced within it. "Someplace safe," Natalie replied without turning around. "Safer than here, anyway." "That's not reassuring whatsoever," Xavier muttered, earning a quick glare from Morgan, the youngest of them.

"It's not supposed to be," Morgan snapped. "You're lucky we found you when we did. If the government got to you first, you'd be wishing for 'not reassuring.'"

They finally came to a stop in front of a plain, unmarked van parked in an underground garage. Natalie opened the back doors, revealing an interior that was cramped but well-outfitted with supplies and basic medical kits.

"Get in," she said, climbing into the driver's seat. Michael slid in beside her while the rest piled into the back.

Nate did not immediately enter, but stopped and stepped inside after Xavier. Then the doors shut with a slam, and the van started with a roar - the motor boisterously echoed off the confined space of the garage.

The group members remained silent while driving in the van through city streets. The van rumbled along the uneven road, its engine's steady growl filling the silence. Nate sat pressed against the window, the cold glass cooling his forehead as he stared out at the blur of city lights giving way to darkened outskirts. He could feel Xavier's presence beside him, a steady, reassuring anchor, but his mind was a tempest of doubt.

The Rogues—Natalie, Michael, Morgan, Ryan, and Ava—sat scattered in the vehicle, their quiet confidence evident in their easy postures and subdued chatter. They knew who they were. They knew what they stood for. Nate wasn't so sure about himself.

His thoughts churned, the weight of his decision settling heavily in his chest. Joining a group like this wasn't just survival. It was a declaration, a choice to be part of something bigger than himself. But was he ready for that? Could he trust them, these strangers who had swept him and Xavier into their fold?

He shifted uncomfortably, his fingers drumming against his knee. A part of him wanted to ask Natalie to turn the van around, to drop him off at some empty street corner where he could disappear into the shadows. Another part, the part that knew there was no turning back, held him in place.

Xavier must have sensed his turmoil because he nudged Nate with his elbow. "You good?" he asked quietly, his voice low enough that the others wouldn't overhear.

Nate hesitated before answering, his gaze fixed on the window. "I don't know, man. This... everything—it's a lot."

Xavier gave a small chuckle, though it lacked his usual levity. "Yeah, no kidding. But what else were we gonna do? Go back to school and pretend like nothing happened?"

"I know," Nate said, his voice barely audible. "But what if we're just trading one danger for another? What if we can't trust them?"

Xavier leaned back, his arms crossed. "I don't trust them. Not yet. But we don't have a choice, Nate. The government's not gonna stop coming after us. At least with the Rogues, we've got a fighting chance."

Nate didn't respond immediately. His eyes drifted to the group in the front of the van—Natalie and Michael in quiet conversation, Morgan sharpening her nails with meticulous precision, Ryan scrolling through a tablet, and Ava glancing nervously out the window. They seemed like a team, bonded by shared experiences and mutual trust. Nate wondered if he and Xavier would ever truly belong among them.

"Do you think we made the right call?" Nate asked, his voice barely louder than the hum of the engine.

Xavier shrugged. "I think we made the only call we could. And hey, if they try anything, we'll handle it. Together."

The word hung in the air like a lifeline, pulling Nate out of his spiral. He let out a shaky breath and nodded. "Yeah. Together."

The van hit a pothole, jostling everyone inside. Michael shot a glare at Natalie, who muttered unapologetically "roads like these aren't exactly smooth."

Nate looked around at the group a bit perplexed "So why are you guys even doing this?" Nate asked, just loud enough for the group to hear. Michael looked down dimly and muttered, "Because someone has to. Government wants us dead or chained. If we don't fight for each other, no one will." His words weren't loud, but they carried weight, pressing into the silence that followed like a vow. Nate couldn't quite formulate a response that felt meaningful.

Meanwhile, Xavier shifted uncomfortably, his stretchy arms snapping back to size every so often as he readjusted in his seat. "So. this base of yours," he ventured. "It's. secure, right?"

"Secure enough," Michael replied without turning around. "We've stayed a step ahead of the government so far. You will be, too."

"Assuming you do nothing stupid," Morgan added, glancing pointedly at Xavier.

Finally, it pulled onto a hidden access road opening into an abandoned factory on the outskirts of town. The structure appeared wholly unremarkable to any casual passer-by, but the moment Natalie ushered the trio inside, in rapid order, it proved anything but-so completely repurposed had it been by the Rogues into ersatz headquarters.

Inside, the room was a jumble of scavenged furniture, high-tech equipment, and improvisations for defense. Maps of the city lined the walls, pinned with notes in sharp, slanted handwriting. A long table dominated the center, the group's planning center point, with scattered papers and electronic tablets.

"This is home," Natalie said rather straightforwardly, waving her arm around. "It's nothing much, but it does the job."

CHAPTER 8: THE ROGUES

Nate and Xavier stood near the door, awkwardly. Whatever else about them, Nate knew this was a tight-knit group-they moved and settled into space as if this was home and they knew instinctively how to function around each other. Natalie issued quiet orders with assumed authority over every member's duty, with Michael setting up defense perimeters. Ava lit a couple of makeshift lanterns, bringing warm, yellow light to flicker through the room.

"Alright," Natalie called out, her voice sharp enough to cut through the chatter. "Everyone, listen up. We've got a situation."

The Rogues and their two new members, Nate and Xavier, formed a loose circle. The air was tense, as though everyone understood the weight of what was about to be said. Nate exchanged a quick glance with Xavier before Natalie began.

"You've probably heard of them," Natalie started, her voice low but commanding. "The Animals."

Nate's brow furrowed. The name wasn't unknown to him. Rumors of an elite group of mutants employed by the government had been flying around for years, but nobody knew much about them.

Michael edged closer, his face grim. "They're not just stories, man. The Animals are out there, and they're among the most powerful mutants alive like Mammal, Crustacean, Reptile.."

"The Pinnacle?" Xavier asked, frowning.

Ryan nodded, his voice clipped. "Yy-yeah. Untouchable, but n-not like the others. Reptile's different—he do-d-doesn't hunt mutants anymore. N-not directly, anyway. He's a-a government operative, sure, but h-his-his focus is on missions f-far above their unusual business." He shook his head. "T-the rest of the Animals... are-are a whole different story."

Morgan crossed her arms over her chest. Her jaw tightened. "Crustacean and Mammal are nightmares. They are whom the government sends when it wants mutants like us dead. And if you get marked as a threat, they'll find you. And they won't just bring you in; they make examples out of you."

"Why would mutants work for them? Hunt their own?" Nate asked, disbelief etched across his face.

Natalie's jaw tightened. "Sometimes they don't have a choice. The government knows how to twist people—threats, blackmail, experiments. You name it."

Michael continued, "And then there are those who truly believe in what they're doing. Crustacean?"

"And Mammal?" Xavier ventured.

Morgan's voice came out low. "He's the enforcer. Cold, methodical, ruthless. He doesn't care about ideals or propaganda. He's just there to do the job, no matter what it takes."

Ava chimed in with a somber voice, "They're the ultimate weapon against us, put at the disposal of the government. And they're effective-terribly effective."

"They're the government's personal executioners," Morgan muttered, eyes dark. "We saw what they did to a group of runaways last year. Crustacean doesn't just kill—he dismantles people like they're insects. And Mammal? He tracked them for weeks, picking them off one by one until there was no one left."

Nate clenched his fists, frustration and fear bubbling just below the surface. "So what happens when they come after us?"

Natalie didn't bat an eye. "We don't make mistakes. We don't get found. Simple. They're strong, but they're not invincible. If we play it smart, we can keep ahead of them."

Michael said, his voice light with a wry grin as he tried to diffuse the moment. "And if they show up? Well, let's just say they haven't seen what this little ragtag group can do."

The others were still for a moment, their faces set in contemplative silence. Then Natalie reached up and rolled her sleeve up her arm, revealing a jagged scar running from wrist to elbow.

"You should trust us," she said in that cool, even tone, "because we know what happens to captured mutants."

Nate hesitated, gaze straying back to the scar. "What... what did they do to you?"

Natalie's eyes hardened. "They treated us like lab rats. Poked, prodded, cut us open to see what made us tick."

"They don't care about registration," Michael said in a low voice, but firmly. "They want weapons. Puppets. People they can control."

Ava crossed her arms, leaning against a nearby table. "Just like that agent you fought- Iron. They train people like him from the moment they're old enough to hold a gun. To them, we're not even human."

Natalie took a step closer to Nate, her face softening. "We've been through hell, and we wouldn't wish that on anyone else."

Natalie's gaze lingered on Nate for a moment longer, her tone softer now. "When I was fifteen, they raided our street. Called it a cleanse. Claimed someone in the neighborhood was harboring a mutant. It was me. But my dad… he stood in the way. They shot him on the porch before he could finish saying my name. That's when I ran. Been running ever since—until I stopped and started fighting back." Natalie looked at Nate and Xavier inquisitively. "So, what's it going to be? You want to keep running? Or do you want to fight back?"

Nate looked at Xavier, their eyes meeting for a moment. Then he turned to Natalie, his voice steady despite the weight of his decision. "We're in. Whatever it takes."

But he gets a little rest; at first light the next morning, the Rogues waste little time in putting Nate and Xavier through their paces-and it is clear they're going to be taken to the breaking point.

Early in the morning, Natalie and Michael, their voices cutting through the haze of his dreams, startled Nate awake. "Get up, kid," Natalie shouted, nudging his shoulder with her boot. "Time to train."

Still groggy, Nate groaned but forced himself up. His body ached from the previous day's events, but he had no intention of showing weakness. To shake off the fatigue, he focused on his power, willing his heart to pump faster. The rush hit him almost immediately, banishing the sleepiness from his mind and bringing his body to full alertness.

As the group gathered in a cleared section of the hideout that they had designated as a training area, Nate scarfed down some spare rations alongside the others. Between bites, Natalie broke the silence.

"So, about those abilities of yours," she started, tilting her head curiously. "From the videos we saw, you're strong, but how does it work exactly? You seem to get bursts of power out of nowhere."

Nate swallowed and shrugged. "It's... kinda weird. My heart beats a lot faster than most people's, and I can push it even further when I need to. I call it Heart Engine. The faster I pump my blood, the stronger and quicker I get. It's taken me years to control it, but when I lose control... Well, let's just say I've had my fair share of heartburn and heart attacks. Probably thousands."

"Damn," Michael muttered, his eyes wide. "That's hardcore. Are you, like... okay?"

"Yeah, I'm fine," Nate replied with a small grin. "I've learned how to manage it better over time, but I still have to be careful."

Michael leaned forward, his expression serious for a moment. "And why does your skin turn red? Like in those videos?"

"Oh, that's from all the blood cycling through me," Nate explained. "It makes my skin tighten and my veins pop."

Michael smirked. "So, basically, you're like a giant—"

"Shut up, idiot," Natalie interrupted, smacking the back of Michael's head with a playful grin.

Nate chuckled, shaking his head. "What about you guys? What can you do?"

"Well, mine's pretty obvious," Natalie said, flexing her massive leg muscles. Her muscles tensed like stone, and Nate could see why she was the powerhouse of the group. "My legs are ridiculously strong. I didn't bother giving it a name."

"I call mine Double Body," Michael chimed in proudly, demonstrating by doubling the size of one arm and then splitting it into two. The sight was as mesmerizing as it was unsettling. "I can double my body mass or duplicate my body parts. Pretty sweet, right?"

"Ryan over there has thermal infrared vision," Natalie added, nodding toward him. "He can see through walls and farther than the rest of us combined."

Ava chimed in softly, "When I touch someone I can sense their emotions... and I'm working on influencing them."

Morgan, who had been quietly sharpening her nails, smirked. "I grow these bad boys," she said, holding up her hands. Her nails extended into razor-sharp, hardened points. "They cut through pretty much anything."

Nate glanced around, taking it all in. Each ability was unique, practical, and, frankly, a little awe-inspiring. He couldn't help but feel a sense of relief, a safety net he hadn't known he needed.

Nate stared at the group, feeling like he was standing at the edge of something huge. These people—they had purpose. A reason to fight. He had spent so long just trying to survive that the idea of something more felt... foreign.

"I don't know if I'm built for this," he admitted, rubbing the back of his neck. "I just wanted to make it through the day, not start a war."

Natalie crossed her arms. "Nobody starts out ready, kid. But with a little training I think you'll do just fine."

Nate nodded in partial agreement as they proceeded to a small training area with mats and workout equipment.

Nate was a natural, considering the increased strength and speed, but he had very little technique to back up his talents. Natalie and Michael took him under their wing, training him through an array of intense drills.

"Use your legs," Natalie said, with a roundhouse kick, powerful.

"That's easy for you to say, you're all legs" Nate joked while trying to sweep Nat's legs.

Nat scoffed "They're the most potent muscles you have in your body. If you're going to take someone down, you gotta know how to use all parts of your body." Nate tried to mimic her form—but overextended and nearly lost his balance. Natalie exhaled sharply. "Okay, maybe not like that."

Meanwhile, Michael centered his training around grappling and close combat, using his powers, which split his body into four arms. With a bunch of boxing pads held by himself, he had Nate moving around him at high speed.

"You're fast," Michael said, dodging a punch. "But speed without control? It's useless. Keep your movements tight. Precise."

Nate gritted his teeth and adjusted his stance, landing a series of powerful strikes that sent shockwaves through the air.

Xavier's training took a different approach. Lacking Nate's physicality, he focused on agility and defense. Ryan and Ava guided him through basic techniques suited to his stretchy body ability.

"Don't fight like a brawler," Ava advised, tossing a foam baton at Xavier. "Fight like a ghost. Slip past their attacks and strike when they least expect it."

Ryan adjusted his sunglasses, smirking. "Y-you're b-burning out, Stretch. I can see it in your body h-hea-heat."

Morgan, typically aloof, sat out of the physical training. She leaned against a wall, observing quietly alongside Matthew, who rarely spoke. When asked why she wasn't taking part, Morgan shrugged. "I'm more of a thinker," she said cryptically.

As the group wrapped up the final round of drills, the subtle hum of drone surveillance and helicopters returned to the edge of Nate's awareness—a distant, almost inaudible buzz above the rooftops. He didn't say anything, but his shoulders tensed. For a second, it felt like the city was watching them. They didn't have the luxury of peace. The Rogues might've been hidden for now, but the government's eyes were always out there, waiting.

Natalie studied Nate like a puzzle she hadn't figured out yet. "You're still keeping one foot out the door," she said, crossing her arms.

Nate leaned against the wall, unimpressed. "I don't see a door."

"Exactly." Natalie stepped closer, her voice lower. "You want in, or are we just a stop on the way?"

Nate held her gaze, unflinching. "I didn't ask to be here. But that doesn't mean I'm not standing with you."

Natalie nodded slowly, as if weighing his words. Then, she extended a hand. "Then stand with us all the way."

For a second, Nate hesitated—but then he took her hand.

By the end of the day, Nate and Xavier were exhausted—but for the first time in a long while, they felt like they belonged to something bigger than themselves.

That evening, Nate found himself alone on the rooftop of the hideout. The city stretched out before him, its lights twinkling in the darkness. He thought of his mother, wondering if she was safe and hoping he'd see her again someday. The weight of everything—the fights, the running, the constant fear—pressed down on him like a physical burden.

"Hey, you're in my spot."

Nate turned to find Morgan leaning against the rooftop access door, arms crossed. Her voice had a teasing lilt to it, but her expression was inscrutable.

"Sorry," Nate mumbled, moving aside. "Didn't mean to intrude."

Morgan lifted one eyebrow. "Relax. I'm kidding." She stood and dropped onto the ledge beside him. "You can stay if you want. Just be prepared to hear me rant."

Nate gave a chuckle, nervously. "Sure. I could use the company."

Morgan smiled softly. "What were you brooding about?"

Nate replied defensively, "Brooding?. I wasn'."

"You're thinking about home, huh?" Morgan asked.

Nate nodded. "Yeah. I just hope my mom's okay. She doesn't... she doesn't deserve any of this."

Morgan sighed, her gaze fixed on the stars. "None of us do. My dad? He called the cops on me the second he found out. Guess there's a limit to unconditional love."

"I'm sorry," Nate said, his voice barely above a whisper.

Morgan shrugged. "It's in the past. But you're here now. And we've got your back. So give us a chance, yeah?"

Nate smiled, and a little of the weight seemed to lift off his shoulders. He let himself cry as Morgan patted his back reassuringly, tugging him into a comforting hug. "I got you," she whispered. And for the first time in a long while, Nate believed it. Maybe… just maybe, he wasn't running anymore.

CHAPTER 9: HIGH ALERT

Morning light filtered through the cracked window panes into the hideout of the Rogues and fell in streaks of golden sunlight on the worn floorboards. The air smelled faintly of cooking bacon, a comfort so rare in their chaotic existence.

Guttural grunts escaped Michael's lips, who further pressed on and never yielded into an endless set of push-ups against the hard concrete. Ava sat cross-legged on a most nondescript worn couch, nose in a thick leather-bound book, periodically setting her gaze sideways to Morgan, who softly hummed on and tended the sizzling griddle. He'd arranged plates beside him, nicely set with fruit, eggs, and bacon—a bit of refinement in contrast to the general roughness.

Natalie and Ryan stood by the map pinned to the wall, deep in an intense discussion about their next move. Their fingers traced routes, marked safe-houses, and noted supply caches. The odd nod or gesture told how vital such plans were in keeping them alive.

Nate stirred on his makeshift bed, a concoction of pillows, blankets, and padded cardboard that little resembled the comfort of his old life. He sat up, and with that, a pang of longing washed over him as he would have risen to breakfast smells from Mom's cooking and the sound of her shuffling around the kitchen. He wondered what she made of all that had happened, if she was safe, whether she worried for him as much as he did for her. A lump formed in his throat, but he swallowed it down, forcing himself into the present.

Stretching, Nate winced slightly as his bruises reminded him why he had slept so much longer than the others. His body still ached from the battle with Iron, but the downtime had helped. He dragged himself up and walked into the main area, rubbing the sleep from his eyes.

The scene wrapped itself around him like a warm hug. For the first time in what felt like an eternity, he was not waking up to an empty bed or masquerading as someone else. He watched the Rogues go about their morning chores: shared purpose, friendly jibes-the sense of being at home rather than a mere hideout.

Xavier was leaning against the wall, waiting patiently for Nate. "About time, man," he said, grinning. "Thought you'd sleep the whole day away."

Nate smirked. "I needed it. My face still feels like it went ten rounds with a steel bat."

"Well, if you're done being a diva, let's head out," Xavier teased. "Got some daylight to burn, and I'm not exactly big on waiting."

Nate shook his head, chuckling. "Alright, let me eat first."

Morgan turned from the griddle and handed him a plate with a soft smile. "Here. Thought you might need this."

"Thanks," Nate said, appreciation heavy in his voice. He ate and looked around the room again, taking it all in. This mishmash group of mutants had given him something he hadn't had in years: belonging.

A nearby compact tv was playing local national news coverage of the incident between Nate and Ironclad from the day before. The news anchor's voice was measured, calm, and practiced as she addressed the camera.

"In breaking news, a dangerous and unregistered mutant wreaked havoc at Lakewood High School, leaving multiple injuries and significant property damage. Footage obtained by officials suggests that this individual may be connected to other violent incidents in the region. Government representatives are urging citizens to report any unusual behavior to their local enforcement offices."

The screen cut to grainy security footage of Nate in mid-fight, his veins bulging with power. The camera angle made him look monstrous.

Then, a statement from a stern-faced government official:

"We assure the public that we are doing everything in our power to contain this growing threat. Mutants operating outside the law pose a significant risk to society. We must remain vigilant."

Nate watched from the shadows of the safe house, his jaw tightening. "Unbelievable. They made me the villain."

Morgan crossed her arms. "Yeah. And the worst part? People are gonna believe it."

The rest of the Rogues sat around finishing their morning routines and food. Nate and Xavier talked with the rest of the Rogues for about 20 minutes when Natalie interrupted them.

"We've been tracking someone," Natalie said, her voice tight. She pointed to a red pin on the map. "Lane… he's a rogue mutant, has severely damaged this area. He's leaving operatives in pieces—mentally and physically."

Xavier leaned back in his chair. "Nightmares, right? That's his thing? Creepy stuff."

Natalie nodded. "He's efficient, ruthless, and impossible to predict. If the government doesn't catch him soon, they'll start lumping all mutants into his category."

Xavier whistled low. "He sounds charming."

Nate frowned, studying the map. "And dangerous."

"He has been killing government agents for well over a year, and the entire government fears him. Having mutants like him out there makes us all look bad," Natalie said with seriousness in her voice, with a pinch of disgust.

Nate always considered it pure propaganda against mutants, but he realized his naivety and that not all mutants act like rogues when cornered.

After breakfast, Natalie showed Nate and Xavier over to a closet with pieces of fabric, sewing materials, pieces of black clothing, and what looked like some tactical gear.

"This is the armory." Natalie joked, pointing impressively at the disarray.

"Armory?" Nate laughed back, questioning what all he was looking at.

"Morgan is the local seamstress. She will take your measurements and make you guys some new outfits that might be more fitting for you guys if y'all are going to stick with us," Natalie said, presenting Morgan

Morgan walked over with some needles and thread in hand. She measured out Nate and Xavier and in only a few hours made them both stark black cloaked hoods matching the ones the Rogues wore when they first met.

The Rogues gathered in the hideout, exhaustion settling over them like a shared weight. Still, something unspoken connected them—something stronger than words.

Nate and Xavier were not to be left behind, either. I worked alongside them, packing equipment and storing supplies. Ava had set up a surveillance system, her fingers flying across a keyboard as he constantly monitored various news feeds and government channels for any signs of danger. Ava was always bubbly and went about checking their arms cache, seeing they were all ready for some action.

"Why do we even have all this if we never use it?" Ava muttered, flipping a sleek but battered baton in her hand.

"We use it when we need to," Natalie replied, her tone firm. "But we're not here to start wars, Ava."

Ava rolled her eyes but didn't argue anymore, muttering something under her breath about how "a good offense is the best defense."

After cleaning up, training continued like the day before. Nate wiped the sweat from his brow, rolling his shoulders as he squared up across from Michael in the underground training room. The Rogues had rigged it together—old mats, reinforced walls, and enough space to spar without breaking the entire hideout.

"You keep relying on your speed," Michael said, cracking his knuckles. His extra arms stretched out, moving like they had minds of their own. "That's gonna get you killed if you don't learn to think ahead."

Nate smirked, bouncing on his feet. "If I'm fast enough, I don't need to think ahead."

Michael grinned. "Bet."

The moment the word left his mouth, he was already moving, all four arms coming at Nate like a flurry of fists. Nate ducked under the first set, weaving between strikes, his footwork keeping him just out of reach. Michael didn't let up, pivoting and catching Nate's ribs with a solid left hook.

Nate stumbled back, exhaling sharply. "Alright," he muttered. "That one hurt."

"Good," Michael shot back, pressing forward. "Get used to it."

Nate didn't have time to respond before Michael's next attack came, forcing him to adapt. He stopped thinking about dodging and instead stepped in, getting under Michael's reach. He launched a quick uppercut to Michael's ribs, following with a snap kick to the knee.

Michael grunted but grinned through it. "Better. Still not enough."

Then he grabbed Nate mid-movement, two arms locking around his waist. Before Nate could break free, Michael lifted and slammed him onto the mat.

The impact knocked the air out of Nate's lungs. He groaned, glaring up at Michael, who loomed over him with an annoyingly satisfied smirk.

"Lesson one," Michael said. "Just because you're faster doesn't mean you're untouchable."

From the sidelines, Natalie chuckled. "He's learning the hard way."

Morgan crossed her arms. "That's the only way he ever learns."

Nate groaned again, dragging himself up. "Alright, round two," he grumbled.

Michael's smirk widened. "Now you're talking."

Still catching his breath. Natalie tossed Nate a bottle of water, watching him for a moment before speaking.

"You're strong," she admitted. "But you hesitate. You can't afford that in a fight."

Nate frowned, twisting the cap open. "I'm not trying to kill anyone."

Natalie studied him carefully. "Neither are we. But hesitation can get you or one of us killed." She crossed her arms. "Trust us enough to have your back, and we'll trust you to have ours."

Later that night, the team all sat down around a small dinner table. It was nothing special, just canned soup and crackers, but it would do to keep their energy up. During the meal, the conversation shifted to the bio-mutants. "I still don't understand how they're even created," Xavier finally said, breaking the silence. "Are they mutants like us? Or something else entirely?"

Michael slumped back in his chair, struck by the thought. "They were people once. At least that's the theory. But something happened-experiments, maybe-that turned them into... that."

"They are dangerous," Natalie added, her voice grim. "And unpredictable. The government says they're trying to contain it, but I don't buy it. They have kept too quiet about where these things come from."

"They're lying to everyone," Morgan said in a low, steady voice. "The bio-mutants aren't accidents. They're projects."

Her words sucked the sound right off the table. Nate gave Xavier a sidelong glance. They were unnerved, both of them, by the implications.

As the night wore on, it would be time for him to patrol the city: a routine matter of keeping sharp, watching for threats, and keeping movements unpredictable. Nate and Xavier tagged along, wanting to prove themselves.

The city was alive with action, its streets humming with people and cars. The Rogues moved through the shadows, sticking to back alleys and rooftops to avoid being seen. Nate was in awe of their precision-each step, each movement coordinated and deliberate.

"Keep up, rookie," Natalie teased, glancing over her shoulder at Nate. He smirked but didn't say a word, matching her pace instead.

As they crossed the rooftops, their phones buzzed all at once. Xavier was the first to pull his phone out, and his face paled as he read the alert.

"Uh… guys? We've got a problem." he said, his voice going tight. "Multiple bio-mutants spotted in the area. Authorities advise residents to stay inside."

The group froze, tension crackling in the air. Natalie stepped forward, her expression unreadable as she scanned the alert. "Location?" she asked.

Xavier tapped on his phone, pulling up a map. "Two blocks east. Looks like they're heading toward the river."

"We're close," Natalie said, her tone decisive. "Let's move. Stay sharp."

The Rogues sprang into action, their earlier camaraderie replaced by a steely focus. Nate and Xavier followed closely, their adrenaline spiking as they prepared for what was to come.

CHAPTER 10: PRESSURE

In state 10 a squad of revolutionary operatives moved in a tight formation through the abandoned factory, weapons raised. Their leader, a hardened veteran named Collins, held up a fist, signaling the unit to halt. The only sound was the drip of water from rusted pipes.

Then, a low growl.

"Movement, west quadrant," one operative reported. "Infrared's picking up something big."

Before Collins could issue an order, the wall behind them exploded. A massive, crab-like claw lashed out, snapping around one soldier's torso. A sickening crack echoed as his body folded unnaturally before being yanked into the darkness.

"Contact! Contact!" another agent screamed, unloading his rifle. The bullets barely slowed the monstrosity emerging from the shadows—a grotesque fusion of human and crustacean, its exoskeleton glistening under the dim light.

Then, from the ceiling, something dropped onto another operative. A blur of fur and muscle. A deafening SNAP as Mammal tore into his target, blood spraying across the concrete. The remaining soldiers opened fire, their screams drowned out by the howls of their attackers.

Collins barely had time to process the carnage before a jagged claw speared through his chest. His last thought was they never stood a chance.

A gray government office somewhere in the world sat dimly lit, its lines of monitors filled with a grimy recording of the mutant incident in State Six: Iron getting knocked out cold by a teenager; the miraculous break-out and, subsequently, bio-mutant attack-replayed and infinite. A few officials sat at a conference table in the middle, their faces stern and serious.

A woman with graying hair leaned forward, fingers steepled. "This isn't just about detaining him," she said. "This is about control. If a teenager can take down one of our elites, what message does that send?"

A younger official hesitated. "But if we push too hard, we risk exposing—"

The woman's eyes darkened. "Then we make an example out of him. We remind the world who holds the leash."

"This isn't just some mutt kid," a senior official growled, gesturing toward the paused screen of Nate knocking Iron out cold. "He took down one of our best. And now we're hearing he's working with the Rogues?"

The other official, with a thin, younger face, leaned forward. "If this kid is as strong as the reports show, he makes up a threat himself. But with the Rogues, though? That is an outright crisis."

"We must act quickly," said the senior official. "How long will it take for the Mammal to be dispatched?"

A spate of silence held as another official scanned a report. "Two days, minimum. He's finishing an operation in State Ten."

The room erupted in piqued murmurs. The grey-haired woman at the head of the table raised a hand to hush the discussion. "Two days is far too long," she said. "What of Knox? Or Nosey?"

"He wouldn't stand a chance," the sharp-featured man replied. "If the Lionstep and the Rogues have joined forces with the kid, we're dealing with a coordinated team of experienced mutants. Knoxx can't handle that. And Nosey is still MIA in State 9."

"And the bio-mutants?" the silver-haired woman pressed. "This isn't the first time they've appeared in the same area as these incidents. What if there's a connection?"

The senior officer shook his head. "We must detain the scum. The instabilities will have to be handled later. If they refuse to register and obey, they had better be dead."

Those words fell like a weight upon the officials as the room hushed in a heavy silence. Everyone understood the meaning of "detaining." It wasn't safety, and it wasn't oversight that the government wanted through its mutant registration program; it was control. Those who would not comply were threatened to be neutralized, no questions asked.

Meanwhile, the Rogues were not sitting idly by, waiting for their next move. The operation was mobile-prepared for, actually in constant evasion from the pursuing governmental elements that followed their every move. The group convened in a sort of common room, the air still thick with the tension from what had just gone down.

"Two bio-mutants," Nat said, pacing in front of the group. Her tone was calm, but the sharpness in her eyes betrayed her concern. "One of them is massive. This isn't going to be like anything we've faced before."

"They've been appearing more frequently," Morgan added, her voice quiet but firm. "It's not random."

Nate leaned onto the edge of an old, battered couch. His words spoke in hesitation. "The bio-mutant I fought. It was human once."

The room fell silent for a moment, quiet. The Rogues shifted in unease before Michael finally broke it. "Wait—what do you mean, human?" Michael asked, his deep voice tinged with surprise.

"I mean, it wasn't some mindless monster," Nate said. "It started transforming during the fight. It was like it didn't want to lose control, but… it couldn't stop."

Nat crossed her arms over her chest, her expression unreadable. "Even if they are human, they're a danger now. We can't risk more lives."

Nate nodded, but to him, this was news heavy with portent. What if these bio-mutants were conscious? Even the thought was sending his stomach roiling.

"Alright, here's the plan," Nat said, continuing as the snap of her voice drew their attention back. "We are going to break up into teams. Michael and I will take the big one. Morgan, you, Ryan, and Ava will take the smaller one. Nate, you support where you're needed and make sure civilians get to safety."

The team nodded as one, believing implicitly in Nat's leadership. Quick, practiced, efficient movements-the way they dressed told it all. There was an unsaid understanding amongst them. Even in the face of such an occurrence, the resolve to protect those who could not protect themselves was implicit.

By the time the Rogues finally arrived, the streets were a chaotic mess of destruction: buildings torn to shreds, cars overturned, smoke and dust filling the air. Already, the smaller bio-mutant was in a rampage, elongated arms bursting through storefronts as it roared in its rage. Farther down the street, the large one loomed over, casting its hulking form over the street as it swung its massive fists into nearby buildings.

And the Rogues would waste no more time. Nat was in the air first, foot extended in a blur of speed and fury, sending the little mutant flying off the ground. Its roar turned to a howl of pain.

The battlefield erupted into chaos as the Rogues clashed with the bio-mutants. Then, in an instant, she unleashed all that pent-up energy stored within her muscles as her feet crackled the air like thunder. The ground shook at every kick that came from her as craters opened on the surface where her foot hit. "Michael unleashed a storm of punches, his four arms moving in a blur. Each blow landed with crushing force, staggering the massive bio-mutant."

Out came Morgan, charging into the chaos, her razor-sharp nails outstretched to deadly points. She moved with a deadly grace, each slash tearing through the smaller mutants as if it was through tissue paper. Ryan and Ava fought as one. Ryan scanned with his thermal vision for weak points and oncoming dangers. Ava used her emotional powers to mislead and confuse the beasts, sending them into disarray.

Nate paired up against a smaller quicker bio-mutant with Morgan, yet both of them looked like toys beside it. It lashed out at them with horrifying speed, but Nate could dance around it thanks to his new reflexes. Quick, strong, he still pulled his punches-which was the weird part-subconscious, as if he was fighting a human thing beneath the grotesque monstrosity.

Nate clenched his fists, heart pounding. He could end this quickly. He knew that. But what if there was still someone in there, trapped?

Morgan sliced into the mutant's flesh with precision and ferocity. With every pass and dodge, gashes were deeper, with blood pouring and splashing onto the street. The sharp, hardened nails gleamed under the faint light of her moving figure as she moved with relentless focus. The mutant roared in agony but lashed out in desperation. Nate stepped in, blocking its retaliatory strikes across his forearms and counter attacking with powerful kicks that staggered the creature.

"Keep it up, Morgan!" Nate yelled, voice strained but determined as he moved in to cover for her. A mighty swing by the mutant just missed Morgan, but Nate met with a fist-to-fist blow against the creature. The impact sounded like a thunderclap, but Nate was weak; he felt conflicted still and could not push his heart beat high enough to give him an advantage over the mutant, and the resulting force sent him flying backward, to skid across the asphalt.

Meanwhile, Nat and Michael confronted the giant bio-mutant. Its guttural roars echoed across the battlefield as it swung its colossal arms in wide arcs, smashing nearby cars and cratering the ground. Darting in, Nat's legs were a blur of motion as she delivered precise kicks against its vulnerabilities. Each strike sounded like the crack of a gunshot, as the sheer force staggered the towering beast.

Michael doubled his mass, turning into a wrecking machine. His four arms pistoned into the mutant's torso, hammering it into submission. "Stay down, you ugly son of a—!" Michael roared, sending the creature to a dazed heap with an uppercut.

Michael stepped in from the left flank, cutting off the mutant's path as Nat darted in from the opposite side. While Nat's strikes distracted it from above, Michael came in low and heavy, his four arms alternating between hammer-like blows and crushing grapples. He kept shifting around the creature's legs, using his bulk to pin its movements, forcing the mutant to keep turning just to keep up.

The smaller bio-mutant, sensing its ally's struggle, turned once more to Morgan. A guttural snarl preceded the powerful lash that sent her flying into a crumpled heap against a wall. She hit the ground with a sickening thud and lay still.

CHAPTER 11: GLORY

"Morgan!" Nate screamed, his voice cracking at the sight of her lifeless form. His heart thundered harder and harder within his chest as his body filled with rage and despair. His blood coursed like fire within him as his skin flushed red from forcing his heart to pump harder, screaming with every fiber in his being to act, to shield the only family he had left.

The words were barely off the mutant's lips when, in a flash of crimson motion, Nate was ahead: easily avoiding the wild swing of the mutant as his senses were high from surging adrenaline. Planting his feet, he put all his strength into one blow: a devastating punch to its torso.

It came down like a shot, echoing across the battlefield, and his chest caved in. Nate's strike cut off the guttural roar abruptly as he crumpled lifeless to the ground, spewing blood and viscera onto the pavement—such was its power. As it wailed, Nate's eyes couldn't help but see a hurting human inside.

Nate still stood over the felled mutant, his chest heaving. As the adrenaline began wearing off, his legs buckled, and he fell to his knees, clutching at his chest. Sharp, searing pain radiated through him; his heart spasmed violently.

"Morgan's down, and Nate's in trouble!" Xavier yelled as he ran toward Nate, an edge of panic lacing his voice.

"Goddamn it, Nate!" Michael yelled, fighting with the larger mutant to buy Nat some time. She leapt high in the air, strong legs coiling before an axe kick smashed into the head of the mutant with a disastrous force that cleaved through the skull, the beast falling to the ground.

The crowd cheered, their phones capturing each second in this fight that mattered. In those seconds, the cloaked figures of the Rogues turned heroes for all to behold-identity aside and risks totally out of sight.

As Michael rushed to restrain Nate and help him breathe, Morgan stirred, coughing weakly. "I'm okay," she muttered, her voice strained. Nate, recovering slowly, looked around at his teammates, his mind swirling with a mix of pride, relief, and the lingering dread.

As the Rogues regrouped, Xavier smirked at the crowd's reaction. "Think we'll go viral for this one?"

Morgan, still wincing from her injuries, shot him a glare. "I'd rather not be trending under 'mutant menace.'"

"Y-you an-and me both," Ryan added, scanning the perimeter with his thermal vision. "But h-hey, at least we look good d-doing it."

"Speak for yourself," Ava quipped, wiping blood off her face. "I'm running on fumes."

"Save the chatter for later," Natalie interjected, her tone sharp but not unkind. "Let's get out of here before someone decides to call in reinforcements."

For a moment, the Rogues stood together, victorious but bruised, the weight of their lives on the run settling once again.

The dust settled, and the city was quiet for one second. Nate straightened himself over the fallen bio-mutant, his chest heaving while trying to catch his breath. His hands were shaking, but that was not out of exhaustion but because of the realization of what he'd just pulled.

Nate couldn't quite grasp what he had just done—or who that bio-mutant might have been. His mind swirled with unanswered questions and images of the creature's eyes, filled with anguish and something painfully human. Was it always like this? Were they all people once twisted into monsters for reasons he couldn't fathom? The victory was bittersweet.

The cheers of the crowd and the hum of recording devices were a distant murmur to Nate, his focus locked on Morgan as she stirred weakly.

For a fleeting moment, they stood as a team—bloodied but victorious. The grim reality of their lives would soon return, but here, in the fractured light of the broken cityscape, they were heroes.

Meanwhile, far from the wreckage, the sterile glow of monitors illuminated a high-tech government control room. Dozens of screens displayed grainy footage of the Rogues' fight, captured from every angle by drones hovering unnoticed in the chaos.

"This is the break we needed," an official said, leaning forward, his expression unreadable as the footage looped endlessly. On screen, Nate's punch shattered the bio-mutant's torso in slow motion, the raw power undeniable.

Another agent nodded, his tone clinical as he responded. "Their location is compromised. Inform Knoxx and Mammal—mobilize immediately."

"We have informed Knoxx and Mammal," said another. "They'll be spearheading a strike team to apprehend them. Orders are clear: take them alive if possible. Eliminate them otherwise."

The only sound in the room for a moment was a pen clicking as the Rogues on the screen tended to their wounded. Finally, a senior official spoke. His voice was ice cold, the best authority can get. "Position drones. Keep tabs on them. Attack first opportunity."

Debate erupted in nearby states once videos of the battle started hitting social media. Local news headlined footage, labeling the Rogues unofficial heroes for rescuing civilians and skillfully felling the bio-mutants.

Newspaper headlines ran as:

Meanwhile, national news told another story. Anchors spoke in alarm, labeling the Rogues as careless vigilantes. Some even said they were no better than the bio-mutants they fought, others a menace to public safety and promoter of anarchy. The public disagreed amongst themselves.

The Rogues' safe house was quiet now, the only lighting dim, filled with the soft murmur of exhaustion. Nate sat cross-legged beside Morgan, wrapping a bandage around her injured arm. His hands shook slightly; his face was a mask of guilt and shame.

"I froze," Nate muttered, his voice thick with regret. "If I hadn't hesitated, you wouldn't have gotten hurt."

Morgan smirked through the pain, her resilience shining through. "You're such a dumbass," Morgan said, smirking as she reached out to smack his shoulder. "Stop sulking. Let me clean this up before you make it worse."

She reached for the bandages from him and started dressing his wounds. Her fingers were so gentle. For moments, complete silence reigned while a shared smile, despite the hurt, released the weight of battle.

The others were around the room; Nat stood before them, her voice firm as she delivered their next briefing. "We move at dawn," she began, laying out a map of the surrounding area. "Lane's trail leads west. Reports say he's been hitting government operatives and leaving no survivors."

She broke off, her eyes scanning the team. "He's dangerous. Said to give people nightmares. If we catch him, we handle with care. Got it?"

The others muttered their agreement, but the mood was palpable.

Xavier sat beside Ava, his usually light nature subdued. As he fidgeted, nervous, Ava-an empath, placed a comforting hand on his hand. When their skin touched, Ava's smile faltered. A wave of darkness hit her-an overwhelming sense of murderous intent, something deeper, more sinister. She gasped, but quickly replaced the gasp with a reassuring smile.

She thought he had been through so much, attempting to brush the unease away. It's only trauma… right?

Still, her hand shook a little as she pulled it away. She said nothing about the sensation, though feelings lingered.

The weight of their growing notoriety hung heavy over the Rogues as they prepared for the coming day. Nate stared out a window, his mind racing with thoughts of the bio-mutant's human origins and his failure to act sooner. Morgan watched him from afar, sensing the turmoil he tried to hide.

In the darkness, forces beyond their understanding closed in: the government mobilizing, Knoxx mobilizing, Mammal mobilizing.

And in those quiet moments before dawn, Ava sat alone, the shaking of her hands a reminder of the darkness she'd felt from Xavier as she whispered to herself, barely audible, "Please…be…nothing".

Yet, deep inside, she couldn't get rid of the feeling that something was drastically wrong.

CHAPTER 12: SHADOWS

The Rogues were all gathered in their shabby hideout, still showing signs of wear and tear from their battle with the bio-mutants. A heavy silence filled the room as Ava, seated in front of her laptop, was telling them news that sent shivers down their spines.

"Lane's close," Ava said, her voice flat but tight. "There've been sightings in the old industrial district. The chatter's picking up."

Nate looked up from wrapping his hands, furrowing his brow. "Lane? The nightmare guy?"

Ava nodded. "Thus far, he has targeted government agents, but that's not what makes him dangerous. The way he fights. it's chaos. He doesn't care who gets caught in the crossfire."

Ryan leaned against the wall, his arms crossed. "H-he's a wild c-card. He doesn't trust anyone, nn-not even other m-mutants. If-if we're not careful, we'll be w-walking into a nightmare—l-literally."

Natalie stepped forward, her expression resolute. "We can't let someone like Lane stay out there unchecked. If the government doesn't get him, he'll keep killing, and that's only going to make things worse for all of us."

Michael popped his knuckles. "What's the game, then? Do we talk him down or take him down?"

"We'll try to talk," Natalie said matter-of-factly. "If he forces a fight, it's over as soon as it starts."

They were going small for this mission: directly Nate, Natalie, and Michael confronting Lane, while Ryan, Ava, Xavier, and Morgan kept their distance to provide information and backup if anything went wrong. It was a serious mission, and one could feel it in the air. "Stay sharp," Natalie warned, her tone unyielding. "Lane's not just dangerous-he's unstable. One wrong move, and it's over."

The abandoned factory loomed like some hulking shadow against the gray sky. It was a building shattered, panes broken and rusting on the outside-perfect for a person not to be seen. Nate approached with Natalie and Michael in tow, his footsteps echoing off the cracked pavement.

Inside, the air was thick with dust, and every groan of the floorboards resounded in the silence. Nate's heart was racing as they moved deeper into the building, his senses on full stretch for any sign of Lane. "Split up but stay in view," Natalie whispered, her voice barely audible. "We need to flush him out."

They fanned out, their movements almost ultra-slow and calculated. Nate could feel the weight of the silence weighing in on him, his heart pounding inside his chest. A sharp whistle sliced through the air—a blade, inches from his skull. Nate jerked back, heart hammering, just as a shadow peeled away from the darkness. Lane materialized from the darkness, his eyes burning like embers, the dim light dancing off the blade in his hand. He wasn't in a rush—because he didn't need to be. His face was hard, a mixture of anger and exhaustion etched into his features. He held a sword in one hand; the blade gleaming menacingly.

"You're either government dogs or fools," Lane growled, his voice low and venomous.

Natalie stepped forward, her hands raised in a gesture of peace. "We're neither. We're here to help you."

Lane let out a hoarse, husky laugh. "Help me? You're no different from those Bio-mutants you fought off yesterday. You are just as much government filth. "

Nate formed his fists, but made himself speak calmly. "We are not going to fight you, Lane. But if you won't listen-"

"I don't take orders from anyone!" Lane roared, the voice ringing off the factory walls. In an instant, he was off-and running his sword in high-speed arcs around himself.

He danced around him, his touches almost calculated and unceasing. Thin shafts of moonlight filtering through the factory's broken windows glinted off his blade as it cut through the air, just narrowly missing Nate's shoulder. Nate's heart thundered in his chest as his blood coursed harder, his powers overclocked. But even with his enhanced speed, Lane's precision forced him into a defensive dance.

Nate ducked under another swing, his back glancing off the rusted support beam. "This guy's relentless!" he hollered, trying to place himself out of reach of the others.

"Stay sharp!" Natalie yelped, launching herself forward. Her heavy legs propelled her in a vicious circle, coming full circle with a powerful kick directed at Lane's chest. But he sidestepped the blow with an unnatural ease, his shining eyes snapping onto her.

"You think brute force will save you?" Lane sneered. "We shall see how brave you are when faced with your worst nightmares."

The next moment, Lane fixed Natalie with a powerful glare. Frozen, her breath stopped, as Natalie collapsed to her knees, her breath coming in ragged, panicked gasps. Her hands clawed at her head, nails digging into her scalp as if trying to rip the images out. Whatever she saw—it was worse than death.

"Natalie!" Nate yelled, his voice hoarse with urgency. He flung himself toward her, but Lane was already wheeling toward his next victim.

Michael flung himself forward, arms outstretched. "Leave her alone!" he thundered in a voice like four growls.

Luminous eyes locked with his, and the response was instant. Michael's towering frame buckled as he stumbled backward, his eyes wide with terror. "No, no, no! It's everywhere-get it off!" he screamed, his arms thrashing wildly at invisible horrors.

Natalie had crumpled near a stack of rusted barrels, her body trembling, knees pressed into the dust-covered floor. Michael was farther off to the left, half-shielding her unintentionally, his massive form hunched in a panic-driven spasm beside a collapsed steel beam. Both were just barely in Nate's line of sight, their bodies twitching and straining as if each second stretched the nightmare longer.

Between gritted teeth, Natalie forced out a desperate warning. "Don't. look at his eyes!"

The words snapped Nate into action. He yanked his scarf up over his face, shielding his vision. Fighting blind wasn't ideal, but it was the only way to avoid falling victim to Lane's nightmarish power.

"Lane, this has to stop!" Nate yelled, his voice echoing in the cavernous factory. "We're not your enemies!"

Lane laughed, the tone cold and hollow. "You're all the same, government, Pinnacles, even your precious Rogues-blind to the truth. You want control. I won't let anyone control me!"

Lane's glare flickered—just barely—and his voice dropped, quieter but heavier. "I've seen what happens when people get too close. When they think they can fix me. It never ends well… for them." He took a slow breath, almost steady as he held his blade tighter. "The government didn't create me, but they made sure I stayed broken. Don't talk to me about CONTROL. I've been on the run for longer than you can imagine…'"

With that, Lane lunged, his blade flashing in the dim light. Nate ducked low, using the sound of Lane's movement to estimate his strikes. Every swing was a gamble, the razor-sharp edge of the blade slicing so close it whispered past his ears. Several strikes grazed Nate's arms and body.

Lane's attacks became more erratic, his frustration mounting. "You're just delaying the inevitable!" he spat, swinging wildly.

Nate took advantage of the opening. Fast, he darted in close and drove a solid punch into Lane's gut. The blow landed with a satisfactory thud, sending Lane stumbling back. But the rogue mutant recovered quickly, a dangerous smile curling his lips.

"You don't get it, do you?" Lane spat, blood trickling down from the corner of his mouth. "You're just as locked in as I am!"

The air around Lane had weighed down turgid with that depressing energy that seemed to seep into the edges of Nate's mind. Even with a scarf over the front of his eyes, the weight of Lane's power leaned on him, threatening to drag him under.

Before he could even think of it, a kunai buzzed past his face, cutting the scarf. As soon as the scarf slipped, exposing Nate's eyes, reality twisted into a surreal nightmare. In a fraction of a second, the dark, damp warehouse dissolved to become the hauntingly known vision of his childhood home. Twisting around him were the walls of the kitchen in some sort of a deformed carousel of memories.

Nate sat at the dinner table, stiff and unmoving. He couldn't speak; his throat felt so tight, as if words were stuck inside. Across the room stood his stepfather-a hulking monster of cruelty and rage.

The man's sharp, venomous voice boomed inside Nate's head, as if amplified by his own worst fears. "You think you're so big, huh? All that strength, and you can't protect your own family!"

The words cut more deeply than any blow ever could have. Nate's chest heaved, trying to move, to speak, to do anything, but his body wouldn't obey. His hands shook with his grip upon the edge of the table, knuckles white with effort.

Nate stood in terror, his stepfather beating into his mother and screaming at her. The cries for mercy pierced the air and keened in Nate's soul. Every stroke came down with the force of thunder, boom-booming into Nate's soul.

"Stop! Stop, please!" The constant noise prevented Nate from screaming, trapping his yell within his mind.

Tears blinded his vision, joining with the swirl of disorientation from the nightmare. The table beneath his hands was real; the air was heavy with the scent of his stepfather's cloying cologne and a faint tang of burnt dinner-pulled from memory, warped into this grotesque manifestation.

He had never felt in so long the bitter sensation of impotence: not impotent against a mutant, not against the government, but impotent in front of his past, which some sort of cruel magic trick produced by Lane had reduced to palpable fears.

The scene ripped backward, snapping into place like a broken cassette tape. Then it happened again. And again. Louder. Faster. The walls warped, the voices stretched, reality buckled under the weight of repetition. His stepfather's voice boomed over everything, drowning out his mother's desperate sobs. The impact of fists sounded like gunfire, over and over and over. Nate wanted to scream, but his voice was trapped in his chest—a prisoner in his own past.

"No." Nate finally whispered, his voice cracking under the strain. His body shook, trembling, as the nightmare pressed in around him, smothering and unceasing.

This isn't real. The thought came like a spark in the dark. His fear wasn't his master. Not anymore. He'd fought monsters, bio-mutants, and government agents. He wasn't that powerless boy anymore.

"Nate!" A voice-a faint, but familiar voice-bruised its way through the storm. It sounded far, far away-from another world.

"Nate, don't give in!" Natalie's voice boomed loud, raw with strain, yet unrelenting.

Like a lifeline, her words hacked through the haze. Gritting his teeth, Nate reached deep inside, forcing himself to focus. His heartbeat thundered in his ears as he pumped more blood, kindling again the fire within his veins.

Suddenly, Lane whirled his sword. Nate wove through the strike, quickness blurring. Dropping low, Nate unleashed a thunderous blow to Lane's midsection, sending him hurtling backward and crashing into the unforgiving stone wall with bone-jarring force. The impact was so devastating that Lane slumped to the ground, unconscious and utterly defeated.

In an instant, the oppressive energy was gone, leaving the factory silent except for the creaking and groaning of old machinery. Natalie and Michael regained consciousness, gasping, faces pale, bodies shaking. Nate stumbled over to them, his legs barely holding him up. "You guys okay?" he rasped, his voice hoarse.

Natalie nodded weakly, brushing dust from her knees as she stood. "Yeah. thanks to you."

Michael groaned, rubbing his temples. "Remind me to never look that guy in the eye again."

As they left the factory behind, Nate looked back to where Lane had lain inert. Something in the man's words stuck with him, nagging at the edges of his mind.

"He's dangerous," Natalie said finally, "But he's not wrong about everything."

Michael let his breath out in a hard whoosh. The resignation was thick in his voice. "If we're gonna survive, we need to be ready for more like him."

Nate didn't say a word. The idea that Lane's nightmare-inducing power was only the tip of the iceberg plagued him.

CHAPTER 13: THE HUNT

The Rogues slipped in and out of the shadows as they made their way from the hideout under the cover of darkness. The Rogues left Lane behind, unconscious but alive. Despite the urgency, Nate could not get the image of Lane's battered form, slumped against the factory wall, out of his mind. A part of him wanted to go back, but he knew it was a risk they couldn't afford.

Inside, the air was heavy with anticipation. Natalie paced across the room, her arms crossed, as her mind juggled every contingency plan they had in store for times like these. Ava moved quietly, taking care of Michael's injuries with her hands, gentle yet hasty. Morgan sharpened her nails on a whetstone in her corner, staring rigidly ahead of herself but somewhere distant, her very stance screaming preparedness for the fateful moment to arrive.

Having been positioned near the perimeter, Ryan entered abruptly, his face tight with tension. "W-we've got company. A-a lot of them. An-and they're c-closing in fast."

The group paused for a second before bursting into frenzied action. Xavier hunched over a map alongside Nate and sharply turned to him. "How many?"

Ryan just shook his head grimly. "To-too many t-to count. They're c-closing in from all sides."

Natalie stopped pacing, her hands now in fists. "It's them, isn't it?"

Ryan's eyes met hers, his confirmation of her worst fears. "T-the Animals. M-mammal's with them."

The room fell silent. The Animals were more than just a government strike force; they were a specialized unit of mutants, trained in tracking and capturing their own kind. Each member possessed unique abilities highly useful in hunting rogue mutants, and Mammal was a living legend among them. His senses, tuned to superhuman acuity, made him an unstoppable tracker, and his combat skills were second to none.

"We need to move—now," Natalie said, her voice slicing through the moment. "Gather only what you need and stick to the plan."

The Rogues were quick to scramble into action as they began stashing essentials in backpacks and duffle bags, weapons, supplies, and every trace of themselves being stowed or destroyed. During that flurry of action, Nate delayed, his eyes going to the door.

"What about Lane?" he asked, the words tight. "If they find him, they'll kill him-or worse." Nate hesitated. Lane was dangerous, but leaving him behind—alone, vulnerable—left a sour taste in his mouth. Was he really okay with that?

Morgan cut in before Natalie could answer, her voice sharp. "And if we stay, they'll do the same to us. We can't save everyone, Nate."

Nate fisted his hands, feeling the weight settle in. He knew she was right; it wasn't any easier to leave a man behind.

"Focus," Natalie said firmly, snapping his attention back. "We stick to the plan. We split up and rendezvous at the secondary hideout."

The Rogues had divided into two groups, their movements nearly simultaneous to devise a plan of escape. Natalie, Michael, and Ryan would take the north way out into a maze of alleys that made up the industrial district. Nate, Xavier, Ava, and Morgan would take their course to the south, where close-in sprawl gave much room to find their hideout for a possible re-conglomeration.

"Stay sharp, stay together, and don't take any unnecessary risks," Natalie instructed as her eyes swept over both groups. The sound of boots finally broke the thick silence of the night, moving, distant, as they came out of the building from different points. It was a hunt that had begun.

Suddenly, facing the grim reality of being surrounded, the Rogues swiftly moved through the hideout. It would appear Ryan's earlier warnings of the heat signatures closing in had been a bit too accurate.

Natalie's eyes darted around, scanning their surroundings. Footsteps echoed from every direction—there was no clear escape. A calculated trap. Her jaw clenched.

The sound of boots crashing through doors made her gut tighten. They weren't just outnumbered. They were hunted. Natalie's pulse quickened as her mind raced. "Damn it... They're everywhere."

Then she made the call. "Split up! Now! Give them too many targets to track!"

The team scrambled into action, began dividing out into smaller groups, and dashed toward the upper floors while others were into the labyrinthine corridors to spread out as much as possible, spreading their scents with the hope it might buy them enough time. That was when crashing glass and the clomping of heavy boots announced their pursuers had finally arrived.

The hideout wasn't big, but it was layered—tight hallways, creaky metal staircases, and rusted catwalks stretching between storage rooms stacked with forgotten crates. Exits led into the alley grid of the industrial district, but each group had to weave through different paths just to avoid overlapping. The place had once been a freight sorting hub, but now it felt like a trap about to snap shut.

Knoxx and his strike force of heavily armed soldiers and genetically enhanced operatives came through the shattered windows with precise ruthlessness that caught Xavier, Morgan, Michael, Ryan, and Ava off their guards.

Mammal intercepted Nate and Natalie as they attempted to regroup. His hulking frame filled the narrow hallway, his sharp claws gleaming in the dim light. The air grew thick with tension as he fixed his predatory gaze on them.

"I've been tracking you for miles," Mammal growled, his voice low and menacing. "You smell like fear... I like that."

Natalie was the first to lunge-powerful legs coiling, launching her forward; her kick connected with Mammal's chest and sent him stumbling back but not off his feet. Nate joined in, his fists a blur as he pushed his blood to its limits. The precision, the ferocity with which the grim knowledge that Mammal had, the relentless strength and endurance of his namesake, met them.

Nate's punches landed like gunshots, each one shaking Mammal's hulking frame, but the beast didn't buckle. Mammal grinned through the pain, swiping out with claws that Nate barely dodged. Mammal's claws raked across Nate's ribs, tearing through flesh like wet paper. A line of white-hot pain erupted, blood already soaking into his shirt.

"You're quick," Mammal acknowledged with an icy smile. "You think you're staying one step ahead, but this is just procrastination."

Nate clamped down on his molars, running hot with sweat. "I procrastinate-I complete."

And with that said, as Mammal sprang anew, Natalie's kick sent Mammal crashing through a doorway, deeper into the structure. She didn't waste a second. 'Move!' she barked, rallying the others.

"No way," Nate shot back. "We do this together."

Through the wreck, the two Rogues hounded Mammal relentlessly.

Michael dove for cover, throwing Ava and Ryan behind an overturned table. "We gotta get outta here!" he yelled, showing his fists ready for a fight. "We have company coming in hot!"

Nodding, Xavier hunched nearby. His tensed, rubber-like material composed his body, making him resilient but far from invulnerable. He didn't want to be hit directly. The chaos happening now around them made every step taken a calculated risk.

Morgan reacted first. Her long nails gleamed in the gloom as she sliced through an oncoming soldier's body armor with surgical precision. "Clear a path!" she yelled, swift and sure in her movements.

"S-south exit!" Ryan shouted while his thermal vision picked up multiple heat signatures closing in on them. "It's our best shot."

The group moved as one tack, dodging and weaving through the debris-littered hallways. Knoxx's team was relentless, firing suppressive shots to pin them down. Morgan took point, carving through the obstacles in their path, while Michael followed suit, providing cover and the occasional dead soldier who got too close.

Ava followed behind, her empathic senses strained to track the chaotic emotions around her. She would yell out directions when danger was near, instinct keeping them a step ahead of their pursuers.

As they closed in on the exit, he lost his footing, catching himself up against a broken support beam. His breathing was in short, ragged gasps-the tension and exertion wearing on him. One soldier marked the momentary lapse and set his sights on the target.

"Xavier, down!" Ava exclaimed.

He reacted slowly; a volley of shots tore through the spot he stood. Xavier twitched with each projectile that hit him, his body lurching. His lips parted—maybe to scream, maybe to curse—but no sound came out.

CHAPTER 14: XAVIER

The building was an explosion of noise: gunfire ringing off walls, shouting and screams, the debris clotted in a dim light bleeding through shattered windows. The Rogues moved like a machine—sharp, calculated, each fighting in sync as they battled Knoxx and his strike force.

Bullets whizzed towards Xavier, strike force rigging an attack to get him out of the way as fast as possible. His rubber-like body absorbed the impact and sent the projectiles careening every which way. Stray bullets hit several soldiers, falling to the ground with moans of pain.

Xavier, still reeling from the chaotic fight, shouted, "Friendly fire! Watch your aim, dumbasses!" He ducked behind a concrete pillar, his chest heaving.

One figure stood defiant amid chaos, uncaring about the bullets that ricocheted and the battlefield crumbling Knoxx. The moment Michael saw him, he knew that this giant mutant was a name whispered in fear in circles of reavers.

"That's Knoxx," Michael muttered to the team, his voice taut. "Be ready."

Knoxx's mutant power was as fearsome as his reputation: he could grow and reshape his bones into weapons, shields, and impenetrable armor. His every movement was a display of controlled power. His tactical gear was well-worn but functional, molded around the jagged protrusions of his natural weaponry.

Standing as tall as Michael, Knoxx was an intimidating monster. His huge bone shield, wide as a car door, glistened in the harsh light of the fluorescent above, edges sharpened to a deadly sheen. Bone claws extended from his hands, each hooked like a scythe, ready to tear through all-anything or anyone-standing in his way.

Knoxx was dark of complexion, scarred from a myriad of battles-the faint scars adding to the terror in his features. Cold calculation seemed to fill his gaze as his eyes locked onto each Rogue, seeming to size up the weak link.

"One chance," Knoxx snarled gruffly. "Step down or you will beg to have."

Michael simply clenched his fists and charged. "Ain't gonna happen."

"Your funeral," he said, diving.

They took full advantage of the momentary confusion. Morgan sprang forward with feline grace, her nails deep into the soldiers. She cut with surgical precision, her movements exact and to the mark. Michael, the tall and resilient tower, continued his battle with Knoxx. Every punch he threw shook the room and made Knoxx shift defensively.

"You think you're tough?" Knoxx snarled, his voice dripping with disdain as he blocked Michael's next punch with a bone-forged shield. "I've killed mutts twice your size."

"Yeah? You'll need twice the brains to keep up," Michael shot back, ducking under Knoxx's blade-like bone arm and slamming a hammer-like fist into his side.

The room they fought in was a half-destroyed warehouse floor, cluttered with crates, toppled shelving, and scattered debris. A support beam had collapsed near the center, splitting the room into two jagged halves. Michael and Knoxx circled each other near the beam while the others darted through broken walkways and cover lining the perimeter. Lighting was scarce—flickering strips above cast more shadows than clarity.

The other soldiers did not go down without a fight. Ryan and Ava moved like clockwork, their teamwork giving the enemy no time to breathe. He yelled out enemy positions, his active thermal vision fitting just perfectly in the smoky surroundings: "Two behind the crates on your left!"

Ava nodded, sidestepped, then leaned into the guard, filling the soldier's mind with jumbled confusion and icy fear; his aim fumbled, finger hesitation stopping them from pulling the trigger. Xavier quickly used the short-lived moment of confusion: one guard had the rifle tugged right out of his grasp and turned back at him. The shot fired and sent him tumbling down.

Michael and Morgan continued to press their attack against Knoxx. Morgan avoided his wild swings. Her razor-sharp nails raked across his bare arms and legs. In a rage, Knoll let out a loud bellow. A wave of projectiles sliced through the air, deadly javelins of bone. A nick in Michael's arm drew blood, but he ignored the pain, pressing his attack as another impaled into Morgan's leg.

Growling, he attacked, dodging another flying bone blade. He caught Knoxx in a grapple, lifting him off the ground. Before slamming him down, Knox grew more jagged bones from his body that stabbed into Michael as they both went down with a thunderous crash. Knoxx groaned, stunned, but still tried to rise. Morgan was on him in an instant, her nails slicing cleanly across his chest. Blood sprayed as Knoxx stumbled back, his breathing in ragged gasps.

Michael fought through the pain and gave the final blow-a powerful punch into Knoxx's jaw. The strike shattered bone and sent Knoxx crumpling to the floor, unconscious.

The dust had finally settled; the group turned to the bodies of the felled soldiers and Knoxx splayed across the floor.

The Rogues moved back into a line. It was a tight and economical movement now. "We have to make sure Nat and Nate are okay," Morgan said, wiping some blood off her face. She then glanced at Xavier, leaning against the wall, not facing them.

"X-xav, y-you good?" Ryan asked, sounding apprehensive.

Forced to nod, Xavier cast an imitation grin. "Yeah, catching my breath."

While the others worked to secure their escape, Xavier stayed behind. His gaze settled on the sprawled figure of Knoxx splayed across the floor. But as he stared at the unconscious mutant, something about the stillness triggered a deeper, older memory—one he'd buried long ago. The room blurred around him, and the sounds of withdrawal and firing grew to be far away in that hollow echo. His face darkened, and shades danced across his features as a memory that he willed not and did not invite.

It hit like a gut punch. The scene unfolded in vivid detail: a sunlit park, warm and serene. Xavier sat on a weathered bench, his legs crossed, a faint smile playing on his lips. Beside him was a boy-no older than ten-his slight frame all but bouncing with excitement. The boy had bright, curly blonde hair, blue eyes, and a birthmark that streaked across his left temple. His face was open and eager, an innocence shining from him like the dappled sunlight through the trees. "It's so cool meeting someone like me!" the boy burst out, his voice full of wonder. Grinning, he stretched his cheek unnaturally far, the skin pulling like rubber before snapping back into place. "See? I can do this! What about you?"

Xavier chuckled softly, though the warmth never reached his eyes. "I've got a trick or two," he said, his voice calm, measured.

The boy beamed, his enthusiasm unbridled. "You're awesome!" he declared, swinging his legs under the bench. He looked at Xavier with pure admiration, completely unaware of the storm brewing behind those composed eyes.

The boy smiled at Xavier, trusting. Completely unaware.

Then—sharp gasp. A moment of struggle. Then silence. The memory cracked like shattered glass.

The park was gone, the sun, the laughter. Now, the quiet of the woods muffled and shrouded the world. There was only the crunch of leaves as Xavier stood over a deep grave, well hidden beneath the thick canopy of trees. The boy's lifeless body lay within; his once bright eyes were now dull and sightless, his small frame shrunken as if vitality had been drained from him.

The grave was shallow, dug in haste, and it reeked of earth and decay. Xavier stood without movement; his face was a mask of cold detachment. His shadow loomed over the boy. The sun was no longer warm, but stark and accusing. Xavier's hands hung at his sides, clenched into fists, the slightest of trembles there to show a storm of suppressed emotion.

He looked upon the grave, an eternity weighing on his shoulders. For a fraction of a second, his fingers twitched—then stilled. If there was guilt, it had long since died with the boy. And yet, without regret, not even a trace of relief crossing his features-just emptiness.

CHAPTER 15: THE REAL ENEMY

Nat and Nate dragged the Mammal deeper into the collapsing structure, using the wreckage to separate him from his allies. Dust rose everywhere, adding an extra load of emotion to any sound. Acute senses, Nat was now leading the fight, observing each move the Mammal would make as he was getting stronger with every pass of time.

The Mammal is this giant amalgamation of nature's most-feared beasts, a high behemoth created from raw, wild fury. Taller than a full ten feet, his body was a dream come true-pressed muscles, thick sinew, flesh formed for little else but brutal combat. The fur stood thickened and scaly, made of hide tanned so it hardened almost to leather. Every inch of his body was a grotesque patchwork of countless beasts, a walking monument to the predators he embodied.

Great curving horns sprout from his skull, like a ram's, their edges rough and apparently whetted against stone; and from below these a pair of massive tusks thrust forward sideways, as if a bull elephant had gone mad, the surfaces of yellowed ivory stained and chipped from countless battles. Between these horns and tusks, a pair of sharp, branching antlers branch out like the crown of some fantastic elk.

A thick unruly mane runs down his neck and shoulder, a wild cascade of fur merging into the muscular contours of his back. His tail is long and whiplike, with a tuft of coarse fur at the end, swishing with an unnerving deliberation.

His limbs are hugely oversized, and the Mammal's clawed hands can easily crush concrete. Every single one of them shone as bright as obsidian, formed in wickedly sharp shapes for flesh tearing. His feet look like the predator's paws with hooves from some kind of mighty ox, and stomp firmly enough to create enormous craters.

But despite the terror of his beastly appearance, it was the eyes of the Mammal that showed unnerving intelligence. Gleaming with a calculating awareness, they betrayed the human mind trapped within the monstrous form. His movements, though heavy and deliberate, were unnervingly precise, each step and strike executed with the strategy of a seasoned hunter.

"Stay on his blind spots," she ordered, her voice firm. "Don't let him corner you."

Nate nodded, and his chest heaved as if his Heart Engine chugged in action. The Mammal snarled, and the towering figure crouched low, ready to pounce into action.

So, Nat struck first, surging forward with the most speed and power she could muster. Her kick landed on the Mammal's ribs, and the louder-than-a-gunshot echo of it reverberated across the empty room. The Mammal hunched over but was up again in a trice, swinging his fist covered in debris towards her. Nat ducked just in time, sending him backward with a spinning kick.

In an instant, Nate seized the opening and plunged deep into the Mammal's torso, flying in smoothly, sure of his precision, a bit too sure and hard enough to crush stones, but for the second time, the mammal was really resilient. All Nate could produce was superficial cuts, using his speed and strength in his attacks.

The Mammal roared, swiping at Nate with his claws. Nate narrowly avoided the attack, his body twisting in midair as he rolled to safety. Nat moved in to cover him, her powerful legs propelling her into a leaping kick aimed at the Mammal's head. The blow landed with a sickening crunch, dazing the creature momentarily.

"Keep pushing!" Nat shouted, sweat dripping down her face. "We've got him!"

But the Mammal wasn't through. He snarled gutturally and swung his paw in a circle, grasping a gigantic piece of debris and slinging it at them. Barely, Nate had time to shield himself. The impact threw him across the floor.

Nat used his preoccupation and nailed him with blow after blow: bone-crushing kicks into limbs. Her final blow at last hit his arm, breaking the bone beneath that thick hide of his. The Mammal whined in pain; his gestures became wild. Every blow sent gusts of winds that barreled towards Nate putting him off balance.

"Stay down!" Nat yelled - words that almost seemed to inject more anger inside him.

Mammal launched himself into Nate, claws flashing through the air. Nate tried to dodge, but it was quicker than he thought. Natalie was quicker, though-she intercepted the Mammal with a powerful kick to his side as his claws barely swiped across Nate's chest, sending Nate folding backwards.

The Mammal was now facing towards Natalie. She was mid-air, fully committed to her attack. The Mammal caught her by the arm, his grip a vice of pure muscle. Then—before she could react, he wrenched her downward and drove a punch straight into her gut. The force sent her flying, but her arm... didn't follow. The sickening tear of flesh and sinew filled the air as her limb was ripped clean from her shoulder, still clutched in the Mammal's massive hand. He hastily advanced towards Natalie to end her life.

Nat screamed as the Mammal knelt down to touch her. This is it. Blood streamed out of her wounds, staining the floor beneath her.

"Nat!" Nate hollered, his voice all wobbly with panic. He struggled to his feet and his Heart Engine blazed back to life as he charged into the fray.

The Mammal spun just in time, his eyes widening as Nate was already barreling towards him. Picking up speed with every step, Nate slammed into the side of the Mammal's head with a vicious dropkick that shattered one of its horns and sent him crashing into the wall.

Nat doubled onto her knee, clutching her shoulder. "Finish it, Nate!" she wheezed out between pained gasps as blood slicked her clothing.

Beyond reason now, the Mammal let out a feral growl and charged at Nate in a blind rage. Nate met him head-on, their fists meeting with a resounding crash that shook the entire room.

The room was in shambles, shattered remnants everywhere. Nate and the Mammal stood facing each other. Their fight boiled into a mad display of tussling bodies, raw power, and furor. He breathed in ragged gasps, his leaden limbs aching with weariness. The Heart Engine drummed in his chest, every pulsation a wrenching mixture of ache and adrenaline.

The Mammal snarled, towering over Nate, his claws swiping inches from his face as he dodged the air humming around the attacks with deadly force. Nate countered with a powerful uppercut, his fist driven with enhanced strength into the Mammal's jaw, and sent him stumbling backward into a wall.

"Get Nat out of here!" Nate yelled the moment he saw the others enter.

Morgan and Ryan barely had time to move, but they hurried. Nat slumped against the wall, her arm dangling loose as blood puddled under her. Morgan and Ryan raised her gently despite weak protests.

"Don't let her bleed out!" Nate yelled back over his shoulder as he refocused his attention on the Mammal.

"We've got her!" Morgan assured him, her tone clipped with urgency.

"We can help." Michael yelled as he approached.

The mammal turned towards Michael and started sprinting on all fours towards the group. Nate caught the Mammal by his tail and slung him backwards away from the group.

"Get out of here, I got this.," Nate yelled, revving up once more. His skin became brighter red and his muscles and veins became more defined. The Mammal lunged at Nate with a cannon of a punch, Nate countered it with a blow of his own that sent a gust of winds that barreled towards Micheal putting him off balance.

Michael hesitated for a moment before ordering everyone else to move Nat and get to the rendezvous point.

The Mammal roared in anger, his eyes aflame as he charged at Nate. His great claws swiped in a wide arc, but Nate ducked under the attack, his movements running on pure instinct. He spun on his heel and delivered a brutal punch to the Mammal's ribs; the force cracking the bone.

The Mammal growled in pain, but it only seemed to fuel his rage. He grabbed a chunk of rubble from the ground and hurled it at Nate, who barely dodged in time. The projectile smashed into the wall behind him, sending shards of concrete flying.

"You're slowing down," Nate taunted, though the strain in his voice betrayed his own exhaustion.

But the Mammal had nothing to say to that, leaping forward and sending Nate tumbling to the ground. It shook his bones, and Nate barely rolled clear before the Mammal's claws tore through the earth where a second before he'd lain.

Nate struggled to his feet, his body protesting in a screaming litany of pains. He heard Morgan and Ryan's retreat as they moved farther and farther away with Nat. It weighed upon him that the fight was done and he was all alone.

The Mammal lurched again, a guttural growl welling up from deep within his chest. Nate sidestepped his attack and delivered a series of quick blows against the creature's torso, each strike a desperate attempt to create an opening. But the Mammal was resilient beyond his expectations.

The mutant countered with a backhanded swipe, his claws raking across Nate's chest. Nate grunted in pain as the force sent him skidding backward, his feet barely finding purchase on the crumbling floor. Blood seeped from the gashes, but he refused to let it slow him down.

"I'm not done yet," Nate muttered through gritted teeth, his Heart Engine pounding in his ears.

He charged forward, confronting the Mammal head-on. Their fists connected in a bone-shaking encounter that shook the room. The force alone shattered what remained of the walls. Nate ground his teeth as his strength failed him.

But the Mammal was tireless, its anger growing hotter. He slashed with his claws wildly. Nate dodged and parried, barely escaping each blow, but knowing he couldn't continue this much longer.

With a last heave of desperation, Nate spun a kick into the Mammal's knee and watched the creature buckle. It was enough to give him the time he needed to jump into the air and slam his knee into the Mammal's chest, sending him flying backward into the ground.

For a few moments, the room was silent but for the heavy breathing of the two combatants as they stared at each other.

"Not bad," the Mammal growled, a twisted grin forming on his face. "But you're running out of steam."

Nate didn't respond. His heart was pounding, his body on the verge of collapse, but he would not give up. Not yet.

The Mammal was rising, its giant body towering over Nate once more. The fight was far from over.

His body shrieked in protest, his muscles strained against the immense effort. He knew he couldn't keep this up much longer. In one last, desperate spurt, he reached out and clutched the Mammal's jaws, holding them apart by force.

The Mammal was thrashing about like a mad thing, his huge hands clawing at Nate. Nate avoided them but as he staggered back, Mammal lunged his massive jaws towards Nate. He barely caught his teeth before they snapped him in half. Nate struggled to keep them open as the mammal pushed Nate backwards with every step. Taking all the remaining strength Nate had, he pushed his hand through the top of his teeth and his foot down on the bottom of his teeth, piercing his own foot. In an instant Nate pushed with all of his might breaking the Mammals Jaw wide open.

The Mammal went back into his stuttering gait, like an animal wounded, bleeding from the mouth as he went down with a thud to the ground, unconscious.

Nate fell back against the wall, chest heaving, trying to catch his breath. Blood streamed down him and onto the floor. Relief washed over him. Briefly.

Dust from the destroyed wall whirled through the air, coloring the devastated area with shades of gray. Nate lunged forward weakly; every breath was hard, blood running from cuts over his face and arms. Fighting with Mammal had taken all of his strength. The sputtering of his weak Heart Engine could barely keep his shattered body upright.

"Xavier?" Nate's voice was hoarse, little more than a whisper. Relief and confusion fought in his head. "What are you-?"

Xavier strode right past him, silent, his eyes fixed on the Mammal's prone body.

"Xavier, stop. I don't know if he's down for good." Nate called, his voice tight, a step forward.

Xavier knelt beside the Mammal, his teeth sharpening into fangs and, in an instant, plunged his teeth deep into the neck of the creature before him, drinking in its life force.

As the gigantic frame deflated, before Nate, the Mammal's body shriveled, while Xavier's grew monstrous. The muscles of Xavier ballooned, his body now completely abandoning all resemblance to what it once looked like, closer to the animal he had transformed from the Mammal. Nate watched in horror as what he saw materialized. All over his body, bone plates began forming, like armor atop this large body of his.

"Xavier, stop!" Nate shouted, his voice filled with desperation.

"You've always been so naive," Xavier sneered, his voice dripping with disdain as he towered over The Mammal's crumpled form. "Thinking you can play hero to the pathetic humans. Do you really believe they'll ever accept us? Mutants won't be tortured and enslaved any longer. Not by them. Not by anyone." His eyes burned with conviction, his words laced with venom. "There will never be an equal world for us unless we make one. And that world? It won't be built by weakness. It'll be forged by power."

Xavier turned to face him, his expression cold and detached, Xavier grew massive bone knuckles around his fist as he stared at Nate. "This is for the best," Xavier said quietly, his voice heavy with something between regret and resolve.

Before Nate could even register the movement, Xavier was already there—a blur of monstrous speed. The punch connected like a cannon blast, an eruption of force that caved in Nate's torso. For a split second, there was nothing. Then—agony. Blood gushed from the cavernous hole where flesh should have been. His body was weightless, flung backward until he crashed against the crumbling wall, his vision darkening at the edges. Above him, Xavier loomed over him, staring at him with his eyes full of dread.

Slumped against the jagged wall, Nate's head slung to the side, his body fought for consciousness. Blood trickled down the temple, mixing into the dirt and rubble below him. There was little rise to his chest; his breathing was shallow.

Xavier stood over him, the distant look in his eyes devoid of warmth and camaraderie that they may have shared. Instead, Xavier mirrored something cold in his eyes—a quiet detachment that chilled the room more than the succeeding silence.

Reaching down, Xavier grasped Nate's wrist in his hand; the hold was firm without being cruel. For one second, he seemed to hesitate. The faint, fading pulse beneath his fingers. A tether to something he did not want to sever.

But the moment passed.

The heartbeat beneath his hand weakened, each beat further apart than the last, until it stopped. Xavier exhaled a soft sigh, shoulders sagging as he released Nate's wrist to fall limply on the ground. He turned away, heavy footsteps against the broken floor.

"You disgust me," Xavier muttered. In one swift move, he propelled himself into the air, his departure whipping the air across the room.

The dust settled, silence once again wrapping the space. Nate slumped against the cool wall, abandoned in the shade.

Everything in the room seemed to hold its breath.

And then, gentle, almost insensible, rose from Nate's chest.

His heart struggled, stuttered, as if uncertain.

Thump.

One beat, soft but sure. Nate's eyes slowly opened. Then closed again.

Thump-thump

INTERLUDE:
THE PINNACLES

CHAPTER 16: DOWNED

The roar of the jet engines filled the cargo hold—a deep, relentless hum that vibrated through the metal floor and into the bones of everyone onboard. The Pinnacles sat in strained silence, each soldier sharpening their focus for the mission ahead. Their destination: State 9. War-torn, unstable, crawling with rogue mutants. No one spoke. Not over the noise. Not over the weight. Near the rear of the hold, one figure sat alone. Back straight. Arms crossed. Eyes half-lidded in thought. The others didn't bother him. They never did. He had that reputation—quiet, ruthless, untouchable. But the arrogance? That was just a mask.

His name had once been Castor. A boy who dreamed of touching the stars—not metaphorically. He wanted to fly, to soar through the clouds and beyond. When his mutation first showed, light bulbs flickered when he passed. The air around him would sizzle faintly, crackling with solar energy as his body pulled in warmth from the sky.

It started as something beautiful—something that felt like it belonged in a comic book. But wonder didn't last long. The government came swiftly. No warnings. No choices. They told his parents it was for his safety. Promised them opportunity. Promised Castor a future. And then they took him. He never saw his family again.

What followed didn't feel like training. It felt like dismantling. They stripped him of his name, his softness, and slowly, his humanity. Compassion was ground out of him like rust. Weakness was scorched away. Every lesson was a punishment. Every breakthrough, a threat. They told him mutants had killed his parents—fed him the lie with a steady hand and a straight face. The rage that followed made him obedient. It made him useful. They stopped calling him Castor and gave him a new name, one brighter and cleaner—something the world could worship, something that sounded like control.

He sat in silence now, eyes fixed on the floor of the cargo hold, letting the engine noise rattle around in his chest. He didn't speak to the others. Didn't need to. None of them dared approach him during the pre-mission flight. Not when he looked like this—tense, unreadable, like a solar flare trapped just beneath the skin. The armor of arrogance wasn't about confidence. It was a lid. It kept the real heat buried. Inside, the boy was still burning.

The others only knew what they'd been told. They saw a symbol, a living deterrent, a sun god wrapped in government colors. They saw strength, precision, power. They didn't know the cost. They didn't know that somewhere, deep under the protocols and programming, Castor was still alive. Still waiting. Still holding the weight of all that loss.

He shifted slightly in his seat, letting the dim red light catch his face. His eyes opened, steady and calm, but behind them was an inferno that never stopped churning. The others only knew him by the name he was given.

Apollo.

Reptile, a towering figure whose reptilian features made him a grotesque blend of man and beast, leaned heavily against the metal wall. His skin, covered in jagged, emerald scales, glinted faintly in the low light. Razor-sharp teeth protruded from his mouth, and his elongated claws tapped rhythmically on the steel floor—a telltale sign of his rising agitation. His yellow eyes flickered over his teammates, watching, always watching.

Tress, with her forest-green eyes and wild, vine-like hair that moved as though alive, sat cross-legged on a crate. Her fingers brushed absently over the strands that coiled and writhed around her like snakes, a physical manifestation of her constant vigilance. She had always been the team's moral compass, the quiet anchor that kept them grounded, even as the world around them descended into chaos.

Atlas was a towering brute, his tan skin stretched over rippling muscles that seemed forged for battle. Tattoos marked his arms and chest like a record of past conflicts, while his short black hair and perpetually gritted teeth added to his intimidating presence. His dark eyes were sharp and unwavering, reflecting a seriousness that left little room for humor. Dressed in scarred tactical gear built for war, Atlas moved with deliberate purpose, every step radiating the quiet menace of a man ready to crush anyone in his path.

Tremor, jittering with barely contained energy, sat beside her. His heavily muscled form was encased in tactical armor designed to withstand the quakes he could unleash at a moment's notice. His fingers drummed incessantly on his knee, a staccato beat that betrayed his nerves. Sweat beaded on his brow, but his jaw was set in determination.

Across the cabin, Angel sat apart from the others, his pristine white wings folded neatly behind him like a shield of serenity. His tactical suit, a blend of ivory and silver, hugged his form, light yet durable, tailored for aerial combat. He adjusted his gloves, his face a mask of calm amidst the rising storm, eyes closed as if in silent prayer.

In the corner, Aero lounged with a deceptive ease. His sleek, yellow-and-black wing suit clung to his lean frame, every muscle coiled and ready despite his relaxed posture. His dark skin shimmered in the light filtering through the jet's small windows, but his amber eyes were sharp, scanning each of his comrades with practiced scrutiny. Aero's ability to manipulate the wind had saved them countless times, and his confidence was palpable.

Apollo, the self-proclaimed solar titan and their begrudging leader, was now absent from the cabin. Instead, he soared alongside the jet, his blue and red suit glowing under the sunlight like a celestial beacon. His suit was lined with thousands of miniature solar panels that helped absorb and store his solar energy. He used this energy to fly using miniature jets built into his feet, wrists, and palms. His blonde hair shimmered like a halo, but the arrogance in his piercing blue eyes undercut any resemblance to a savior. His voice crackled over the comms, smugness dripping from every word.

Tress broke the quiet first, her voice cutting through like a whip. "Let's get one thing clear—we're not the first ones sent to handle this mess." She leaned forward, her green eyes darting between her teammates. "And judging by the radio silence, the last team didn't fare so well."

Angel's wings shifted behind him, feathers brushing the cabin wall as he frowned. "How many?" His voice was calm, but held a note of apprehension.

Tress crossed her arms. "Five. Strike force agents sent days ago. They haven't checked in since."

"Any idea who they sent?" Aero asked, leaning back against the wall, his sharp amber eyes narrowed.

Tress nodded, her vine-like hair curling slightly as she spoke. "Scarlet was one of them. Redhead. She's got a nasty ability to manipulate blood—short range, but effective. One wrong move, and she can stop your heart without blinking."

"Scarlet?" Aero raised an eyebrow. "Yeah, that's a cheerful addition."

"Then there's Nosey," Tress continued, ignoring Aero's sarcasm. "A tracker. His sense of smell is so sharp he can pinpoint someone from miles away."

"Great," Tremor muttered, his fingers drumming nervously on his leg. "We'll just add 'sniffed out by a government bloodhound' to the list of ways we might die today."

Tress's gaze darkened. "And Coil. A mutant with a spine that can stretch and snap like a whip. He's brutal—uses it to strangle, impale, whatever gets the job done."

Reptile growled low in his throat. "That one's bad news. Fought beside him once. Ruthless bastard."

"Don't forget Maxxy," Tress added. "Martial artist. Spiked knees, elbows, and fists. Not just enhanced strength—he's tactical, precise. Hits like a freight train."

"And Glade," Angel said softly, his brow furrowing. "The cold-blooded one."

Tress nodded. "he's a double threat. Can freeze anything or anyone on contact, and his water jets lets him freeze people solid from a distance."

Reptile's claws scraped against the steel floor. "Five agents like that, and they still vanished?"

Tress hesitated. "Exactly." Her fingers tightened into fists. "And that's not even the worst part."

Aero raised an eyebrow. "Oh, good. What's worse than five top-tier agents getting erased?"

She took a slow breath before speaking. "There's a rumor about an unidentified mutant leading the uprising. No files. No known powers. No one even knows what they look like."

A heavy silence fell over the cabin.

"Wait," Tremor said, frowning. "You're saying we're flying blind?"

Tress nodded. "I'm saying we don't know what we're walking into."

Apollo's voice crackled over the comms, interrupting the conversation. "Sounds like they couldn't handle the heat. Don't worry—I'll clean up their mess." His arrogance practically bled through the earpiece. "You know, if I wasn't stuck babysitting you lot, we'd have been done with this mission already," Apollo taunted, his voice tinny but unmistakably condescending.

Reptile's claws dug into the metal wall, leaving faint grooves. His voice, a guttural growl, rumbled through the cabin. "Not all of us pretend to be gods, Apollo. Some of us know the value of teamwork."

Before the comms could devolve into further bickering, Tress intervened, her voice cutting through the tension like a blade. "Enough," she snapped, eyes like green fire. "We've got a mission. State 9 is in chaos, and we're here to end it. We do this together, or we don't do it at all."

The cabin fell into a tense silence, the weight of her words pressing down on them. Tremor muttered something under his breath, glancing anxiously at the loading ramp. Angel merely inclined his head, acknowledging the truth in Tress's statement, while Aero's mouth quirked in a fleeting, wry grin.

Suddenly, the aircraft jolted violently, throwing them against their restraints. The shriek of metal tearing filled the cabin, and red emergency lights flared to life. Outside, the rhythmic beat of gunfire clattered against the hull, tracer rounds streaking past the windows in fiery arcs. Below, the twisted remnants of State 8 loomed—a wasteland littered with burned-out vehicles and skeletal buildings. White-eyed soldiers surged from the shadows, their movements unnervingly mechanical, their weapons a hodgepodge of scavenged armaments.

"We're taking fire!" the pilot's panicked voice crackled through the speakers, barely audible over the din. "Brace for impact!"

Apollo's voice followed, sharp and commanding. "I see them. Hold the damn jet steady."

But the warning came too late. Another salvo of bullets pierced the fuselage, and the aircraft began a nauseating spiral, engines sputtering as smoke filled the cabin.

"Brace yourselves!" Reptile bellowed, wrapping his massive arms around Tress and Tremor. His scales dug into their suits, anchoring them as the jet bucked wildly. Atlas grew massive muscle fibers around himself creating a shield. Aero and Angel, reacting instinctively, flung themselves from the cargo bay, wings snapping open to catch the turbulent air.

Outside, Apollo was a streak of blue light. He zipped beneath the plummeting jet, his hands pressing into the metal as solar energy surged through his suit. With a herculean effort, he slowed its descent just enough for the remaining team members to leap free before the aircraft crashed into the ground, a fiery blossom of smoke and shrapnel.

The Pinnacles regrouped in the smoking crater left by the jet's crash, their bodies bruised but intact. Apollo landed heavily beside them, his suit scorched, his face twisted in irritation. He surveyed the treeline, where the white-eyed soldiers emerged once more, their rifles leveled, their faces blank slates of inhuman obedience.

Apollo's jaw clenched, his fists sparking with residual energy. "Humans," he spat, eyes glowing with a fierce, golden light. "Puny. Weak. Insolent."

Before anyone could stop him, Apollo launched himself forward, a blur of motion that left the air crackling in his wake.

Apollo was a force of nature, almost godlike.

He ripped through the first soldier's chest with a single punch, a shockwave splitting the man's ribs outward like broken twigs. His solar beams didn't just incinerate bodies—they cooked them from the inside out, skin bubbling, eyes liquefying before they collapsed into charred husks.

He grabbed another by the throat, his grip so tight it crushed the man's windpipe into pulp before hurling him into his comrades like a human cannonball. Limbs tore free from sockets as Apollo ripped through them, each strike sending bodies flying in gory arcs.

The battlefield stank of burning flesh and ruptured organs. Blood sizzled as it hit his super-heated suit. He barely noticed. Limbs flew as his fists struck with unrelenting force, each punch reverberating like thunder. Blood sprayed the battlefield, painting the already scorched earth in grotesque streaks of crimson.

The Pinnacles watched from their position, momentarily stunned by the sheer brutality of Apollo's assault. Reptile's claws flexed reflexively, his scales bristling as he took a step forward.

Angel's wings trembled slightly as he surveyed the carnage. He had fought in wars before, but this—this was different.

Tremor stared at the remains of a man who had been cut clean in half by Apollo's solar beam. His stomach twisted violently. He swallowed hard and turned away, breathing deeply through his nose.

"Apollo, stop!" Reptile roared, his deep voice cutting through the chaos. "You're going too far!"

Apollo didn't so much as flinch. His focus was singular, his golden eyes blazing as he ripped through another line of soldiers, his hands coated in blood. He focused the solar energy in his eyes through his specialised contacts, making them into focused beams burning anything in his path. A final solar blast left a wide swath of destruction in its wake, silencing the last of their attackers.

A single groan rose from a dying soldier—a boy barely past twenty.

He wasn't trying to fight anymore. His rifle had fallen from his hands. The soldier's fingers twitched over his wound, as if trying to push his guts back in. His white-glazed eyes flickered, unfocused.

He wasn't dead yet.

Apollo barely acknowledged him. His golden gaze locked onto the boy, impassive. Detached.

The boy tried to mouth something —"please" — but Apollo's solar beam cut through his skull before the word left his lips.

His body slumped, motionless.

Silence.

Angel's wings twitched at his back, his usually calm face pale. "This isn't what I signed up for," he muttered under his breath. His voice trembled, barely audible over the crackle of scorched earth. He didn't even realize he'd taken a step back.

Aero let out a breath he didn't realize he'd been holding. "Jesus," he murmured. "Dude was already down."

Apollo barely spared him a glance. "And now he's not getting up." Panting, Apollo turned to face the team, his suit charred but still glowing faintly with residual energy. His face was a mask of disdain, his lips curling into a sneer. "They shot at us," he said coldly, his voice dripping with venom. "They deserve worse."

Reptile stepped forward, his massive frame casting a long shadow across the battlefield. His yellow eyes burned with barely contained fury. "They were human. Brainwashed or not, they weren't a threat to you. You didn't have to slaughter them."

Apollo scoffed, wiping a streak of blood from his cheek. "Spare me the lecture, lizard. You think mercy will save you when the real monsters show up? These humans chose their side."

Reptile's claws scraped against each other as his hands curled into fists. He opened his mouth to retort, but Tress interceded, placing a firm hand on his arm. Her vine-like hair swayed gently, calming him just enough to make him step back.

"We don't have time for this," Tress said, her voice steady despite the tension crackling in the air. "We're still miles from our target, and if this is what we've seen at the border, the uprising will only be worse, deeper in."

Apollo's glare shifted to Tress, but her unflinching expression silenced whatever barb he'd been ready to hurl. Instead, he turned away, his cape billowing as he began walking toward the horizon. "Fine," he spat. "Try not to slow me down."

CHAPTER 17: FIRST STRIKE

Apollo streaked through the sky, his solar-powered suit radiating an ethereal glow against the ashen backdrop of State 9. From this altitude, the land below was a grotesque panorama of destruction. Entire city blocks lay in ruin, skeletal remains of buildings jutting up like broken teeth against the smoky horizon. Fires dotted the terrain like scattered embers, their orange light flickering ominously through the haze. Even at this distance, Apollo could feel the oppressive heat rising from the ground, mingling with the acrid scent of burning debris and death.

Switching his contacts to thermal vision, Apollo scanned the city. The display hummed to life, revealing clusters of bright heat signatures concentrated around a central point: bio-mutants and armed humans—an army bristling with weapons and abilities. A smirk tugged at the corner of Apollo's mouth.

"Found them," his voice crackled over the comms, self-assured and biting. "Bio-mutants, armed humans, and a pathetic excuse for an uprising. I'll take care of it. Try to keep up."

Before anyone could respond, the line went dead, and Apollo dove toward the epicenter.

Far below, the rest of the Pinnacles moved cautiously through the devastated city. Atlas ran and leaped about the debris. Reptile carried both Tress and Tremor effortlessly on his massive shoulders, his scaled hide reflecting the faint light that filtered through the smoky air. His hulking frame moved with surprising grace, his claws tapping lightly against the ground as he sniffed the air.

Tress's vine-like hair tendrils twitched restlessly, sensing the tension in the air. Her green eyes darted across the shadows of the ruins, searching for any sign of movement. Tremor, perched beside her, clutched his weapon tightly, his armored leg bouncing anxiously as he surveyed the crumbling structures around them.

Above them, Angel and Aero flew in tandem, their wings cutting silently through the heavy air. Aero used massive gusts of wind he conjured from his mouth in order to fly using his wingsuit. Angel's pure white feathers contrasted starkly against the grim backdrop, while Aero's dark figure darted ahead, his sharp amber eyes scanning for threats.

"He's going to get himself killed," Aero muttered through clenched teeth, breaking the uneasy silence.

Tress frowned, her voice calm but firm. "He won't die, but he'll make everything worse. Stay sharp."

Reptile growled low in his throat. "Arrogant prick's going to drag us into his mess."

The group quickened their pace, urgency propelling them forward. They all knew Apollo too well. His recklessness had a way of escalating even the most manageable situations. The sound of distant gunfire suddenly cut through the air, followed by the faint rumble of collapsing debris.

Apollo had arrived.

Apollo slammed into the street like a bomb, concrete buckling beneath his boots. Shockwaves blasted outward, chunks of pavement flying like shrapnel. A few unlucky soldiers were sent sprawling, crushed under debris, or straight-up buried in the rubble. His entrance was met with immediate resistance: a hulking bio-mutant, its body encased in thick, armored plating, barreled into him at full speed. The two crashed through a crumbling building, the force of the impact shaking the ground.

Apollo grunted as he hit the ground, the bio-mutant's massive weight pinning him. The creature roared, raising a spiked fist to strike. The monster tore into Apollo, rag-dolling him about inside the smoldering building. The bio-mutant slammed into Apollo, dragging him through the charred remains of a storefront, rubble collapsing around them. Once they stopped, the beast lunged, thick claws driving toward Apollo's throat. He tilted his head slightly; the attack was missing by inches. Before the creature could reset, Apollo's hand shot forward, clamping onto its wrist. The mutant snarled, trying to wrench itself free—right before Apollo twisted.

A sickening pop rang out as bone separated from the joint. The mutant howled, its arm going limp. Apollo tightened his grip, squeezing—cracks webbed through its armored forearm as Apollo crushed it like brittle rock. His eyes flickered, sending a thin, concentrated beam through the mutant's shoulder. It reeled back, clutching the burned wound, but Apollo was already moving. His knee shot up, caving in the creature's ribs with a single sharp blow.

"Is that all you've got?" Apollo sneered, his voice laced with derision.

The bio-mutant charged blindly, swinging a jagged fist. Apollo didn't dodge—he stepped forward. The blow crashed against his shoulder, barely staggering him.

Apollo's response was instant. His hand clamped onto the mutant's face, fingers digging into its thick hide before he drove it through the wall, sending rubble and dust flying. The mutant screeched, its claws scrambling uselessly at his wrist.

Apollo exhaled, rolling his eyes. "Pathetic."

His grip tightened. The mutant's skull started to cave inward. Its legs kicked weakly, barely clinging to life.

"Keep squirming," he muttered, lifting the creature off the ground like it weighed nothing. His other fist slammed into its ribs again—and again—until bone cracked and blood spewed from its mouth.

Apollo yanked his hand away, ripping out a chunk of the creature's shattered jaw. With a brutal motion, he plunged his hand into the mutant's torso, tearing out its heart in a grisly display of dominance. It collapsed at his feet, twitching, and Apollo straightened, blood dripping from his gloved hands as he crushed the heart.

His victory was short-lived. An icy barrier erupted in front of him, cutting off his line of sight to the advancing army. The air grew frigid, and frost began to creep along the ground toward him. Apollo narrowed his eyes, his irritation growing.

"Really? Ice?" he muttered, shaking his head. "Pathetic."

The moment the icy barrier rose, Apollo felt it—a sudden, unbearable tightness wrapping around his ribs. His chest seized, his breath hitched, and a deep, suffocating burn spread through his veins like wildfire. He took a step forward, but his limbs didn't obey the way they should. Scarlet wasn't hitting him. She was pulling him apart from the inside. Blood pressure spiked in his skull, hammering against his temples. His vision blurred at the edges, his muscles locking up in spasms. Scarlet stepped into view, her lips curving into a slow, knowing smile. Her eyes were white.

Scarlet's fingers twitched, and Apollo's body rebelled against him. His breath hitched, his muscles locking in an unnatural spasm. His chest felt like it was in a vice, his ribs tightening as if trying to crush his own heart. He tried to step forward, but his limbs dragged, unresponsive, sluggish. The pain was unlike anything he'd felt before—not from an external force, but from the inside out. His own blood had turned traitor.. His knees bent involuntarily, a staggering motion that almost looked like submission.

It wasn't just the pain—it was the familiarity of it. That feeling of something crawling under his skin, muscles locking, blood turning foreign. The sensation gripped him like the old days—when machines used to clamp down on his spine, pump volts through his nerves, and make him feel every single twitch, every scream he didn't allow himself to let out.

His chest tightened. Ribs contracting like they were being crushed inward. He staggered, not from weakness but because it felt like back then—like the early government trials, where every failed upgrade felt like being pulled apart and stitched back wrong.

Scarlet tilted her head, voice laced with venomous amusement. "That's it," she mused. "I can feel your heart struggling. You're not so untouchable, are you?" She clenched her fist, twisting the blood in his veins like puppet strings. Apollo shuddered involuntarily.

Scarlet let out a soft chuckle. "I wonder what happens if I squeeze just a little harder?"

Apollo's knees buckled, but he refused to fall. His body felt like it was imploding—veins swelling, muscles locking like they were ripping themselves apart. Apollo's vision blurred at the edges, but he gritted his teeth, refusing to let her see him break. His hands trembled before he forced them into fists.

"Cute trick," he growled, voice strained. "Let's see how long you can hold it."

With a burst of energy, his suit flared, solar reserves disrupting her control momentarily. Apollo lunged forward, his fist aimed at her chest. But before he could reach her, a hail of bullets ricocheted off his suit. More bio-mutants surged forward, their monstrous forms closing in.

Apollo smirked, his eyes glowing fiercely. "Finally, a challenge."

Apollo moved forward, not waiting for them to react. His fist caved in a man's sternum, the impact sending him flipping backward over his allies. Another bio-mutant lunged—Apollo caught its wrist mid-swing, ripping its entire arm from the socket before using it as a club.

A gunman fired. Apollo barely turned—the bullet hit his cheek and ricocheted off harmlessly. He reached the shooter in a single step, grabbing him by the throat and slamming him face-first into the pavement.

His fists didn't just connect; they tore. His knuckles drove through ribs, caving in chests with every blow. A skull shattered against his forearm, blood spraying up his sleeve. Another mutant lunged—Apollo gripped its head and twisted until the snapping stopped.

Heat beams weren't wasted on wide destruction—they were knives, carving through flesh precisely where it would hurt the most. Soldiers began dying in droves, their bullets did little more than aggravate Apollo more. The ground trembled as explosions rippled across the battlefield, Apollo's sheer presence commanding chaos.

But the enemy's numbers were growing, and even Apollo's boundless confidence couldn't ignore the strain this would take on his body. Scarlet regrouped, her glowing hands readying another attack, and the remaining bio-mutants encircled him, their eyes completely whited out.

Apollo's chest heaved as he scanned the growing swarm surrounding him. Scarlet's crimson glow intensified, her control over his blood causing a searing pain to ripple through his veins. Ice began forming at his feet again as Glade stepped forward, her hands outstretched, sending frost crawling up his legs and torso. The bio-mutants, sensing an opportunity, closed in like wolves circling wounded prey.

"Giving up already?" Scarlet sneered, her smirk widening as Apollo faltered under her manipulation. "The mighty Apollo brought to his knees. Poetic, isn't it?"

Apollo licked blood from his split lip—not his, theirs. He cracked his knuckles, eyes glowing. "Come on." His smirk widened. "You wanted a god? Start praying."

CHAPTER 18: REINFORCEMENTS

The chaos of the battlefield was deafening, a cacophony of screams, gunfire, and the clash of raw power. Angel and Aero arrived just as Apollo stood on the brink of being overwhelmed, his blue suit battered but still glowing faintly with solar energy. The bio-mutants swarmed him, their coordinated attacks like a relentless tide.

Angel dove into the fray, his wings slicing through the air as he aimed to turn the tide. His graceful descent was cut short when a sharp spine pierced through his leg, the pain shooting up his body like fire. Angel's cry echoed through the ruins as he was slammed into the pavement. His pristine wings crumpled beneath him, now smeared with blood and dust.

"Angel!" Aero's voice rang out, sharp and panicked. Fury ignited in his chest as his amber eyes locked onto Coil, the spined mutant responsible. Aero swooped low, conjuring a powerful gust of wind that sent debris spiraling toward his target. The force collided with Coil, but the mutant anchored himself by driving his spines into the ground, resisting Aero's attack with ease.

The rest of the Pinnacles arrived like a storm. Reptile and Atlas led the charge, his massive forms crashing into the enemy lines like a battering ram. Reptiles claws tore through flesh and armor alike, leaving a wake of destruction. He roared as his tail lashed out, sending bio-mutants flying like rag dolls. Atlas, now wrapped in massive muscle fibers, began making his way to Apollo. He reached down, grabbed the twisted frame of an overturned truck, and heaved it overhead like it weighed nothing. With a roar, he hurled the entire vehicle into a crowd of charging bio-mutants, the impact erupting in flame and debris. "Cover the left flank!" he barked, voice thundering across the field as he charged behind the blast.

Glade, the ice-wielding mutant, stepped forward with a calm precision that contrasted sharply with the surrounding chaos. With a flick of his wrist, Glade unleashed a wave of frost that encased Reptile's limbs in thick, unyielding ice. Reptile struggled, his claws scraping against the frozen bonds, but the cold seeped into his muscles, slowing his movements. Because of his cold-blooded nature, Reptile quickly began losing energy because of the extreme cold.

Tress and Tremor moved to cover him. Tremor's seismic waves rippled across the battlefield, creating small chasms that swallowed soldiers whole. The ground quaked under his feet. But Scarlet, the blood manipulator, had been waiting for this. Her crimson eyes glowed as she stretched out her hands, seizing control of Tremor's blood. His body froze mid-motion, and then violent spasms wracked his form, dropping him to his knees.

"All of their eyes are white, even the bio-mutants," Tress commend to the team.

"Tremor!" Tress yelled, her vine-like hair snapping to attention. She turned just in time to block an attack from Maxxy, the spiked mutant. His elbows and knees hardened into lethal weapons, struck with terrifying speed and precision. Tress countered with her tendrils, which lashed out like whips, deflecting his blows and slashing at his exposed skin. The two engaged in a deadly dance, each strike more ferocious than the last.

Above, Aero continued his aerial assault, weaving between the bio-mutants' projectiles with practiced agility. Spotting Glade distracted by Reptile, Aero dived sharply, heaving a mass of hot air toward the frozen bonds. The gust melted the ice, freeing Reptile with an explosive crack.

Reptile roared, his yellow eyes blazing with fury. With a single swipe of his clawed hand, he sent Glade sprawling. But the cold had taken its toll on him, his movements slower and more deliberate as he closed in on his icy adversary.

Meanwhile, Scarlet moved closer to Apollo, her hands glowing with a sinister crimson light. She smirked, confident in her ability to bend even the solar titan to her will. But Apollo was not so easily subdued. His suit pulsed with renewed energy, and with a guttural shout, he unleashed a focused beam of heat vision. The attack forced Scarlet to dive for cover; her smirk replaced with a glare of frustration.

The battlefield was a storm of clashing abilities and relentless violence. For every mutant the Pinnacles struck down, two more seemed to rise in their place. The ground was a chaotic tapestry of scorch marks, shattered ice, and craters littered with the bodies of the fallen.

Aero's voice crackled over the comms, his breath ragged. "They just keep coming! We're running out of ground to stand on!"

The fight raged on. Each member of the Pinnacles pushed to their absolute limits, their bond as a team tested like never before.

Reptile's claws scraped against the frozen ground as he lunged at Glade, his rage fueling his every motion. The icy mutant responded with a spray of water jets, each freezing midair into deadly projectiles. Reptile dodged most, but one sharp shard pierced his shoulder, causing him to stagger. With a guttural growl, he ignored the pain and lashed out with his tail, catching Glade in the chest and sending him sprawling across the rubble.

Tress, meanwhile, danced through Maxxy's onslaught. His spiked elbows and knees came at her like battering rams, but her long hair acted like a second set of limbs, wrapping around his strikes and pulling him off balance. With a sharp flick, she sent Maxxy tumbling to the ground, pinning him briefly as her hair tightened around his throat.

"Stay down," she hissed, her voice low and dangerous.

Maxxy grinned through the pressure, blood seeping from a cut above his eye. "Not a chance," he spat, his hardened elbow striking her in the arm. Tress recoiled in pain, but she quickly regrouped, her hair snapping back like a whip to keep him at bay.

Above, Aero circled the battlefield, his sharp amber eyes scanning for opportunities. He spotted Scarlet preparing another assault on Apollo and dove toward her, unleashing a concentrated blast of wind. The force knocked her to the ground, disrupting her focus.

"Annoying little pest," Scarlet muttered, pushing herself up. She turned her attention to Aero, her hands glowing crimson.

Before she could unleash her power, Aero narrowed his eyes and took a deep breath. Instead of force, he went for precision. A concentrated blast of sub-zero air struck Scarlet's hands, numbing her fingers instantly. She yelped, stumbling back as her control over the battlefield wavered.

"Try harder," he taunted, his voice dripping with defiance.

Scarlet snarled, her frustration mounting as she struggled to maintain control over the battlefield.

Apollo, meanwhile, was holding his own against the swarm of bio-mutants. His fists moved like pistons, each punch sending shockwaves through the air. His heat vision carved through the ranks, leaving smoldering craters where enemies once stood. But even he was beginning to show signs of wear. His movements, though powerful, were slightly slower, and the glow of his suit had dimmed just enough for the others to notice.

Apollo's fists slammed through bone and muscle, but every hit was costing him. His shoulders ached. His breath came sharper. Apollo's vision blurred at the edges. His suit, once radiant, was now flickering, the solar reserves struggling to keep up.

A bio-mutant's claw raked across his ribs—the first to land a real hit. Then another struck his shoulder, sending him stumbling back.

Scarlet smiled. She saw it too. "You're not invincible," she called, her voice cutting through the chaos. "You'll burn out, Apollo. Just like the rest of them."

Apollo's gaze snapped to her, his blue eyes still burning with fury—but his breath was heavier now. Slower.

He clenched his fists. Not yet. "Then let's see who burns first," he growled.

CHAPTER 19: THE PUPPET MASTER

The battlefield, already chaotic with the sounds of clashing abilities and the groans of fallen combatants, fell unnervingly silent. The air thickened, heavy and oppressive, as if the world itself were holding its breath. A low, almost imperceptible hum spread across the field, drawing every eye toward a shadowy figure emerging from the haze.

Hypno.

He was tall and wiry, his every movement deliberate and unnervingly calm. His eyes glowed, swirling with hypnotic patterns that seemed alive, twisting and spinning like vortices pulling the unwary into their depths. He was a predator radiating control, expertly manipulating the surrounding chaos.

Apollo narrowed his eyes at the mutant. His bloodied fists clenched, and the faint hum of solar energy rippled across his battered suit. "Finally," he muttered under his breath, his voice edged with both frustration and relief. "The Puppet-master shows himself."

Hypno smiled faintly, his tone disarming but dripping with malice. "Impressive work, Apollo. You and your little team almost turned the tide. Almost." He stepped forward, his movements unnervingly smooth. "But you didn't think it would be that easy, did you?"

Before Apollo could retort, Hypno's swirling gaze locked onto Tress and Tremor. It was as if an invisible string snapped taut between them, pulling them under his control in an instant. Tress froze mid-strike, her deadly vine-like hair dropping limply to her sides. Tremor, whose seismic powers had been creating rippling destruction moments ago, stood still, his fists slack and his eyes blank.

"Tress! Tremor!" Aero's voice crackled over the comms as he darted through the air. The panic in his tone was unmistakable.

Hypno's glowing eyes shifted skyward, meeting Aero's sharp amber gaze. The spinning patterns caught Aero mid-flight, and his powerful wings faltered. He hovered for a moment, his movements erratic, before descending unsteadily to the ground. His wings drooped like a bird caught in an unseen net.

"Stay with me!" Reptile roared, his deep voice cutting through the rising panic. But Hypno's gaze turned on him next. Despite his reptilian strength and cold-blooded resistance, Reptile's movements slowed, his claws falling to his sides as he took an involuntary step back.

One by one, the Pinnacles succumbed to Hypno's influence, their expressions eerily blank. Even the once-ferocious bio-mutants stopped their assault, their aggression evaporating as they joined the growing ranks behind Hypno.

Apollo's jaw tightened as he stood alone at the epicenter of the battlefield, surrounded by the nine mutants he called his team. His breathing was heavy, each inhale sharp and ragged as he tried to process what was happening.

"You see?" Hypno said, spreading his arms theatrically. "This is what real power looks like, Apollo. Control. Unity. My army obeys without question. Can you say the same for yours?"

Apollo ignored the taunt, his fists igniting with golden light. "Release them," he growled, his voice low and dangerous.

Hypno tilted his head, his smirk widening. "Why would I do that? They're so much more... effective this way."

Before Apollo could make a move, Hypno raised a hand, and the Pinnacles attacked.

Aero launched a powerful gust of wind that sent debris flying toward Apollo. Reptile followed close behind, his claws swiping with lethal precision. Tress's hair lashed out like snakes, their sharp edges slicing through the air, while Tremor's fists slammed into the ground, sending violent shockwaves rippling beneath Apollo's feet.

Apollo barely dodged the combined assault. He leapt into the air, his heat vision slicing through the oncoming gusts. Reptile's claws scraped against his suit as Apollo twisted mid-flight, countering with a solar beam that sent the reptilian mutant staggering back.

Scarlet stood at the edge of the chaos, her hands glowing crimson as she prepared to manipulate Apollo's blood. He felt the familiar, nauseating pull in his veins, his strength faltering for a moment. Gritting his teeth, he channeled his solar vision, it grazed her shoulder forcing her influence away as she dropped to the ground.

"You're hesitating," Hypno's voice echoed mockingly through the battlefield. "You can't fight them at full strength, can you? That's the difference between us, Apollo. You care. I don't."

Apollo snarled, unleashing a blinding wave of stellar energy that forced everyone to stagger back. The sheer intensity of the light momentarily broke their formation, giving him a brief reprieve.

But it was short-lived. The Pinnacles regrouped, their movements mechanical yet coordinated. Scarlet raised her hands again, her crimson glow intensifying as she locked onto Apollo. Glade stepped forward next, frost creeping along the ground as she aimed icy jets at his legs, threatening to immobilize him.

Apollo dodged, but not without effort. The constant onslaught was taking its toll. His suit's energy reserves were depleting, and his movements grew sluggish.

"Give up, Apollo," Hypno taunted, stepping closer. "This is a battle you can't win."

"Not while I'm still standing," he spat, the defiance in his voice unwavering.

Hypno smirked, his eyes glowing brighter. "Then let's see how long you can stand."

The circle tightened around Apollo as the next wave of attacks began.

Apollo stood at the center of the battlefield, sweat dripping down his face and his suit flickering weakly. His team—no, the people he was stuck leading—stood against him, their bodies still and their expressions hollow, like puppets waiting for their master to pull the strings. Surrounding them were the bio-mutants and remaining insurgents, forming a suffocating circle of enemies.

"Release them," Apollo growled, his voice more annoyed than desperate as his gaze fixed on Hypno. "I don't have the energy to waste fighting through all these idiots."

Hypno smirked, his glowing, swirling eyes gleaming with amusement. "But where's the fun in that? You like to pretend you're unstoppable, Apollo—let's see how you handle the odds when they're stacked against you."

Apollo's fists crackled faintly with solar energy, the golden glow barely hanging on as he raised them into a loose stance. "If you think this is going to break me, you're dumber than you look."

The hypnotized Pinnacles moved first. Aero unleashed a powerful gust of wind that sent debris and rubble flying in every direction, forcing Apollo to shield his face. The instant his guard dropped, Reptile surged forward, claws slashing in a brutal arc. Apollo ducked under the first swipe but caught the second across his shoulder, sparks flying as his suit's armor took the brunt of the attack.

"Really?" Apollo muttered, pivoting sharply and delivering a massive kick to Reptile's chest. The blow sent the reptilian mutant staggering back, but Apollo's frustration only grew as Tress and her razor-sharp hair tendrils closed in.

The hair whipped at him from every angle, slicing through the air with deadly precision. Apollo dodged and deflected as best as he could, his movements less fluid than usual, thanks to his drained reserves. One of Tress's hair nicked the side of his helmet, sending a sharp metallic screech ringing in his ears.

"Ugh, I don't have time for this!" Apollo snapped, grabbing one of her hair and yanking hard enough to pull her off balance. With a quick, calculated strike, he knocked her unconscious and let her crumple to the ground.

From the corner of his eye, Apollo saw Scarlet raising her glowing hands. He felt his blood tighten in his veins, a nauseating pull that sent waves of heat and cold through his body.

Apollo moved to counter, but his foot dragged slightly. His body felt heavier, slower.

Scarlet's grin widened. She saw it. She felt it.

"Oh, you're breaking down," she whispered, her voice giddy. "I can feel it in your blood."

Apollo gritted his teeth and forced his fist forward, catching her in the stomach, shattering ribs and sending her crumpling to the ground.

The ground rumbled beneath his feet as Tremor stepped in, slamming his fists into the earth and sending a shockwave that nearly toppled Apollo. He leapt into the air just in time, avoiding the worst of it, but as he landed, Aero hit him with a gust of wind that sent him skidding backward.

"Alright, fine, you want a fight?" Apollo barked, cracking his neck. "Let's do this."

Atlas joined the fray next, his muscles swelling grotesquely as he charged at Apollo with relentless force. The ground cracked beneath his footsteps as he hurled a massive fist at Apollo's midsection. The punch connected, sending Apollo flying into a pile of rubble.

"You actually hit me," Apollo muttered, coughing as he climbed to his feet. His voice was flat, but his smirk hinted at something dangerous. "Not bad. Let's see how long that lasts."

Apollo surged forward, his speed almost too fast to follow. He feinted to the left, forcing Atlas to overextend, before landing a heavy blow to his ribs. The impact echoed across the battlefield, but Atlas absorbed the hit with a snarl, countering with a crushing overhead strike. Apollo sidestepped at the last moment, delivering a hard jab to Atlas's knee that made the massive mutant stagger.

"Big and slow," Apollo said with a smirk. "Classic."

Before he could finish Atlas off, Reptile and Aero rejoined the attack, forcing Apollo to stay on the move. The fight devolved into a chaotic free-for-all, with Apollo dodging and countering against multiple opponents, his solar beams cutting through the dim haze but never quite landing a decisive blow.

"Getting tired, Apollo?" Hypno's voice rang out, smug and infuriating.

Apollo didn't bother to respond. Instead, he unleashed a blinding stellar flare, forcing everyone to pause as the intense light washed over the battlefield. He took the opportunity to catch his breath, his hands resting on his knees as his suit dimmed further.

Hypno clapped slowly, stepping closer to the battered solar titan. "Is that all you've got? I was expecting more from the great Apollo."

Apollo's head snapped up, his blue eyes blazing despite his exhaustion. "I'm just getting started," he lied, forcing himself upright.

Hypno's smile widened. "We'll see about that."

The remaining Pinnacles began to rise again, their movements slow and methodical as Hypno's control tightened. Apollo could feel the weight of the battle pressing down on him, his body aching with every movement, but he refused to let it show.

Apollo surged forward—or tried to.

His foot barely left the ground before his knee gave out. The shift in momentum sent him staggering, his suit crackling and flickering. He caught himself just before he hit the rubble.

No. He forced himself upright, ignoring the scream in his muscles. His vision dimmed at the edges.

Hypno's smile widened. He saw it.

"You're not a god," Hypno taunted, his voice dripping with malice. "You're just a man playing pretend. And now, your team—your failures—will be the ones to take you down."

Apollo's fists clenched, his glare burning hotter than his suit.

"Keep talking," he growled, forcing his body back into a stance. "Let's see how smug you are when I rip that stupid grin off your face."

CHAPTER 20: APOLLO'S WRATH

The battlefield was chaos. The mutants attacked in unison, their movements synchronized as if driven by a singular, malicious intent. Reptile surged forward first, his massive, scaled arms wrapping around Apollo's torso like constricting steel cables. The crushing force was immediate, his claws digging into the solar titan's armor with a screech of metal.

"Stay down, Apollo," Reptile snarled, his voice guttural. "You're not as invincible as you think."

Apollo grunted under the pressure, his ribs straining as Reptile's grip tightened. "Cute," he muttered through gritted teeth. "But you're going to need a lot more than bad breath and lizard arms to stop me."

Before he could break free, Tress's hair lashed out from behind, the sharp tendrils slicing into his suit's solar panels. Sparks flew as one tendril wrapped around his arm, yanking it back with enough force to dislocate it. The pain was sharp, but Apollo didn't flinch—his pride wouldn't allow it.

"Scarlet, now!" Tress shouted.

Scarlet stepped forward, her hands glowing with an eerie crimson light. With a flick of her wrist, Apollo felt his blood twist unnaturally in his veins. A cold, suffocating sensation crept through his chest, and his heart stuttered as if caught in a vise.

"Can't take the heat?" Scarlet sneered, her voice laced with venom.

Apollo stumbled, his vision narrowing as nausea rolled through him. Frost crept up his legs as Glade stepped into view, her breath misting in the frigid air. The ground beneath Apollo froze solid, the ice climbing his body and locking him in place.

The pressure, the pain, the cold—it was all-consuming. For the first time in a long time, Apollo felt the weight of his enemies bearing down on him, their combined powers threatening to snuff out his own.

From the sidelines, the remaining Pinnacles could only watch, their battered bodies too weak to intervene. Aero struggled to lift himself from the rubble, his amber eyes filled with worry as he saw Scarlet's grip on Apollo tighten.

"Come on, Apollo," Aero whispered under his breath. "Get up."

Apollo's teeth clenched as his suit's solar reserves flickered weakly. Scarlet's manipulation burned through his chest, and the ice biting into his legs left him almost immobile. His mind screamed at him to act, to fight back, but his body rebelled against every command.

Then he heard Reptile's mocking laugh, low and guttural, in his ear. "You're nothing but a fraud," he growled. "All that power, and you're still just a scared little man hiding behind a suit."

Something inside Apollo snapped.

"No," he growled, his voice low and dangerous. The glow of his suit intensified as he forced himself to stand against the ice's grip. "I'm not just some scared human. I'm Apollo."

With a roar that shook the battlefield, Apollo unleashed his suit's emergency solar reserves. A blinding wave of heat and light erupted outward, the force of it shattering the ice, encasing him and sending Reptile flying backward. Scarlet screamed as the energy disrupted her control, the glow in her hands flickering out. Glade was thrown to the ground, steam rising from her body as the frost melted away in an instant.

Tress's hair burned away in the explosion, her tendrils falling limp as she hit the ground with a pained cry. The blast carved a smoking crater into the battlefield, scattering bio-mutants and allies alike.

Apollo stood at the center of the destruction, steam rising from his battered suit. His glowing blue eyes locked onto the bio-mutants who still remained standing, their monstrous forms hesitating in the face of his raw power.

"Who's next?" Apollo spat, his voice cutting through the chaos like a blade.

Scarlet, trembling as she pushed herself to her feet, glared at him with fury. "You think this makes you a hero?" she shouted. "You're nothing but a monster!"

Apollo smirked, the blood dripping from his hands a grim testament to the destruction he had unleashed. "Call me whatever you want," he said coldly. "I get results."

From the edge of the battlefield, Hypno stepped forward, his spinning eyes gleaming with amusement. "Impressive," he said, his voice smooth and mocking. "But brute force only gets you so far."

Apollo turned to face him, his expression unreadable. "You talk too much," he said flatly.

Hypno tilted his head, a smirk playing on his lips. "And you rely too much on power. Let's see how well you fight when you're out of energy."

Before Apollo could respond, Hypno's gaze locked onto him. His eyes spun in their sockets, the spinning patterns in his eyes started drawing Apollo in. For a brief moment, the solar titan's glowing eyes flickered, and his movements slowed.

"You're losing your edge," Hypno taunted, his voice dripping with malice. "Even gods can kneel."

The remaining mutants seized the opportunity. Reptile, still smoldering from Apollo's earlier blast, charged with a guttural roar. His claws raked through the air, aiming for Apollo's throat. Tress, though weakened, lashed out with what remained of her tendrils, their frayed edges snapping like whips. Glade emerged from the steam, her frigid breath condensing into a flurry of ice shards that she launched with pinpoint precision.

Atlas finally stepped forward, his body swelling as his muscles expanded with terrifying speed. His tactical gear stretched taut, veins bulging along his arms as he grew into a hulking figure of raw power. With a thunderous stomp, he cracked the ground beneath him, the tremor sending a ripple of destruction toward Apollo.

Apollo stumbled, his mind clouded by Hypno's influence. He gritted his teeth, forcing himself to focus as the mutants closed in. Reptile's claws grazed his chest plate, leaving deep gouges in the armor. Glade's ice shards struck his side, the freezing impact numbing his ribs. Tress's tendrils coiled around his arms, holding him in place as Atlas loomed closer, his massive fists raised high.

"You can't fight forever," Hypno said, his voice echoing inside Apollo's head. "You're outnumbered. Outmatched. Just give in."

Atlas roared, his fists slamming down toward Apollo with the force of a collapsing building. At the last second, Apollo's instincts kicked in. With a burst of energy, he broke free of Tress's hold and dodged, the impact of Atlas's fists creating a crater where he had stood.

"Nice try," Apollo spat, his voice strained but defiant.

Spinning on his heel, he delivered a swift kick to Atlas's knee; the force cracking the ground beneath them. Atlas grunted but remained standing, his muscles rippling as he swung a massive arm. Apollo ducked, using his heat vision to blast a searing beam at Glade, forcing her to retreat.

Reptile lunged again, his claws slashing through the air. Apollo caught his wrist mid-swing, the scales burning under his grasp. With a twist, he threw Reptile into Atlas, the two colliding with a thunderous crash.

"You call this a fight?" Apollo snarled, his glowing eyes locking onto Hypno. "This is just a waste of my time."

But Hypno's grin only widened. "And yet, you're still struggling."

Suddenly, Scarlet appeared behind Apollo, her hands glowing with crimson light. He barely had time to react before she sent a wave of blood manipulation through his veins. Pain exploded in his chest, and his knees buckled as his body seized up.

"I'm tired of your games," Apollo growled, his voice strained.

With a furious shout, he released another pulse of solar energy; the shockwave forcing Scarlet and the others to retreat. The ground beneath him cracked and crumbled, the heat radiating from his suit scorching the air.

But the strain was beginning to show. Apollo's breathing grew heavier, and the glow of his suit dimmed slightly. The relentless assault was taking its toll, and Hypno's voice continued to worm its way into his mind.

"You're not invincible, Apollo," Hypno said, stepping closer. "You're just a man pretending to be a god. And now, you'll fall like one."

Apollo staggered but refused to kneel. He clenched his fists, the faint hum of his suit's remaining energy pulsing around him. "You talk too much," he muttered.

Apollo's breath came in ragged gasps as the surrounding chaos momentarily stilled. His suit flickered faintly, its solar reserves nearly depleted. The battlefield was a wasteland of scorched earth and smoldering corpses, the once-relentless mutants now reduced to scattered remnants. But at the center of it all stood Hypno, untouched, his smug smile as sharp as a blade.

"You've burned through your strength, your team is useless, and even now, you hesitate to finish this."

Apollo wiped a smear of blood from his lip, his glowing blue eyes narrowing. "Let's cut the monologue, shall we? Release them. I've got better things to do than waste my time dealing with puppets."

Hypno chuckled, the sound low and mocking. "Why would I do that? I've got you exactly where I want you."

Before Apollo could respond, Hypno's spinning eyes flared brighter, their glow spreading like tendrils of light across the battlefield. Apollo tensed, bracing himself as the energy washed over him—but nothing happened. He blinked, his body steady, his mind clear. A slow, arrogant grin spread across his face.

"Hypnosis? Really?" Apollo scoffed, tapping the side of his temple. "These contacts? State-of-the-art tech. Blocks all that psychic mumbo jumbo. Did you honestly think that would work on me?"

Hypno's smile faltered, just for a fraction of a second, before his confidence returned. "Technology won't save you from me, Apollo. You can't stop what I've done."

Apollo tilted his head, his grin widening. "Then stop it yourself. Call this whole circus off."

Hypno sneered, his voice dripping with disdain. "Over my dead body."

Apollo's smirk disappeared, replaced by cold resolve. "If you insist."

In an instant, Apollo surged forward, moving faster than Hypno could react. The ground beneath his feet cracked from the force of his acceleration. Hypno raised a hand, his eyes spinning furiously in a last-ditch effort to ensnare Apollo. But the hypnotic glow fizzled harmlessly, his protection rendering Hypno's power useless.

"Nice try," Apollo said, his voice cutting like a blade.

His fist collided with Hypno's skull, the force obliterating bone and brain matter in a single, sickening blow. Blood sprayed in a gruesome arc as Hypno's lifeless body crumpled to the ground, his once-powerful eyes dimming into nothingness.

Apollo straightened, shaking the gore from his gloved hand as he glanced down at the body with detached indifference. "Guess that's that."

The battlefield fell silent, the oppressive weight of Hypno's influence shattering like glass. One by one, the Pinnacles collapsed, their bodies slack as they gasped for air. Tress clutched her head, her tendrils weak and lifeless. Tremor groaned, his hands trembling as he pushed himself up from the dirt. Reptile staggered to his feet, his scaled form battered and bruised.

Apollo surveyed them briefly, his expression unreadable. To him, they were merely collateral damage—necessary sacrifices for the greater goal.

Reptile was the first to confront him, his voice a low growl. "You didn't have to kill him like that. We could've—"

"Could've what?" Apollo interrupted, his tone sharp and dismissive. "Talked him down? Negotiated with the guy who turned you into his puppets? Spare me the lecture, Reptile."

Reptile's claws flexed, his fury barely contained. "You don't care about anyone but yourself, do you?"

Apollo stepped closer, his glowing eyes meeting Reptile's without flinching. "Care gets you killed. Results keep you alive. Remember that."

The two stared each other down, the tension crackling like static electricity. Before the confrontation could escalate, Tress stepped between them, her voice firm but weary. "Enough. We've already lost too much today."

Apollo let out a huff, turning away as he adjusted his battered suit. "Fine. We're done here."

As the Pinnacles began tying up the remaining mutants and waiting for backup, the weight of the battle hung heavy in the air. For all their power, their victory felt hollow, the cost etched into the scorched earth and their battered bodies.

Apollo, standing apart from the others, stared into the horizon, his cape flickering in the smoke-filled wind. The fires burned on, but for him, the flames were nothing more than background noise.

The aftermath of the battle was heavy with tension. The Pinnacles worked in grim silence, binding the captured mutants—Scarlet, Maxxy, Glade, Nosey, and Coil. Their hands were tied securely behind their backs, but their exhausted, hollow expressions revealed they had no fight left in them. Though Hypno's influence was broken, its effects lingered in their sunken eyes and trembling bodies. Though Hypno's influence was broken, its effects lingered in their sunken eyes and trembling bodies.

The prisoners sat huddled together, their expressions a mixture of fear and exhaustion. Scarlet's red hair clung to her sweat-soaked face, her hands trembling despite the defiant glare she directed at the Pinnacles. Glade remained eerily composed, her icy demeanor betraying no emotion. Nosey sniffed the air occasionally, his sharp sense of smell seemingly searching for an opportunity to escape, while Coil hung his head low, his elongated spine coiled tightly around his waist like a grotesque belt. Maxxy sat in silence, his spiked joints flexing slightly, as if testing his bonds.

Tress knelt in front of Scarlet, the fiery-haired mutant who sat slumped against a piece of rubble. Tress's voice was firm but not unkind. "You were part of the strike force, weren't you? Sent to take down Hypno?"

Scarlet nodded slowly, her bloodshot eyes flickering up to meet Tress's. "We didn't sign up for this," she said, her voice hoarse. "We were sent here to capture him. Five of us. Strong, capable. But the moment we got close…" she trailed off, her hands trembling in their bindings.

"He got into your heads," Tress finished for her, her tone softening.

Scarlet gave a bitter laugh, shaking her head. "It wasn't even a fight. One look, and we were gone. Puppets on strings. I don't even remember most of it. Just flashes—things I did, things he made me do." Her voice cracked, and she swallowed hard. "He used us like tools. Turned us into his personal enforcers."

Reptile loomed nearby, his yellow eyes narrowing as he listened. "You didn't stand a chance," he muttered. "None of us would've."

Scarlet nodded again, her gaze falling to the ground. "We didn't. And I don't think the bio-mutants did, either."

At that, Tress straightened, her brows furrowing. "What do you mean?"

Scarlet hesitated, glancing at the other prisoners. Maxxy looked away, his jaw tight. Glade remained silent, her icy demeanor unreadable. It was Nosey who finally spoke, his sharp gaze flicking between the Pinnacles.

"They weren't just bio-mutants," Nosey said quietly, his tone heavy with implication.

Tress turned to him, her expression hardening. "What are you saying?"

Nosey inhaled deeply, his nose twitching as if sniffing out the truth. "Hypno could only control humans, right? That's what everyone says about his power. But he controlled the bio-mutants, too. Which means…" He paused, his voice dropp

ing to a near whisper. "They must've been human. Once."

Like a shroud, the weight of his words settled over the group. The Pinnacles exchanged uneasy glances; the implications gnawing at them. Even the prisoners seemed rattled, their gazes darting nervously between the Pinnacles.

"That's insane," Tremor muttered, his fists clenching. "Bio-mutants are engineered. They're not—"

"They're not supposed to be human," Aero cut in, his voice tight. "But if they were... if Hypno could control them because they used to be..."

"Then they were turned into this," Reptile growled, his claws flexing. "Twisted. Deformed. Stripped of everything they were."

The silence that followed was suffocating, broken only by the faint crackle of distant fires. Tress ran a hand through her hair, her vine-like tendrils curling restlessly. "What kind of monster would do that?" she asked, her voice barely audible.

Apollo, who had been standing apart from the group, finally spoke. "Doesn't matter," he said, his tone cold and dismissive. "They were enemies. Human, mutant, bio-mutant—it's all the same. They're dead now. Problem solved."

The others turned to him, their expressions a mix of disbelief and anger. Reptile stepped forward, his voice low and dangerous. "You don't get it, do you? They were people. Innocent people who were turned into weapons."

Apollo shrugged, his golden eyes gleaming faintly. "Innocent or not, they're gone. What's the point of this debate?"

Before anyone could respond, a faint hum cut through the air—a sound that grew into a sharp, sizzling crack. The group turned just in time to see a beam of golden heat shoot from Apollo's eyes, striking Nosey in the head. The tracker's body jerked violently before slumping forward, lifeless. Smoke curled from the charred remains of his skull.

For a moment, the world seemed to stop.

Tremor took a step back, his fists still clenched, but his face drained of all color. He opened his mouth as if to say something—then closed it, swallowing hard.

Scarlet let out a sharp, involuntary breath, her lips parting slightly in stunned silence. For once, she had nothing to say.

Tress froze, her breath catching in her throat. Her vine-like hair, usually restless, went eerily still, as if even they had gone into shock. "What the hell are you doing?!" Tress shouted, her voice shaking with fury and disbelief.

Apollo straightened, his expression calm, almost indifferent. "He was speaking out of line," he said simply. "We don't need distractions."

Reptile's growl rumbled deep in his chest. In one swift motion, he lunged at Apollo, tackling him to the ground. The impact sent a shockwave through the clearing, scattering ash and debris. Reptile pinned Apollo beneath him, his claws digging into the ground on either side of Apollo's head.

Apollo's eyes flared brighter, his body heating up like a furnace beneath Reptile's claws, but Reptile didn't let go. His grip only tightened.

"You're a goddamn psychopath," Reptile snarled, his voice trembling with barely contained rage. "He was tied up. Helpless. And you killed him for telling the truth?"

Apollo's glowing eyes locked onto Reptile's, unflinching. "He was weak," he said coldly. "And weakness has no place here."

Reptile roared, raising a clawed hand as if to strike, but Apollo's voice cut through. "Do it. Prove you're just like me."

Reptile hesitated, his claws trembling. The moment's pause was all Apollo needed. With a burst of energy, he drove his fist upward, slamming it into Reptile's chest and sending him staggering backward. Apollo rolled to his feet, his suit flickering faintly as he squared off against the reptilian mutant.

"You think you're better than me?" Apollo spat, his tone laced with contempt. "You're a disgusting creature pretending to be human."

Reptile snarled, charging forward again, but Tress stepped between them, her vine-like tendrils snapping out like whips to hold them back.

"Enough!" she shouted, her voice sharp and commanding. "This isn't the time for this!"

Apollo held his ground, his fists clenched, but he didn't advance. Reptile, breathing heavily, flexed his claws but stayed where he was, his yellow eyes burning with fury.

The group stood in tense silence, the weight of what had just happened pressing down on them like a suffocating fog. The trust between them, already fragile, now felt irreparably shattered.

Apollo turned away first, his cape flicking behind him as he began walking toward the horizon. "We're done here," he said coldly, his tone devoid of any emotion. "Let's wrap this up."

Tress exhaled slowly, her hands still shaking, but she clenched them into fists—steadying herself.

Tremor stared at Apollo's retreating form, then down at Nosey's body, his jaw tightening. He didn't say a word, but his shoulders slumped, something breaking inside him.

Aero was the last to move. He watched Apollo disappear into the haze, then turned to Tress, his voice quiet. "So what now?"

Tress didn't answer immediately. She just stared into the firelight, watching the embers burn.

As the group watched him go, their expressions ranged from anger to disbelief to quiet resignation. The firelight danced across their faces, illuminating the fractures in their once-unshakable team.

ACT 2: GRANGER HEIGHTS

CHAPTER 21: INTOLERANCE

Nate lay sprawled across a jagged pile of rubble, his chest heaving as if every breath were a battle. His skin glistened with blood, a massive gash carving across his stomach, exposing the raw, torn flesh beneath. The cool air stung the wound like a thousand needles. Dust coated his face, sticking to the streaks of sweat and blood that trailed down his temples. His vision blurred, the flickering streetlight above him casting dancing shadows across the faces of his enemies.

Encircling him were government strike force agents, their figures faceless behind dark visors and thick combat suits. The barrel of every weapon pointed directly at him, unflinching in their precision. Nearby, a few agents poked and prodded at the grotesque remains of Mammal's corpse, their expressions hidden but their body language, a blend of fear and disgust.

"Did that kid do all of this?" Agent José's voice was low, quivering just enough to betray his unease.

"I have no fucking clue," Agent Simon muttered, his voice barely audible over the low hum of their equipment.

Captain Michele, a woman whose every movement exuded control, stepped forward, her sharp tone slicing through the tension. "Not likely. His file mentions enhanced strength, stamina, speed, reflexes—nothing that could explain... this." She gestured toward the remains of Mammal, now little more than shredded, withered tissue. "Besides, if he did... where's the mass? Guts don't just vanish into thin air."

"It's… weird," José added, hesitating as he crouched next to the remains. "There's barely any blood, let alone the amount of mass this thing should've had."

Michele straightened, her gloved hand tightening around her rifle. "Alright, enough. Whatever happened here, he's coming with us. Get him shackled, drugged, and out of here before he wakes up."

The order sent a ripple of movement through the circle. Several agents raised their tranquilizer rifles, firing dart after dart into Nate's already motionless form. His muscles twitched faintly, as if trying to fight even in unconsciousness, but the drugs quickly overwhelmed him. A few agents cautiously approached, their boots crunching against the rubble.

As one agent leaned down to secure his wrists, Nate's eyes shot open, wide and wild. Nate's body jolted awake, as if he'd been ripped out of a nightmare. A sharp gasp tore from his throat, his limbs sluggish and unresponsive at first. His breaths were shallow, uneven, his chest rising and falling in rapid bursts. For a moment, the world around him was a haze of white—blinding and sterile. He blinked hard, his head pounding, and slowly his surroundings came into focus.

Padded walls. No windows. A single light fixture embedded in the ceiling cast a harsh, artificial glow over the small, suffocating room. The floor was cold against his skin, and every movement sent sharp pain radiating from the massive scar stretching across his stomach. His hand instinctively went to the wound, fingers brushing against the ridged, puckered skin.

"Oh, shit…" The words slipped out in a whisper, barely audible over the pounding in his head. His voice cracked, raw and strained.

He stumbled to his feet, the room spinning as he steadied himself against the wall. His legs felt like lead, trembling under his weight. A dull ache throbbed in his stomach, each breath tugging painfully at the fresh scar tissue. Pulling up his shirt, he stared at the wound—an ugly reminder of Xavier's betrayal. His mind raced with fragmented memories: Xavier's cold expression, the sharp pain of being impaled, the sound of his own blood dripping onto the floor.

He staggered to the corner of the room, his back against the padded wall, and slid down until he was sitting. His thoughts spiraled. How did I survive that? How long was I out? Did… did he really try to kill me? His jaw clenched, his fingers curling into fists. After everything we've been through?

The memory hit him like a physical blow.

"Xavier, wait!" Nate's voice echoed in his head, desperate and cracking with disbelief. He could still see the way Xavier had turned, his face cold and devoid of any warmth.

"This is for the best," Xavier had said, his tone chillingly even, as if he were explaining something mundane.

Before Nate could react, he felt the searing pain—the sensation of bone piercing his stomach. He gasped, choking on his own blood, his vision blurring as he fell to the ground. Xavier had stood over him, his expression unreadable.

"You're strong," Xavier had murmured, almost to himself. "But you're not what I need."

Nate's hand tightened into a fist, the memory fading but leaving a bitter taste in its wake. His chest felt heavy, a mix of betrayal and anger coursing through him. He had trusted Xavier—relied on him. And Xavier had left him to die.

What's the point of trusting anyone? He thought bitterly, his eyes staring at the padded walls. What's the point of trying to protect anyone if they'll just stab you in the back the moment they get the chance?

His musings were interrupted by a sharp beep. The sound was shrill, mechanical, and it sent a jolt of adrenaline through him. Before he could move, the heavy metal door to his cell swung open with a groan, revealing the shadowed figure of a guard.

The facility loomed like a fortress of despair, its concrete walls stretching high into the sky, lined with razor wire that glinted ominously under harsh floodlights. Granger Heights wasn't just a prison—it was a statement. The surrounding air was oppressive, filled with the faint hum of security drones and the mechanical whirr of automated turrets perched along the perimeter.

Inside, it was no better. The hallways were cold, sterile, and filled with the sounds of muffled screams echoing from the distant cells. Guards patrolled in pairs, their boots clanging against the metallic floors in a rhythm that was both precise and unrelenting.

They escorted Nate down one of these hallways for testing. His body was stiff with tension. Two guards flanked him, their rifles held at the ready. His scarred stomach throbbed with every step, and the collar around his neck chafed against his skin. The weight of it—the threat of instant death—kept him from trying anything reckless. Yet his eyes darted to every corner, every security camera, cataloging the layout. Even now, his mind raced with possibilities.

The air inside Granger Heights carried a heavy stench—sweat, blood, and something chemical that burned Nate's nostrils. He caught glimpses of other inmates as he passed, their faces hollow and gaunt. One of them, a wiry man with sunken eyes, pressed his face against the bars of his cell and hissed, "New meat. You're not gonna last a week, kid."

"Back off, Wallace!" one guard barked, slamming the butt of his rifle against the cell bars. Wallace recoiled, retreating into the shadows with a sinister grin.

Nate's stomach churned. Every instinct screamed at him to run, to fight, to do something—but the memory of the scar on his stomach reminded him of what had happened the last time he underestimated his opponent.

A sudden wave of dizziness hit him, his vision narrowing at the edges. His knees buckled, and he barely caught himself against the wall.

"Move it," the guard snapped, shoving him forward.

Nate grit his teeth and kept walking. He wouldn't give them the satisfaction of seeing him weak.

Miles away in State 5, wheelchair District, under a sky thick with storm clouds, a different kind of battle was brewing.

Inside a dimly lit hideout, the air was thick with tension. The flickering glow of an old portable monitor cast ghostly shadows across the walls as the Rogues gathered around a cluttered table. The atmosphere was suffocating, weighed down by exhaustion, grief, and the unspoken question lingering on everyone's minds: What the hell do we do now?

Ava's hands trembled as she pressed them against Nat's wounded shoulder, eyes squeezed shut in concentration. The effort was taking a toll on her, but she pushed forward, determined to keep Nat stable.

Meanwhile, Michael paced the length of the room, frustration leaking into every heavy step.

The air inside the small, dimly lit hideout was tense, the weight of their loss pressing down on the group. Morgan worked methodically, dressing Nat's wounds with blood-stained bandages, her jaw set in a grim line.

"This is why we can't go around getting attached to everyone we meet, Nat," Michael said, pacing the room. His voice was sharp, frustration dripping from every word. "It's exactly what I warned about. Look where it got us."

Michael's jaw tightened, but there was hesitation behind his frustration—a flicker of something softer buried beneath the anger. He wasn't just lashing out at Nat. He was scared. Scared of what losing people again might do to them all. He didn't say it out loud, but the thought kept gnawing at him: if they kept risking everything for strays, eventually there'd be no one left to carry the weight.

Nat shot him a glare, her voice weak but resolute. "No one deserves their fates, Michael. Not Nate. Not Xavier. And not the kids we save. It's our job to protect them—because no one protected us."

Michael scoffed, but there was a flicker of guilt in his expression. "And how many of us have to die before you get that we can't save everyone?"

"Michael, shut up!" Morgan snapped, her voice cracking. She stood abruptly, fists clenched at her sides. "They're not dead. Nate and Xavier—they're not dead!"

Michael sighed, running a hand through his hair. "And what are the odds they made it out of there alive, huh? If they did, they're probably at Granger Heights by now, and you know what that means."

"I-I might know how to f-find out," Ryan interjected, his voice quiet but steady.

All eyes turned to him. "How?" Morgan and Ava asked simultaneously, their desperation evident.

Ryan hesitated, then gestured to the map laid out on the table. "I-I've been t-tracking heat signatures from government vehicles in the a-area. If they'd kk-killed Nate and X-Xavier, they'd have flown north to S-Shoetrees M-Military Hospital for testing. But a-all the trails lead ea-east—toward Granger Heights."

The room fell silent. Ava's expression shifted, a glimmer of hope breaking through her tears. Michael frowned, his arms crossed as he stared at the map.

"Even if that's true," Michael finally said, his tone skeptical, "how are we supposed to get them out of a place like that?"

No one had an answer. The weight of Ryan's words hung heavy in the air as the group exchanged uncertain glances.

The tension inside the hideout lingered, unspoken fears pressing down on each of them like a vise. The discussion had ended, but no one moved. The weight of their next decision was suffocating, settling into their bones like cold lead.

A distant rumble of thunder broke the silence, the storm clouds outside rolling in thick and heavy. It was fitting, really.

Ryan tapped a few final keys on his monitor, the soft clicks barely audible over the howling wind outside. The map's glowing screen reflected in his narrowed eyes, and for a brief moment, he looked as though he was searching for something more than just a plan—some reassurance that they weren't walking into a death sentence.

Nat exhaled, wincing as she adjusted her posture. "Then it's decided," she said, her voice steady despite the exhaustion in her limbs. "We move soon."

No one spoke, but they didn't need to.

Far away, across miles of steel and silence, another prisoner stirred in the depths of his cage.

When the guards finally shoved him back into his cell, the heavy door slammed shut with a deafening clang. Nate staggered forward, catching himself on the padded wall. His breaths came in short gasps, and he pressed his forehead against the cool surface, trying to steady himself.

Nate's fingers curled against the firm mattress beneath him, his body instinctively reacting to the faint hum of electricity running through the walls. His breath hitched as he shifted, the wound at his stomach reminding him of its presence with a sharp sting.

His mind was groggy, but his survival instincts were sharpening by the second.

I can't be here. I can't.

His hand went to the collar around his neck, fingers brushing the intricate technology. He didn't need to guess its purpose. One wrong move, and it would detonate. They'd probably already programmed it with his vitals.

He forced himself to stop thinking about Xavier. About the betrayal. Survival came first, everything else could wait.

What do the Rogues think happened to me? What are they going to do to me here? His musings were interrupted by a loud beep.

The heavy metal door of his cell swung open.

CHAPTER 22: CLOSE QUARTERS

The round table in the Pinnacles' meeting room felt less like a symbol of unity and more like a stage for brewing conflict. The air hung thick with tension, illuminated by the stark overhead lights that cast long shadows across the room. Apollo stood at the center, his solar-powered suit gleaming faintly as he scanned the faces of his team. His piercing blue eyes settled on Reptile, whose hulking, reptilian form loomed at the far end of the table.

"You're really going through with this?" Apollo's voice cut through the silence, sharp and disdainful. His blonde hair gleamed under the lights, and his confident stance screamed authority, even if it grated on the others.

Reptile leaned back in his chair, his jagged scales catching the light. His yellow eyes narrowed as his claws scraped faintly against the armrest. "I've told you already. I'm done following orders that lead to nothing but destruction."

Apollo sneered, stepping closer. "So what, you're leaving to play a glorified security guard? Guarding the weak and helpless? That's what you're running off to?"

Reptile's growl was low and dangerous, reverberating through the room. "I'm leaving because I'm tired of the senseless slaughter. There's more to life than tearing apart bio-mutants and playing your little god complex game."

Apollo's smirk faltered, replaced by a cold glare. "A coward, then. Hiding behind some ridiculous idea of morality. You're just a slimy, disgusting creature pretending you're better than me."

The room tensed. Aero shifted uncomfortably in his seat, his amber eyes darting between the two. Tress's vine-like hair twitched as if reacting to the growing unease, and Atlas sat motionless, his massive arms crossed but his jaw tight with disapproval. Angel, seated in the corner, unfurled his wings slightly, a subtle gesture of tension as he watched the exchange with sharp focus.

Reptile rose from his chair slowly, his massive frame towering over Apollo. His slit-pupil eyes burned with anger, but his voice remained measured. "Immature as usual, Apollo. And you still think you're fit to lead us?"

The jab struck a nerve. Apollo's fingers twitched, his jaw tightening. The tension stretched for a single unbearable moment. Before anyone could react, Apollo launched himself over the table, his fist a glowing blur aimed straight for Reptile's face. The impact sent them crashing through the wall, debris raining down as the room erupted into chaos.

Reptile retaliated with raw strength, slamming Apollo into the ground with a deafening crash. The floor cracked under the force, and Reptile's claws came dangerously close to Apollo's throat. "You don't scare me," Reptile snarled, his voice low and threatening.

Apollo grinned despite the situation, his glowing eyes locking onto Reptile's. "You should be." With a burst of solar energy, Apollo freed himself, the force sending Reptile sprawling backward.

The two charged at each other again, their blows colliding with thunderous force. Apollo's strikes were precise and blindingly fast, while Reptile's raw power and durability allowed him to absorb the hits and keep coming. Apollo's attacks were a blur, but every blow against Reptile was like striking a wall of armored flesh. He absorbed the hits with a slow, deliberate grin, his muscles coiling like a predator waiting for its moment.

Golden arcs of plasma surged around Apollo's fists as he wrenched free, the heat warping the surrounding air before he blasted Reptile backward.

Tress stepped forward, her hair extending like tendrils to separate the two combatants. "Enough of this!" she shouted, her voice commanding as her tendrils coiled around Apollo's arm and Reptile's shoulder, pulling them apart.

"That's enough," Atlas growled, moving to flank Apollo with Aero, each grabbing one of his arms "Unless we're shifting to cannibalizing our own roster, maybe put your dick-measuring contest on pause." Aero yelled out.

while Angel stepped in to help hold back Reptile. "You're better than this, Reptile." He said softly. Both men were breathing heavily, their postures still aggressive despite the intervention.

"This isn't how we solve things," Tress continued, her voice sharp as her green eyes flicked between them. "If we're supposed to be a team, then start acting like one."

Reptile let out a frustrated growl but stepped back, shaking off Angel's grip. "This isn't a team," he muttered, his gaze lingering on Apollo. "It's a circus."

Without another word, he turned and stormed out of the room, leaving the rest of the team in tense silence.

Atlas sat down slowly, rubbing the bridge of his nose. "That was a shitshow."

As the doors shut behind Reptile, Apollo exhaled, flexing his fingers. The surrounding air shimmered with heat.

"He thinks he can just walk away from us," he muttered.

No one responded. But Aero and Tress exchanged glances. They knew that tone.

A few days later, in the depths of Granger Heights, the air was suffocating.

Nate's cell was jarring. The cramped, dimly lit space smelled of damp metal and despair. Nate sat on the edge of the cot, his thoughts racing as he tried to piece together his next move. The sound of heavy footsteps approaching his cell snapped him out of his haze.

A shadow loomed outside the bars, and Nate's heart skipped a beat as he looked up. Standing before him was a massive figure, his scales glinting faintly in the dim light.

"What the hell…," Nate muttered, eyeing the mutant warily. "Didn't expect to see one of the Pinnacles in here."

"Didn't expect to end up here either." Reptile tilted his head slightly, a faint smirk curling his lips. "So you're the one who killed the Mammal?"

The calm demeanor caught Nate off guard, and he stuttered out a response. "No—I didn't… He was killed by… by someone I knew."

Reptile's smirk vanished, replaced by a skeptical glare. "And why would anyone believe you?"

Nate hesitated, searching for the right words. "Because he'll show his real face again. I'm sure of it."

Reptile studied him for a moment, his yellow eyes narrowing as if trying to read Nate's soul. Then, to Nate's surprise, the towering mutant chuckled. "Well, until then, you're stuck in hell. And it's lunchtime."

Reptile turned and gestured for Nate to follow. The corridor was dimly lit, the flickering fluorescent lights casting eerie shadows on the walls. Each step felt heavier than the last as Nate passed rows of identical cells. The atmosphere was suffocating, a dark aura of despair hanging over the place.

Nate's stomach churned as they entered the mess hall. The room was vast but oppressive, with long tables stretching across the space. Dozens of mutants sat hunched over trays of food, their eyes hollow and suspicious. Conversations ceased as Nate entered, and he felt the weight of their stares on him.

Whispers rippled through the room, the inmates murmuring about him. His battles with Iron and the Mammal had earned him a reputation, and he could feel the mix of awe and resentment in their gazes.

Scanning the room, Nate spotted familiar faces. Lane sat alone at a distant table, a high-tech blindfold strapped over his eyes. His posture was rigid, his body language screaming with disdain. Nearby, Iron slouched in a corner, his body battered and bruised. The once-intimidating mutant now looked broken, his aura of dominance reduced to bitterness.

Grabbing a tray of food, Nate ignored the open seats left for him and walked directly to Lane's table. He set the tray down and sat across from the blindfolded mutant, ignoring the tension that settled over the room.

Lane tilted his head slightly, his blindfold hiding his expression but not the edge in his voice. "Do you think you're funny?"

"If you're just going to be mad at me, I can sit somewhere else," Nate replied, smirking despite the unease twisting in his gut.

Lane leaned forward slightly. "You're the reason I'm in this hellscape."

Nate met his accusation with a flat stare. "You brought this on yourself the second you attacked us."

Lane's lips curled into a bitter grin as he leaned back, his body language radiating disdain. "You think you're so righteous. You have no idea what you've done. And now, you're here, trapped in the same hell you threw me into."

Nate didn't flinch. "We gave you a chance—more than most ever would. You chose to fight us."

Lane's grin twisted into a scowl, but he remained silent for a moment. Finally, he sighed, leaning back and crossing his arms. "You don't get it, do you? This place… it isn't just a prison. It's a playground. For them." He gestured vaguely toward the guards patrolling the room, their faces cold and impassive.

"What do you mean?" Nate asked, his voice low but steady.

Lane tilted his head, his tone turning dark. "This isn't Granger Heights—it's hell. A facility built for creatures like us, mutants they don't know how to deal with. They keep us here, caged like animals, and when they get bored… they make us fight."

Nate frowned, his stomach sinking. "Fight?"

Lane nodded, his blindfolded gaze piercing through Nate. "Every year, they host the Gauntlet. It's not a tournament. It's a culling. They pit us against each other—mutant against mutant, power against power—until only the strongest are left standing. The rest? They're just meat for the cleanup crew."

Nate's chest tightened. "And… everyone here has to participate?"

Lane's grin returned, more sinister this time. "Everyone. You don't get a choice. And lucky for you, you showed up just a few months before this year's event. That means you'll have plenty of time to train—or to watch and hope someone else kills you before it begins."

Nate clenched his fists, his mind racing. The thought of being forced to fight for his life against other mutants who had been broken and hardened by this place was enough to make his heart pound. But he wouldn't let Lane see his fear.

His voice takes on a dark edge. "Maybe I'll get the chance to kill you this time."

"Can't wait," Nate replies distantly, staring off into the suffocating expanse of the prison.

Lane chuckled, the sound low and mocking. "You're a cocky one, aren't you? We'll see how long that lasts."

The tension between them was broken by the loud clanging of a guard's baton against a metal railing. "Lunch is over!" the guard barked, his voice echoing through the mess hall.

The mutants began to shuffle out, their trays clattering as they stacked them by the doors. Nate stood, glancing one last time at Lane before following the crowd.

As they moved back toward their cells, Nate couldn't shake the weight of what Lane had said. The Gauntlet. A tournament of death, designed to entertain their captors and cull the weakest among them. His thoughts were interrupted by a low growl behind him.

Reptile's towering form loomed just a few steps away, his yellow eyes fixed on Nate. The other mutants gave him a wide berth, their heads lowering as he passed.

"You'll get used to it," Reptile said, his voice a deep rumble.

Nate glanced back at him, confused. "Used to what?"

"The feeling," Reptile replied, his tone grim. "Of being watched. Of knowing that everyone here either wants to kill you or use you to survive."

Nate frowned, his gaze narrowing. "And what about you? What do you want?"

Reptile stopped walking, turning to face Nate fully. His towering frame cast a shadow over the smaller mutant, and for a moment, the room seemed to hold its breath.

"What I want?" Reptile said, his voice low but filled with conviction. "I want out. And if I have to crush anyone who gets in my way, so be it."

Nate held his ground, his heart pounding in his chest. "Then maybe you're no different from the guards keeping us here."

For a moment, Reptile's expression hardened, his claws flexing at his sides. But then he let out a dry chuckle, shaking his head. "You've got guts, I'll give you that. Just don't let it get you killed."

With that, Reptile turned and continued down the hall, leaving Nate standing alone in the suffocating shadows of Granger Heights.

Reptile stepped into the corridor and let the door hiss shut behind him. The hall was narrow and suffocating, lined with matte gray walls that drank in the overhead light. No windows. No signs. Just a repeating pattern of numbered doors and corner-mounted cameras that tracked every movement with silent, red-blinking judgment. Even the ceilings were gridded with motion sensors—so sensitive, a sneeze could trigger a lockdown. He paused at the intersection and let his eyes scan upward. The turret ports above hadn't moved in days, but he knew better. They never blinked, never slept. The prison watched you like it wanted you to try something. Just to remind you what would happen next.

The floor vibrated faintly with the hum of the ventilation system and the ever-churning machinery beneath. This place didn't have guards so much as handlers—people in thick, featureless suits who barely spoke unless it was a command. Everything about Granger Heights was designed to erase identity: no personal effects, no natural light, no sound but your own breath echoing off concrete. The cells weren't cages. They were slabs—sealed, magnetized, and powered by a grid that pulsed like a heartbeat.

He'd seen mutants cry in silence behind those walls. He'd seen others laugh until their throats went dry. But no one talked about escape. Not seriously. Not anymore. Not here.

Back at the Pinnacles' headquarters, the mood was no less tense. Tress stood by the window, her vine-like hair trailing idly along the floor as she gazed out at the sprawling cityscape. Aero lounged in the corner, his sharp eyes flicking toward Apollo, who was pacing back and forth, his frustration radiating off him like heat.

"Reptile's gone," Tress said quietly, breaking the silence.

Apollo stopped pacing, turning to face her. His piercing blue eyes burned with irritation. "He'll be back," he said dismissively. "He always comes crawling back."

Aero snorted, crossing his arms. "Maybe this time he's serious. Can't blame him, really. You're not exactly the easiest person to work with."

Apollo's glare shifted to Aero, but Tress stepped between them before he could respond. "This isn't the time to argue," she said firmly. "We need to focus on what's happening in State 9. The uprisings are only getting worse."

"Then let's crush them," Apollo said coldly. "If Reptile doesn't have the stomach for it, that's his problem. The rest of us will do what needs to be done."

Tress frowned, her green eyes softening. "It's not that simple, Apollo. We're not just fighting mutants—we're fighting people. Innocent people who've been caught in the crossfire."

Apollo scoffed, turning away. "Innocent or not, they're in the way. And if they think they can stop us, they're wrong."

CHAPTER 23: RELENTLESS

Nate woke up to the same stark white walls, the same stale air, the same suffocating weight of the collar locked around his neck. Every morning felt like a cruel loop, a never-ending cycle of confinement and suffering. The hum of the overhead fluorescent lights was constant, a dull drone that had wormed its way into his subconscious. The only variation was the occasional distant scream—some poor bastard enduring another round of the facility's experiments.

He lay on the hard cot, staring at the cracks in the ceiling, letting the background noise fade into white static. The scent of disinfectant and sweat lingered, mixing with the coppery tang of dried blood. It was inescapable, just like everything else in Granger Heights.

His mind wandered to the Rogues. Were they still out there fighting? Did they think he was dead? The thought gnawed at him. Not just because of the uncertainty, but because of the guilt. He hadn't just failed to protect himself—he had failed them, too.

And then there were the lives he had taken. The bio-mutants, the government soldiers, the guards he'd crushed in the heat of battle. Their faces flashed through his mind like a cursed slideshow, each one bringing a fresh pang of regret. He told himself they were enemies, that they would have killed him without hesitation. But was that really justification?

He squeezed his fists, feeling the heat rise in his chest. No. It wasn't about justification. It was about survival. And if the government thought they could break him, they were wrong.

If he was going to be thrown into the Gauntlet, he wasn't going in as easy prey.

Nate threw himself into training with an almost obsessive intensity. There was no gym, no proper equipment—but that didn't matter. He pushed his body in every way possible, his muscles screaming as he forced them past their limits.

Push-ups. Sit-ups. Squats. He used the metal bed frame for resistance, lifting it as if it were a makeshift barbell. The concrete floor was his personal training ground, and he left pools of sweat behind as he worked.

More than anything, he focused on refining his control over Heart Engine. It wasn't just about brute force anymore—he needed precision. He experimented with micro-adjustments, shifting the blood flow in specific muscles to see how it affected his endurance, his speed, his recovery.

One night, he pressed his hand against a bruised rib, focusing his power. He slowed his heart rate, directed the blood flow to the injury, and within minutes, the pain dulled. His healing wasn't instantaneous, but it was faster—more efficient.

His body adapted faster than he expected. His movements became sharper, his reflexes more explosive. The guards took notice. They wanted to break him.

The cafeteria was always tense. The air was thick with unspoken grudges, shifting alliances, and the ever-present threat of violence. It didn't take much to spark a fight—a wrong look, a careless bump, an insult muttered under someone's breath. But today, the tension felt heavier than usual, like something was about to snap.

Nate sat in his usual spot, watching as Cinder made his way through the crowded mess hall. Built like a brick wall, his burned skin stretched taut over corded muscle. He had a reputation—a temper like a wildfire and fists just as deadly. He had been here longer than most, long enough to know the rules. But something about his posture, the way his shoulders were squared, told Nate he didn't care about rules today.

The guards watched from their stations, their hands resting near the detonators strapped to their belts. Every prisoner knew what those meant. Step too far out of line, and they wouldn't bother dragging you away. They'd end you where you stood.

Cinder stopped at the food line, staring down one of the guards—a thick-necked bastard with dead eyes and a shock baton holstered at his hip. The two of them locked gazes for just a second too long.

Nate knew that look. Cinder was going to do something stupid

The moment came when the guard bumped Cinder's tray off the counter, sending food splattering across the floor. The room went silent. Conversations halted. Every inmate knew this wasn't an accident. It was a power move.

Cinder exhaled through his nose. "Pick it up." His voice was low, controlled—but barely.

The guard smirked. "Or what?"

Nate tensed. There were only two ways this ended—Cinder backed down, or he died.

Cinder moved first. His right fist ignited, a wave of heat rippling through the air. He swung at the guard's head, but the bastard was quicker than expected. The shock baton came up, cracking against Cinder's ribs with a burst of electricity. Cinder staggered, his teeth grinding as the charge ran through his body.

But he didn't drop.

With a snarl, he caught the guard's wrist, forcing the baton away. His other hand—still burning—clamped onto the man's throat. The smell of scorching flesh filled the air as the guard choked, struggling against the searing grip.

For a moment, it looked like Cinder might actually win.

Then came the beep.

Nate barely had time to register it before Cinder's head exploded.

A deafening crack echoed through the cafeteria, followed by the sickening wet splatter of blood, bone, and brain matter coating the floor. His body dropped instantly, like a marionette with its strings cut, the stump of his neck still sizzling.

The cafeteria was dead silent.

A sickly wet sound splattered against the floor, the blood pooling near Nate's boots, still steaming from the heat of Cinder's flame. No one moved. Not the prisoners. Not the guards. The scent of burnt flesh, raw meat, and iron clogged the air. Then came the sound—a single drop of blood hitting the linoleum, then another, and another, like rain before a storm.

Cinder's body twitched once. A reflex, nothing more.

The guard who had killed him sighed, wiping his burned throat with the back of his sleeve, before kicking Cinder's corpse away like it was garbage.

A slow, deliberate clap echoed through the cafeteria.

Warden Lariks stood at the edge of the room, watching with an amused smirk. His uniform was crisp, his boots polished to perfection. Unlike the guards, he didn't flinch at the carnage—he welcomed it.

"Ah, such a shame," he mused, stepping closer. "I had a bet going that Cinder would last at least another month."

He eyed the remaining prisoners, his expression dripping with condescension. "Let this be a reminder mutts," he said, spreading his arms like a preacher before a congregation. "You are nothing but dogs in a cage. And I—" He gestured toward the decapitated corpse, the blood pooling at his feet. "I hold the leash."

No one moved. No one spoke.

Nate clenched his fists beneath the table, his nails digging into his palms. He knew that wouldn't be the last time he saw someone die in here.

The tension in Granger Heights grew thicker with each passing day. The inmates whispered about the Gauntlet, their voices hushed, their eyes filled with barely concealed fear.

Most had heard the stories. The Gauntlet was the government's twisted form of entertainment—a blood-soaked spectacle where mutants were forced to fight for survival. Only a handful ever made it out. The rest became corpses.

Nate listened to the rumors. He heard about past champions, about prisoners who had found ways to cheat the system—only to be executed later. He heard about alliances, betrayals, and the brutal reality that awaited him.

One night, he overheard two inmates talking in the corner of the mess hall.

"I heard last year's winner didn't even get a chance to celebrate," one muttered. "They put him down like a dog."

"No way. They always let the winner join the military."

The first inmate shook his head. "Not this time. He tried to escape. Didn't even make it past the first wall."

Nate clenched his jaw. "There had to be a way out." Nate said under his breath.

Days passed. The guards became lazier, confident in their control. The scientists grew more comfortable in their sadistic experiments.

And in that monotony Nate started noticing things.

The way one guard hesitated when giving orders, like he didn't fully agree with what was happening.

The patterns in the patrol routes, tiny gaps where movement wasn't monitored for a few seconds.

The collars—flawed, imperfect. They weren't as invincible as the government wanted them to appear.

And then there was Reptile.

Nate had seen the former Pinnacle before, back when he was free. Reptile had always worn the same collar in public appearances, but it had never registered as strange.

Why would a government enforcer still be wearing a prisoner's collar?

That night, Nate sat across from Iron during dinner. The former government soldier looked worse for wear, his bruises fresh from another round of "discipline."

Nate took a bite of his tasteless meal before speaking. "Your collar's different from before."

Iron barely reacted. "What of it?"

"How long have they had you under their control?" Nate pressed.

Iron's expression darkened. "Too long."

Nate studied him carefully. "You ever think about getting out?"

Iron's lip curled. "You looking for allies, brat? I'm just biding my time until I get the chance to beat you into the dirt. Nothing more."

Nate smirked. "Good talk." He stood up, his mind already working through the next steps.

Iron might have been reluctant, but he wasn't the only one with doubts.

There was a crack in the system. And Nate was going to exploit it.

The days blurred together, a relentless grind of training, pain, and survival. Every meal tasted like ash. Every hour was a battle against exhaustion. Nate barely slept. When he did, his dreams were haunted—faces he had fought, people he had lost. He woke up each morning with a pounding heart, drenched in sweat, fists clenched like he had to fight for every breath.

His vision blurred, his arms shook, but he kept going. Pain didn't matter. Nothing mattered except getting stronger. Because if he stopped, if he let himself feel it for even a second, the weight of it all would crush him.

He gritted his teeth, digging his fingers into the cold floor. Again. One more set. Again. If he couldn't fight his way out of here, he'd die trying.

The experiments were the worst. At first, they only took his blood—vials upon vials, drawn until he felt lightheaded. Then came the injections, foreign chemicals forced into his veins, burning like acid, meant to test his mutation's limits. But the actual nightmare began with the endurance trials. They strapped him to machines, hooked electrodes to his skin, and pushed his body to the breaking point. Nate barely felt the first electric shock. His muscles locked, his body jerking against the restraints, but he refused to scream.

A slow chuckle came from the viewing deck above.

"Oh, this one's got spirit," Warden Lariks mused, watching like a man admiring a work of art. "Tell me, Doctor, how long do you think he can last before he breaks?"

The scientist beside him hesitated. "His mutation is… unusual. His heart is compensating for every test we run. The longer we push, the stronger he becomes."

"Then we push harder," Lariks interrupted, his tone sharp. "He will break. They all do."

He ran until his legs collapsed, fought until his muscles tore. Once, they submerged him in a water tank, laughing as they timed how long he could hold his breath. He clenched his jaw, ignoring the panic clawing at his chest. His Heart Engine kicked in, maximizing oxygen efficiency. Eighteen minutes passed before he blacked out.

They revived him with a sharp electric shock. He woke up choking, gasping for air, his body trembling with exhaustion. The scientists murmured to each other, taking notes like he was some lab rat they could break down and rebuild. Every session, every experiment—they only hardened him. The pain, the exhaustion, the torment—it became fuel. He wasn't just surviving anymore. He was preparing.

Nate wasn't the only one suffering. Every day, he saw other mutants dragged into the labs, only to return broken, twitching, half-alive. Not all of them survived. But some fought back. Two of them caught his attention: Echo and Manny.

Echo was wiry and jittery, with short black hair and a dark complexion. He was always twitching like he had too much energy to contain. His mutation allowed him to generate high-frequency sonic waves, from echolocation to piercing screams that could rupture eardrums. He had sharp, calculating eyes that rarely blinked, and he moved like a bird too anxious to perch. A natural scout, Echo kept his head down but had clearly been around long enough to know how the system worked. Beneath his skittish movements, Nate sensed a controlled fury, barely suppressed.

Manny was the opposite. Towering and broad, with a square jaw and a hulking frame, he looked like someone bred to break bones. His mutation gave him a thick, muscular tongue that could shoot out like a whip and coil with crushing force—he could pin someone or snap a limb before they could react. But despite his monster-like strength, Manny had a laid-back charm. He cracked jokes constantly, even during fights, earning him the nickname "Man Man." Where Echo was edge and tension, Manny was comic relief and controlled chaos.

Nate started sitting with them at lunch, their conversation low, careful.

"Word is, they're moving up the Gauntlet schedule," Echo muttered one day, glancing around the mess hall. "They're bringing in new Gauntletiers. Fresh meat."

Manny raised an eyebrow. "Why? We're already packed like sardines."

Echo shrugged. "Who knows? Maybe they're running low on entertainment. Maybe they just want to see us rip each other apart."

Nate frowned. "That means less time to prepare for the bloodbath."

"It's not just a bloodbath," Echo muttered, his voice tight with disgust.

Nate frowned. "What do you mean?"

Echo's hands clenched. "The Gauntlet isn't just for their entertainment. It's a fucking business. The high rollers, the government bastards—they bet on us. They watch the fights like we're nothing but dogs."

Nate's stomach twisted. He could see it in Echo's face—the shame, the rage. "They bet on us?"

"They don't just bet," Manny said, his usual grin nowhere to be found. "The winners? The strong ones? They don't 'win' shit. They're sold."

Silence.

Echo nodded. "Military, mercenary work, black ops. If you survive, they break you down, force you into service. No one leaves free."

Echo leaned forward, voice dropping lower. "There's another thing. Rumor is, there's someone else here. Locked up. Codename: Fire."

Nate's stomach tightened. "Fire?"

Echo's expression turned serious. "They keep him on the second floor. No one knows what he did to get isolated, but if they won't even put him in the general population, he's gotta be dangerous."

Manny grinned. "Let's go meet him then."

Echo smacked the back of his head. "Man Man, shut your toad ass up. You trying to get us all killed?"

Nate stayed quiet, filing the information away. If Fire was being kept separate, it meant he was either incredibly valuable or incredibly unstable. Either way, he was worth investigating.

Fights were common inside Granger Heights. Sometimes, they were scheduled sparring matches—a way for the guards to gauge who was Gauntlet-ready. Other times, they were for entertainment. One afternoon, the guards threw Nate into the center of the training yard. A crowd of prisoners gathered as the guards barked orders.

"New rules, boys," one of them sneered. "No powers. Hand-to-hand only. Winner gets an extra meal."

The other fighter stepped forward—a mountain of a man, covered in scars, eyes cold and dead. Dredge. Nate had seen him before. A pit fighter, undefeated, his body a wall of raw muscle.

Dredge cracked his knuckles. "You're small."

Nate rolled his shoulders. "You're ugly."

Dredge charged. Nate barely dodged as a massive fist came swinging at his head. The air rippled with force. The sheer power behind it would've cracked his skull open if it landed. He ducked low, driving a quick punch into Dredge's side. The impact was solid, but the bastard barely flinched.

Dredge snarled, launching another punch. Nate dodged again, weaving through the barrage of attacks, his mind working through possibilities. Dredge was too strong to trade blows with. If he was going to win, he needed to end this quickly. He waited for the next attack, watching the way Dredge overextended with each punch, leaving his ribs exposed just for a second too long.

Nate's fist shot forward like a piston, slamming into Dredge's solar plexus. The impact sent a shockwave through his opponent's body, forcing the air from his lungs. Dredge wheezed, staggering back. Before he could recover, Nate swept his leg out from under him, sending him crashing to the ground.

The guards banged on the glass, signaling the end of the match. Dredge glared up at him, coughing. "You little—"

Nate just walked away.

That night, Nate sat on his cot, thinking. The Gauntlet was coming too fast. If he waited, if he let them control the timeline, he'd be dead. He needed a way out, and he wasn't the only one. Echo and Manny sat across from him, their voices barely a whisper.

"I talked to Agent Ron," Echo murmured. "There's a guard. Not like the others. Might be... persuadable."

Nate's jaw clenched. "How persuadable?"

Manny grinned. "I'd say about two rations and a favor's worth."

Nate exhaled. It wasn't much, but it was something. They had two options—go through with the Gauntlet and hope to survive, or find a way out before it even started. Neither was ideal, but one thing was certain. If they wanted to live, they couldn't afford to wait for the system to decide their fate.

CHAPTER 24: CALM

Nate couldn't tell if hours had passed or just minutes. Time in Granger Heights was slippery—thin, stretched, and strangely repetitive. There were no clocks, no sunrises. Just lights that dimmed when they wanted and humming generators that never stopped. He lay flat on the cold floor of his cell, eyes fixed on the little black circle in the corner—the camera. He swore he saw it blink once. Maybe it didn't. But it felt like it did.

He hadn't heard Reptile in a while. No voices. No guards. Just silence. That was the worst part. Not the pain. Not even the fear. It was the quiet. Like the prison was waiting for them to break themselves before it had to lift a finger.

He rolled to his side and stared at the concrete wall. It wasn't just a building. It was a system. Designed to contain, to erase. Even breathing felt like resistance.

Every day, Nate was escorted to the lunch hall by Reptile. The towering mutant moved with a quiet authority, his reptilian eyes scanning the corridors with sharp precision. At first, he barely spoke, his silence as imposing as his monstrous form. But as the weeks passed, the tension between them softened, and though their exchanges were brief, there was something simmering beneath the surface—a history, a weight, a reason why Reptile wasn't with the Pinnacles anymore.

Nate studied him whenever he could. Reptile wasn't just a former enforcer—he had been one of the best. Yet here he was, shackled with the same explosive collar as the rest of them, taking orders from the same guards he once fought beside. There was something off about that. One day, as they walked, Nate decided to push a little harder.

"You know, that collar on your neck…" Nate said, keeping his voice casual. "It looks bigger than it did on TV."

Reptile stopped dead in his tracks. Before Nate could react, he was slammed against the cold, metallic wall with terrifying force. Clawed fingers pressed against his throat, not enough to cut, but enough to make it clear—one wrong word, and he'd be bleeding out on the floor. Reptile's sharp teeth bared in a snarl, his pupils narrowing into deadly slits.

"You have no idea what you're talking about, kid," he growled, his voice a low, venomous hiss.

Nate barely flinched. He had seen the way Reptile handled himself, controlled but restrained. If he had wanted Nate dead, he would have done it already. Reptile's claws tapped against the wall as he spoke, his voice slower now, more deliberate.

"You think the Pinnacles are heroes? I used to think that too," he muttered. "Then I saw what they do to people who don't follow orders." His claws flexed, digging into his palms. "I used to believe in them. I was one of them. Hell, I was proud of it."

He let out a slow breath, but it was almost shaky, like he was trying to hold something back. "Then I learned the truth."

"They don't save lives—they control them. And if you step out of line…" He trailed off, baring his teeth again. "Let's just say I've got the scars to prove it."

Nate kept his breathing steady, feeling the weight of the moment pressing down on them. Reptile wasn't just angry—he was haunted.

"What happened?" Nate asked.

Reptile's grip on his collar tightened for a moment before he let go, stepping back. He studied Nate with an unreadable expression before exhaling through his nose.

"There was a mission," Reptile said finally. "Classified. We were sent to deal with a mutant insurgent group—small-time rebels. Nothing we hadn't handled before. But they weren't just rebels. They were kids. Starving, scared, running from the same people we thought we were protecting." His claws curled into fists. "We were ordered to wipe them out. No survivors. When I hesitated, they sent someone else in to finish the job."

The way his voice tightened told Nate everything. Someone important had died. Someone Reptile had tried to protect.

"Who was it?" Nate pressed.

Reptile didn't answer immediately. His gaze flickered away for a second before he finally spoke again.

"Her name was Talia." His voice was quieter now, as if just saying the name was an effort. "She wasn't a fighter. Just a kid who got caught in the crossfire. I—" His jaw tightened. "I tried to stop it, but Apollo made sure she didn't make it out."

Nate's breath hitched. Apollo. That was the first time he had heard that name in here.

Reptile saw the recognition in Nate's eyes and smirked, but there was no humor in it. "Yeah. That Apollo." His voice was almost mocking. "The golden boy. The Pinnacle's prodigy. Strong, fast, untouchable." He flexed his fingers, and his claws glinted under the artificial lighting. "He made sure I knew my place before they threw me in here."

"So that's why you left," Nate murmured.

"I didn't leave," Reptile muttered. "I was removed."

Nate folded his arms. "And now you're playing enforcer for them, anyways?"

Reptile's eyes flashed, but instead of anger, something else surfaced—something almost like regret. "You think I have a choice?" He scoffed. "You're young. You still think choices mean something. They don't. You survive, or you die. And surviving means doing the job." His gaze lingered on Nate for a moment before he shook his head. "Even if you knew the truth, what could you do about it?"

"I could do a lot more if I wasn't stuck here," Nate said.

Reptile stared at him for a long time before something almost resembling a smirk crossed his face. It was small, barely there, but it was the closest thing to amusement Nate had seen from him.

"You'd need a lot of help to do something that stupid, kid," he muttered, turning and continuing down the hall.

Nate rubbed his throat, watching the hulking figure walk away. He had been right. Reptile wasn't here by choice.

And maybe, just maybe, that meant he wasn't completely lost yet.

Nate spent the rest of the day thinking about the encounter. It stayed with him through training, through the endless mental calculations of escape routes, through the dull, tasteless meals. When he finally sat down at his usual table with Echo and Manny, his mind was still racing.

Manny smirked, shoving a tray of food toward Nate. "Man, this stuff makes prison worse. Back in the day, I had this spot near my place—an old-school diner, greasy as hell, but they made waffles that could fix your soul. Me and my little sis used to hit it up every weekend. She'd pile on so much whipped cream, the waffles barely stood a chance."

Nate raised an eyebrow. "What happened to her?"

Manny's grin faded slightly, his tone growing quieter. "Government scooped her up a while back. Probably stuck in some place like this, just trying to survive." He tapped the side of his tray and forced a small smile. His eyes clouded for a moment. "But hey, once we're outta here, maybe I'll take her back there. First stack's on me."

Nate didn't know what to say. There was a lot of bravado in a place like this, but every now and then, the walls cracked just enough to show the truth. They were all fighting for something. Some for revenge, some for escape. Some just to see someone they loved again.

Time passed slowly. Nate's days were consumed by training, reconnaissance, and piecing together the fragments of information he had gathered. He had never seen the outside of the facility, but through cryptic hints from Reptile and Echo's echolocation scouting, he began to form a rough idea of the layout. The prison was on an island, surrounded by miles of water. Escape on foot was impossible, and even if they made it out, the question of what lay beyond the coastline loomed large.

The collars were the biggest obstacle. Nate had spent weeks observing how the guards activated and monitored them, but he still couldn't determine how to disable them without triggering an explosion. He needed to find a way to communicate with the Rogues, to coordinate a rescue. But with no access to the outside world and no clear means of sending a message, the plan seemed like a distant dream.

One night, as Nate lay in his cell staring at the ceiling, he felt a strange sensation in his arm. At first, he thought it was a muscle spasm from over-training. But as he sat up and looked closely, he saw his veins moving under his skin, shifting in response to his thoughts. Intrigued, Nate began experimenting.

Nate had always been able to manipulate his blood flow with precision, but this was different. He found he could direct his veins to specific areas of his body, engorging them with blood to reinforce his muscles or redistribute weight. He theorized that he could use this ability to strengthen his punches, reduce blood loss from injuries, or even absorb impact more efficiently.

He trained this new technique relentlessly. His next fight was coming.

And he wasn't going to lose.

The atmosphere inside Granger Heights had changed. Conversations were quieter, eyes more calculating. The inmates could feel it—the Gauntlet was coming, and the weight of it pressed down on them like a storm on the horizon.

Nate trained harder than ever, pushing his body beyond its limits. He didn't just want to survive. Nate wanted to be stronger, faster, sharper. He had discovered a new layer to Heart Engine, the ability to manipulate his veins, shifting blood flow to different parts of his body. It wasn't just about enhancing his strikes anymore—he could redirect damage, lessen impact, and keep himself standing longer in fights where endurance meant life or death. But he needed more than just raw ability.

He needed to understand his enemy.

On the eve of the Gauntlet, Nate sat in his cell, muscles aching from the day's training. The tension in the air was suffocating. The loudspeakers crackled to life, the static buzzing through the prison's cold walls. Then, the voice of Warden Lariks filled the cells, slow and dripping with amusement.

"Good evening, my lovely little freaks. I hope you're all enjoying your stay in my humble home."

Silence. No one spoke. No one dared.

"I just wanted to remind you that the Gauntlet is coming. Your chance at glory. You're one shot to prove that you are worthy of existing a little longer." He chuckled. "And the best part? Only one of you will get that chance."

Nate clenched his fists, jaw tightening.

"So get comfortable. Train hard. Kill your fellow prisoners if you must," Lariks continued. "But remember—in the end, you all lose."

That's when a guard approached his door and slipped a folded piece of paper through the slot.

Nate grabbed it cautiously, unfolding the thin, crumpled page. It was a list of matchups.

His eyes scanned the names, recognizing some, dreading others. Then, his gaze landed on his own opponent.

Nathan Mercer vs. Knight.

His stomach turned. Knight. He had heard a name whispered in hushed voices around the prison. A former Pinnacle. A fighter who was once considered unstoppable. But unlike Reptile, Knight had disappeared years ago. Most assumed he was dead. Apparently, that wasn't the case.

Nate leaned back against the cold wall, forcing himself to breathe. He had seen old footage of Knight, had watched him move with impossible speed and precision. His ability allowed him to harden his skin into sharp, jagged scales, making him a living weapon. Even without that, the man had been a soldier, a tactician, a war machine disguised as a man.

But there was something off about this matchup. If Knight was so dangerous, why was he still here? Why wasn't he out there, working for the government like the rest of the Pinnacles?

Nate had questions. And he knew exactly who to ask.

That night, Nate spotted Reptile patrolling the halls. He waited until the towering mutant was near before speaking. "I need to know about Knight." Nate said quietly

Reptile didn't stop walking. "You're not ready for that fight."

Nate followed him, lowering his voice. "Then tell me how to be ready."

Reptile finally stopped, turning to face Nate. His yellow eyes glowed faintly under the dim prison lights.

"You don't fight Knight head-on," Reptile muttered. "You survive him."

Nate crossed his arms. "That bad?"

Reptile let out a slow exhale, his expression unreadable. "Knight was one of us once. One of the best. Then something changed. He stopped following orders, stopped listening. The government tried to break him, same as they're trying to break you. The difference is, it worked."

Nate frowned. "What do you mean?"

Reptile hesitated, then leaned in slightly. "You ever seen someone fight because they want to? Not because they have to, not because they're forced, but because it's all they have left?"

Nate didn't respond. He didn't need to. He had seen that look in people's eyes before.

Reptile straightened. "They turned him into something worse than a soldier. A weapon with nothing left to lose." He paused, then added, "If you want to survive, don't try to win. Just make sure you're the one still breathing when it's over."

With that, Reptile turned and walked away, leaving Nate standing in the dimly lit corridor.

The next day, Nate sat with Manny and Echo in the cafeteria. It was the last meal before the Gauntlet. The food was the same disgusting slop as always, but today, no one complained.

Manny was the first to break the silence. "I know we all got our fights coming, so let's make a deal. No hard feelings. If we have to go against each other, we go all out. We make it a fight worth remembering."

Echo smirked. "That's if you even make it past round one, Man Man."

Manny grinned, but there was a shadow behind his usual carefree demeanor. "You'll see, bat-boy. I've been holding back."

Nate poked at his food. "If we're making promises, then I'll add one. If I make it out of here, I'm coming back."

Echo raised an eyebrow. "To rescue us?"

Nate shook his head. "To burn this place to the ground."

Manny chuckled. "Now that's a promise I can get behind."

No one rushed to finish their food. No one cracked jokes. It was the slowest meal they had ever eaten, and every bite tasted like their last.

For a few minutes, they weren't prisoners. They weren't fighters being sent into an arena to kill for entertainment. They were just people, sharing a meal, talking like they had something more than survival waiting for them. But the moment was short-lived.

The prison speakers crackled, then wailed—a long, grating sound that echoed off the cold concrete walls. The entire cafeteria went silent. No movement. No last words. Just the sound of hundreds of prisoners holding their breath, waiting to see which of them would survive the night.

Then the guards came.

CHAPTER 25: STORM

Near a military port city in White Water, State 5, the Rogues had never felt so powerless.

Huddled together in the dim light of a run-down warehouse, they sat in tense silence as the glow of a small, flickering television cast long shadows over their faces. The place smelled of salt, rust, and engine grease, remnants of whatever industry had once used this forgotten space. Now, it was just a shell—a temporary hiding place while they tried to plan the impossible.

On the screen before them, Granger Heights loomed like a tombstone, its towering walls and floodlights giving it the appearance of something more war zone than prison. Millions of people around the world were watching this broadcast, cheering for the bloodshed to come. For the Rogues, it was something else entirely. It was a nightmare they couldn't wake up from.

"I can't believe they still run this ancient murder trap," Nat muttered, her arms crossed tightly over her chest as she stared at the screen. The disgust in her voice was obvious, but beneath it, there was something else—fear.

Ava, who had barely blinked since the broadcast started, shifted uncomfortably. "Nat, how are we even supposed to get to them if they're inside that place? It's not like we can just walk in."

"There's bound to be a ship docked in White Water we can commandeer," Nat replied, her voice sharper than before. "Once we get to the island, we'll come up with a plan to retrieve them."

Michael, who had been leaning against the warehouse's rusted metal wall, let out a dry laugh. "That's your plan? Steal a boat and wing it?"

Nat's glare cut toward him. "We don't have the luxury of a detailed strategy, Michael. It's not like Granger Heights leaves blueprints lying around for us to study. We go in, we improvise, and we don't leave without them."

No one responded right away. The flickering light from the television made their shadows stretch long against the warehouse walls, distorted, fractured—just like their options. Morgan's fingers dug into her arms, her nails pressing against her skin hard enough to leave marks. Ava shifted her weight, opening her mouth to speak, then closing it again. No one wanted to say it out loud, but they were thinking the same thing. What if we're too late?

Morgan, who had been the quietest so far, suddenly leaned forward, eyes widening as she pointed at the screen. "Wait, wait—it's starting!"

Everyone turned their attention back to the television, and the weight in the room grew heavier.

With dramatic camera angles and orchestrated music, the broadcast shifted to a highly produced introduction. The government had turned this into an event, a worldwide spectacle. The aerial view of Granger Heights made it look even more suffocating, its concrete walls towering over the surrounding wasteland. Massive spotlights illuminated the bloodstained battleground where the condemned would fight for their lives.

One by one, the prisoners were paraded across the screen. And then Nate appeared. The warehouse fell into complete silence.

Morgan exhaled slowly. "He's gotten a lot bigger since we saw him last, huh?" Her voice was soft, almost hesitant, like she was afraid that speaking too loudly might shatter the moment.

Michael, for once, didn't have a sarcastic remark. His arms were still crossed, his jaw tight. "He better have been training his ass off if he wants to last long enough for us to get him out of there."

Ava hugged herself, trying to steady her breathing. "At least we know he's alive," she whispered.

Their momentary relief was quickly drowned out as the announcer's voice boomed through the speakers as he listed off the matches for the day.

"And for the second to last round… The Blood Curdle, HEARTBEAT versus the Shattered Pinnacle, KNIGHT!"

The words hit like a sledgehammer.

Nat's body stiffened. She had hoped Nate wouldn't be thrown against someone too overwhelming in the first round. But this? Knight?

Michael let out a slow exhale, shaking his head. "Shit."

The warehouse seemed to shrink around them. Morgan gripped the edge of the table, her knuckles turning white. Ava's lips parted like she wanted to say something, but no words came. Even Michael—who always had something to add—just exhaled slowly, rubbing a hand over his face.

Ava's hands curled into fists. "That's really fucking bad. How the hell is he supposed to beat a Pinnacle?."

"I trust Nate's abilities," Nat said, though her voice was quieter than before, "but Knight might be too much for him."

On the screen, Nate was standing motionless.

There was no time for him to process what was happening. The Gauntlet had begun.

The prisoners were corralled like cattle, forced into a massive open, holding area just outside the arena's battlefield. Nate moved with the others, his collar heavy around his throat, the thick steel walls pressing in on all sides. The air inside was suffocating—a mix of sweat, blood, and damp rot, like something had died in here and never been removed.

Everywhere he looked, he saw faces hardened by suffering. Some prisoners stood tall, their expressions blank, unreadable. Others hunched their shoulders, avoiding eye contact, their bodies tense with the knowledge that they weren't leaving this place alive.

The guards watched from raised platforms, rifles locked and loaded. But it was the detonators strapped to their belts that held the real power. The collars around each prisoner's neck ensured that resistance meant instant death. A guard strolled lazily past the prisoners, his fingers tapping the detonator at his hip like it was a toy.

Click. Click. Click.

Every press let out a faint beep—just enough to make the collars light up, just enough to remind them that any second they could be next. Some flinched. Others didn't even blink. They had learned there was no point.

In the center of the battlefield, a colossal metal capsule had been wheeled in, its reinforced plating glinting under the floodlights. Murmurs spread through the prisoners.

"That has to be Fire," someone whispered.

"They're really letting him out?" another muttered.

Nate stared at the capsule, his stomach twisting. The way the guards were positioned, the way their fingers hovered closer to their weapons, made it clear—whatever was inside, even they were afraid of it.

A mechanical whir signaled the start of the first match. The massive steel gate at the far end of the battlefield began to rise, and the guards pulled two names from the roster.

The Deathloop, Echo and The Sickening, Weezer.

Nate's muscles tensed as Echo stepped forward, his face neutral, his wiry frame looking almost too small compared to the battlefield he was walking into.

Across from him, Weezer slouched into position. His skin was sickly pale, almost translucent, his posture hunched, his breathing ragged. But Nate knew better than to underestimate him. Weezer's ability was deadly—a toxic gas expelled from his lungs capable of suffocating anyone within range.

The announcer's voice rang out through the arena.

"BEGIN!"

Weezer lurched forward the second the match started. His mouth stretched unnaturally wide, a thick, green cloud pouring out from his throat like a living thing. The gas spread rapidly, curling through the air, moving with a disturbing unnaturalness.

The moment it reached Echo, he moved.

A sharp inhale, a shift in his stance—and then, with a force that seemed impossible for someone his size, he let loose a deafening supersonic scream.

The sound wave ripped through the battlefield, tearing the toxic gas apart in an instant. The sheer force of it sent shockwaves through the air, knocking some prisoners off balance even from the sidelines.

Weezer stumbled, clutching his head. His skin cracked, his ears began to bleed.

Nate clenched his jaw. He knew what was coming next.

For a moment, deathly silence filled the arena. The force of Echo's scream had torn through the battlefield, splitting the gas apart like a hurricane scattering smoke. The impact had been enough to send a vibration through the ground, even making some of the prisoners in the holding area shift uncomfortably.

Weezer clutched his head, his hands trembling as thick blood poured from his ears. His whole body swayed, his balance destroyed by the ruptured eardrums and the aftershock of Echo's attack.

He blinked, disoriented. Then he collapsed onto his knees, shaking. Nate, still standing among the other prisoners, felt his stomach twist. Echo had won. But that didn't mean Weezer was walking away. One guard tapped something on his wrist. A barely audible beep echoed across the arena.

The beep echoed for half a second. Not long enough to react. Not long enough to plead. Not long enough to realize he was already dead. Then—

A flash of red, a wet explosion, and silence.

His head vanished in an instant, replaced by a violent, red explosion of bone, brain, and blood. A wave of warm gore splattered onto the ground, and his body slumped forward, twitching for half a second before going completely still. The smell of burned flesh and iron saturated the air.

The crowd erupted.

Nate barely blinked. The smell of burnt flesh filled his nostrils, thick, putrid, almost suffocating. He had seen death before, had caused it, had survived it—but this? This wasn't a fight. It was a slaughter. He looked at the guards. Not a single one reacted. No acknowledgment of the body, no hesitation in resetting the collars for the next match. Just routine.

The spectators—rich, powerful, safe behind layers of security and comfort—cheered like it was a damn halftime show. They roared, clapped, some even laughing as the cameras zoomed in on the headless corpse twitching in the sand.

Nate barely heard them. He couldn't stop staring at Echo's face.

There was no victory in his expression. Just cold, bitter understanding. Echo had fought well, flawlessly even, but in the end, it hadn't mattered. The Gauntlet wasn't about skill. It was about control.

Echo turned away from what was left of Weezer's body and made his way back toward the waiting area, his hands clenched so tightly his knuckles were white. No words were spoken between the prisoners. No nods of acknowledgment.

Nothing.

Because there was nothing to say. The system had reminded them all of their place.

The warehouse felt suffocating. No one spoke. No one moved.

The TV flickered with the Granger Heights logo, an overlay flashing across the screen with Weezer's name crossed out in thick red letters.

Morgan was the first to react, her voice quiet, shaken. "They didn't even hesitate."

Michael exhaled slowly, rubbing a hand down his face. "They never do."

Ava had turned away from the screen, her arms wrapped around herself. Her breaths were slow, deliberate, like she was trying to push back whatever emotion threatened to surface.

Nat's jaw was clenched so tightly that the muscles in her neck were tense. "This isn't a game. This isn't a fight for survival. It's a goddamn execution line."

Morgan swallowed hard. "Echo didn't even kill him. He just won."

Michael scoffed, shaking his head. "Winning is losing in this place. If you don't die in the fight, they kill you for putting on a bad show."

Ava suddenly turned, her voice sharp. "Then why the hell do they even bother?"

Nat didn't answer right away. Her eyes were still glued to the screen. The camera had switched angles, now showing the other contestants waiting for their turn. Their faces were unreadable, their postures tense. They had just seen the same thing the Rogues had. And now, they had to step into that same slaughterhouse.

Nat exhaled through her nose, her voice quiet but unwavering. "Because if they make you believe there's a chance, they can get everyone to fight for them."

The prisoners were forced to stand in the holding area as the blood from Weezer's corpse seeped into the sand. No one made a sound.

Nate's heartbeat pounded in his ears.

He had seen death before. He had killed before. But there was something different about this.

It wasn't the violence itself. It wasn't even the fact that a man had just been executed in front of him. It was the way no one reacted.

No horror. No protest. Not even a flinch.

The Gauntlet had done its job. It had broken these people so thoroughly that a human being blown apart was nothing more than an expected result.

The metallic stench of blood was thick in the air. Nate could still hear the wet sound of the collar detonating, the way the remains had splattered against the sand. He forced himself to breathe evenly.

They wanted blood. They wanted fear. They thought they had broken him. They hadn't. Not even close.

CHAPTER 26: MERCY-LESS

The midday sun was merciless, bearing down on the bloodstained sand with unrelenting heat. There was nowhere to escape it—no shade, no shadows, just open ground surrounded by towering metal walls. The air was thick with sweat, blood, and scorched heat. Even breathing felt like a chore.

Above the pit, massive holographic screens displayed the faces of the competitors, their names appearing beside them in bold, stylized letters. Drones hovered overhead, their tiny engines humming as they recorded every movement, every drop of blood, and every broken body. The Gauntlet wasn't just a battle. It was a global event, a carefully crafted spectacle meant to keep the world entertained.

Nate sat in the holding area, his back against the cold steel barricade that separated the waiting competitors from the battlefield. Around him, fighters of all kinds were preparing themselves. Some paced anxiously, their eyes darting to the arena with nervous energy. Others sat in silence, mentally bracing for what was about to come. A few exchanged quiet words, forming brief alliances that would shatter the moment survival took priority.

One man near Nate muttered under his breath, rocking slightly. "You don't fight a Pinnacle. You survive them."

Someone else let out a low chuckle. "If you're lucky."

Nate didn't respond.

A loud chime rang through the arena.

The announcer's voice echoed across the battlefield, dripping with manufactured excitement.

"And now, our second match of the day—The Unwavering Ironclad versus Bedrock Lexar!"

The crowd erupted in a deafening roar.

Ironclad stepped onto the battlefield first, rolling his shoulders, his expression unreadable. Despite his time in the prison, he still carried himself like a soldier—calm, precise, and confident. Across from him, Lexar entered the arena, towering over nearly everyone. His body was a fortress of thick, rock-like skin, his sheer size making him look like a moving mountain.

Nate had fought plenty of big guys before, but Lexar was something else. He wasn't just large. He was built like a siege weapon.

The horn sounded.

Lexar moved first, fast for his size. His massive fist swung through the air, the force alone kicking up sand as he tried to crush Ironclad in one devastating blow.

Ironclad dodged, just as Lexar's punch crashed into the ground, sending tremors through the arena floor. Instead of retreating, Ironclad stepped in, closing the distance with ruthless efficiency.

His first punch connected with Lexar's ribs, sending cracks through the rock-like exterior. The second strike followed immediately—a vicious uppercut to the jaw. Shards of hardened stone broke away from Lexar's face, revealing raw skin beneath.

Lexar grunted but didn't back down. He swung again, using his entire weight, but Ironclad weaved under the strike and retaliated. His fists moved with calculated precision, each hit targeting the weak spots he had already exposed.

The crowd cheered wildly as the fight turned into a brutal exchange of blows.

Lexar, growing frustrated, tried to grab Ironclad in a bear hug, but the smaller man slipped free, using his agility to stay one step ahead. It was clear now—Lexar wasn't used to an opponent that didn't just try to overpower him.

Ironclad ducked another slow, powerful swing, then went for the finish.

With a sharp pivot, he drove his fist into the weakened section of Lexar's head.

A deep crack echoed across the arena.

Lexar staggered, his massive form swaying for a moment. Then his body gave out. He crumpled forward, his enormous frame crashing into the sand, sending a cloud of dust into the air.

The announcer's voice cut through the noise. "Ironclad advances to the next round!"

The crowd erupted, but Nate barely heard them. Inside the holding area, no one spoke. Because everyone knew what came next. The tension didn't ease as the next names appeared on the massive screens.

Lane sat in silence, his fingers tracing the edge of the blindfold in his lap. The fabric was worn; the edges frayed from years of use. He had never needed it before Granger Heights. Before this place, he had control—or at least something close to it. Now, he barely recognized himself.

"I've killed more people than I can count," he muttered, the words barely escaping his lips. "And for what? A world that'll never accept me?"

A sharp knock rattled the bars of his holding cell.

The guard outside smirked, his voice filled with mock amusement. "Let's go, nightmare boy. You're up."

Lane inhaled slowly, letting the breath steady him before pulling the blindfold over his eyes.

The crowd's noise hit him like a wall the moment the waking nightmare stepped out. He could feel them watching. Thousands of eyes locked onto him. Across the battlefield, his opponent stood waiting—a mutant named Blaine the bleeder, his arms and legs covered in jagged bone spikes. He grinned, tapping one of the sharp protrusions against his palm.

The horn sounded.

Blaine rushed forward, moving fast despite his bulky frame.

As Blaine closed the distance, Lane's visor slowly slid down, revealing his glowing ember eyes.

Blaine's sprint slowed, then stopped altogether. His cocky grin vanished. His chest heaved, his fingers twitching involuntarily. Blaine's eyes widened in sheer terror. Blaine let out a wheezing sob. His body convulsed violently, spasming as if unseen hands were tearing him apart from the inside. Blaine's mouth stretched wide in a silent scream—only a strangled gurgle escaped as his mind fractured. His fingers dug into his own skin, raking deep grooves into his face as if he could claw the terror out of his skull.

Nate watched from the sidelines as Blaine's entire body trembled violently, his breath coming in short, ragged gasps. He clawed at his own face, eyes darting wildly as if he were trying to escape something only he could see.

Lane took a slow step forward. Blaine fell to his knees.

The crowd, once deafening, fell into an uneasy silence.

With one fluid motion, Lane reached out, grabbed one of Blaine's own bone spikes, and drove it straight into his chest.

A strained gasp escaped Blaine's lips, his body jerking violently before going still. Blood poured into the sand, dark and endless.

The silence in the arena lasted only a moment. Then the spectators erupted—half cheering, half murmuring in horror.

Lane could hear the murmurs, even through the cheers. The fear. The discomfort. They loved bloodshed, but this? This was something else. He wasn't just another killer in the sand—he was a walking nightmare, and even the bloodthirsty bastards in the stands didn't know how to cheer for that.

Lane didn't react. He turned, wiped the blood from his fingers, and walked away.

As he sat back on the bench, wiping his hands clean, Nate stepped in front of him.

"You don't have to keep killing," Nate said, his voice steady. "You can be better than this."

Lane scoffed, shaking his head. "Better? In this world? You're naive."

Nate folded his arms, watching him carefully. "Maybe. But I'd rather be naive than a monster."

Lane didn't reply. His jaw tightened for a moment, something flickering behind his expression, before he turned away. The next set of names appeared on the screens.

Manny stood, cracking his knuckles.

The next fight began with no hesitation. His opponent, Snowy, moved like a blur, the frost coating her hands, leaving a thin mist in her wake. She lashed out first, releasing a burst of freezing mist toward Manny. He didn't even try to dodge.

His tongue lashed out, moving faster than Snowy could react, wrapping around her midsection. A sharp crack echoed through the arena. Her body went limp.

Manny swung her into the ground with brutal force, the impact sending sand flying. The blood pooling beneath her was instant, deep red soaking into the golden grains.

The crowd's cheers were deafening.

Manny's face was unreadable.

Manny stood over Snowy's lifeless body, his breathing steady despite the brutality of what had just happened. The blood pooling beneath her body spread quickly, staining the golden sand beneath their feet. The crowd roared, but Manny barely acknowledged them.

The Gauntlet wasn't about winning—it was about surviving.

The announcer's voice cut through the noise, smooth and enthusiastic. "And with that, The Tongue of Terror moves on to the next round! What an absolutely dominant performance against the Winterlight Snowy!"

The cheers that followed were loud, almost deafening. But inside the holding area, no one said a word.

Manny walked back toward the waiting section, shaking out his arms like he had just finished a routine workout. He sat down, stretching his shoulders, his expression carefully blank.

Manny flexed his fingers, wiping Snowy's blood on his pant leg, but for the first time, it didn't feel like just another win. The fights had always been fun before—dangerous, yeah, but fun. Now, all he felt was exhaustion. He wasn't sure when the switch had flipped. Maybe it was when the collars had gone on. Maybe it was when the first head exploded. Maybe it was now.

Nate watched him closely.

He had seen Manny fight before, had even trained with him, but there was something different this time. There had always been a playfulness to Manny's battles, an edge of cocky bravado that made it seem like he was having fun, even when things got serious. This wasn't that. This was calculated, efficient. A kill.

Nate leaned forward. "You good?"

Manny looked at him, his expression unreadable. For a moment, it seemed like he was about to say something, but then he just shrugged. "What does it matter?"

Nate didn't have an answer. The next competitors were already being called. The fights continued, each one more brutal than the last.

Some were over in seconds—a quick snap of a neck, a blade through the ribs, a broken skull caved in with a well-placed strike. Others stretched longer, brutal exchanges that left both fighters barely standing until one of them finally collapsed.

One match lasted nearly ten minutes, the two competitors locked in a grueling brawl that left the sand soaked red. The winner barely managed to stay on his feet after delivering the final blow, and the moment he did, his collar beeped. A second later, his head was gone.

The crowd barely reacted to the execution, already more interested in who was next.

Nate clenched his fists, his nails digging into his palms.

The reality of the Gauntlet was fully sinking in now.

There was no real escape here, no way to game the system. If you didn't die in the fight, you'd die later. The only people who left this place were the ones the government decided to keep alive.

And Nate was willing to bet that even the winners weren't really free.

Nate glanced around the holding area. No one spoke. Even the ones who had fought and won barely acknowledged their victories. They just sat there, staring at the sand, at their hands, at nothing. Some muttered under their breath, repeating names or prayers to gods who weren't listening. Others clenched their fists so tight their knuckles were white. No one smiled. There was no celebration. The only thing waiting for them was the next fight—and the realization that survival wasn't the same as freedom.

At the top of the stands, separated from the roaring crowd, a handful of officials sat watching the games unfold.

A man in a crisp military uniform leaned back in his seat, watching the fights with mild interest. "We have some strong Gauntletiers this year."

Another official, an older woman with silver-streaked hair, nodded. "Ironclad performed as expected. The others..." Her eyes flicked toward Lane, Manny, and Echo, who were still waiting in the holding area. "We'll see."

A third official, younger, with sharp eyes, folded his hands together. "HeartBeat is the one I'm watching."

The military officer smirked. "You and the rest of the world."

"And if HeartBeat wins?" the younger official asked, barely concealing his amusement.

The military officer smirked, swirling the whiskey in his glass. "Then we make sure he doesn't."

The older woman barely looked up from her notes. "Knight will handle it."

On the holographic screens, Nate's face flashed for a moment, reminding the audience that his fight was still to come.

The crowd cheered just at the sight of his name. The next fight ended in less than thirty seconds.

A mutant with razor-sharp claws lunged at his opponent, only to have his arm snapped at the elbow before he even got close. He screamed, staggering backward, but his opponent—a thin man with unnervingly sharp features—didn't let him retreat.

He grabbed the injured arm and tore it free from its socket.

Blood sprayed across the sand. The man collapsed instantly, writhing in agony.

The crowd went wild. Nate forced himself to keep watching, but his stomach churned. This wasn't a fight. This was a performance.

Every move, every action, every kill—it was all designed to entertain. The audience didn't care who lived or died, as long as they got their blood.

The crowd's energy wasn't just excitement—it was hunger. They didn't just cheer for death; they craved it. The ones in the front rows leaned forward eagerly, their faces illuminated by the screens replaying the carnage. Some of them weren't even watching the fights anymore. They were watching the holding area, waiting for the next victim to step into the sand.

The moment the match ended, the drones zoomed in on the victor's expressionless face, broadcasting it to the world.

The announcer's voice rang out, as cheerful as ever. "And another incredible match! Let's keep this momentum going, shall we?"

Another name flashed on the screen. Nate took a slow breath. His fight was next.

Back at the warehouse, the Rogues sat frozen, their eyes glued to the screen.

Morgan's hands were clenched together so tightly her knuckles were white. "It's him."

Ava exhaled sharply. "Finally."

Nat stared at the TV, her jaw set, her expression unreadable. "He better be ready."

Michael leaned forward, resting his arms on his knees. "He's been ready."

The screen zoomed in, capturing every detail of Nate's face as he walked toward the battlefield.

Morgan swallowed hard. "I don't think that matters."

The sound of the horn blaring filled the room.

The fight had begun.

CHAPTER 27: KNIGHTHOOD

"This will be interesting," the military officer murmured in the VIP stands, swirling his whiskey. "We need a replacement for Reptile. If Knight wipes the floor with HeartBeat, we move on."

"And if HeartBeat surprises us?" the older woman asked, raising an eyebrow.

"Then we have a problem," the younger official muttered, arms crossed. "Knight is supposed to be our control variable. If this kid actually gives him trouble, we might have to reassess everything."

"Or recruit him," the older woman mused, eyes never leaving the screen.

The military officer's smirk faded slightly. "We don't need another wild card. Reptile already burned us once."

The air inside the arena was thick with dust and sweat, the once golden sand now a battlefield littered with the evidence of past fights—scars carved into the earth by fallen competitors, dark stains where bodies had been broken. As the day dragged on, the intensity of the fights had only increased, and now, with only two matches left, the entire crowd seemed to be holding their breath in anticipation.

Then the announcement came.

"And now, the fight we've all been waiting for! The newcomer, HeartBeat, against the legend himself—KNIGHT!"

The stadium erupted. Cheers, chants, and the rhythmic pounding of fists against the metal railings above echoed across the arena. This was the fight they had been waiting for. Nate was shoved forward, his boots scraping against the sand as the guards dragged him into position. He barely noticed them. His focus was locked on the man standing across the battlefield.

Knight.

Towering, built like a fortress of flesh and armor, his razor-sharp scales glinting in the dying sunlight, Knight stood with the effortless confidence of a man who had done this more times than he could count. He didn't move right away, just watched, studying Nate with the cold efficiency of a predator who already knew the outcome. There was no tension in his stance, no sign of hesitation or anticipation—just a quiet certainty that this was already over.

"You look nervous, kid," Knight called out, voice smooth but laced with condescension. He took a slow step forward, his heavy boots pressing firm imprints into the sand, his movements measured and unhurried. "You should be. I've fought hundreds like you. Fast, desperate, overconfident. You know what happens to them?" He gestured lazily at the surrounding battlefield, at the blood-soaked sand and shattered bodies. "They don't last."

Nate said nothing, forcing himself to keep his breathing steady. Knight wanted a reaction, but he wouldn't get one. Nate's mind was on something else entirely. His eyes flicked downward, scanning the sand beneath his feet, calculating the space he had to work with. If he could last long enough, he might be able to carve a message for the Rogues—his only chance to signal when to move. But it meant staying on the defensive against a man who could tear him apart the second he slipped up.

The horn blared.

Knight moved first, and he was fast. Too fast for a man his size. Nate barely had time to react before Knight's fist tore through the air, aiming directly for his skull. Ducking at the last second, he felt the wind from the missed punch stir the sand beneath him, the sheer force of it alone enough to tell him what would happen if Knight ever actually landed a clean hit.

Knight didn't slow. He pressed the assault immediately, fists coming in rapid succession, each one cutting through the space where Nate had been just moments before. His armored skin shifted as he moved, forming jagged, scale-like protrusions along his knuckles and forearms—a built-in set of blades designed to tear flesh apart on contact. Nate kept moving, forcing himself to focus only on dodging, each step dragging subtle lines into the sand.

The air pulsed with every missed strike, the raw power behind Knight's attacks carving small craters into the ground. He fought like someone who had nothing to prove, his movements clean, efficient, free of unnecessary force. Every punch, every kick was a calculation, meant to end the fight in as few moves as possible.

Then Nate miscalculated. His foot caught uneven sand, throwing his balance off for half a second—half a second too long. Knight saw the opening instantly and took it.

Before Nate could recover, a massive fist slammed into his ribs. The impact was like getting hit by a wrecking ball. Pain detonated through his body as the blow lifted him off his feet and hurled him backward across the arena. He hit the sand hard, skidding before coming to a stop. His breath ripped from his lungs. Every nerve in his torso screamed in agony.

Knight exhaled, flexing his fingers as he walked toward Nate, unbothered, unhurried. "You can't run forever," he mused, his smirk widening. "But I'll give you credit—you lasted longer than most."

He lifted his foot and slammed it down, kicking up a massive wave of dust and sand, obscuring everything in a thick haze. The world blurred, and for a brief second, Nate lost sight of Knight.

Panic almost set in, but then he realized—this was his chance.

Under the cover of the dust, he dragged his foot through the sand, completing the markings he had started earlier. The symbols were quick, simple—just enough for the Rogues to understand.

As the dust settled, the symbols became visible. "12"

Miles away, in their hideout, the Rogues leaned in closer to the flickering screen.

"That's it," Nat whispered, her voice barely audible over the tension in the room. "Twelve o'clock tonight. He's telling us when to move."

Michael's fists clenched, his eyes locked on the screen. "Then we'll be ready."

Back at the arena, the dust settled, revealing Knight's imposing silhouette, standing motionless like a statue, his piercing gaze locked onto Nate. He had figured it out. Nate wasn't fighting to win. He was fighting to buy time.

The realization flickered across Knight's expression, and the shift in his stance was immediate. The amusement was gone.

His eyes darkened, his shoulders squared, his muscles tensed. This fight was no longer entertainment to him.

"You're not even trying to fight me," Knight said, rolling his shoulders. His tone had lost the amusement—now, it was something else. Calculation. Annoyance. Maybe even a little curiosity.

Nate exhaled, wiping blood from the corner of his mouth. "I don't need to."

Knight's smirk returned, but this time, it was different—sharper, edged with something almost resembling excitement.

"Then let's see how long you can last," he said.

This time, he didn't hold back.

He lunged, closing the gap between them in an instant. Nate barely dodged the first strike, but Knight was already pivoting into the next. A brutal kick slammed into Nate's side, sending him staggering. He recovered just in time to block an incoming fist, but the impact sent a shockwave through his bones, knocking him back several steps.

He couldn't keep this up.

Knight's strength was overwhelming, his unrelenting attacks chipping away at what little stamina Nate had left. His muscles screamed, his ribs ached, and his breathing was already becoming labored. There was only one option left.

Nate closed his eyes for a fraction of a second, focusing inward, reaching for the one thing that could turn this fight around. His Heart Engine.

He pushed it past its normal limits. Heat surged through his veins, his pulse hammering like war drums. His body tensed, his skin glowed faintly, and steam curled from his shoulders as his blood circulation skyrocketed. Every beat of his heart felt like a drum being slammed against his ribcage.

The moment he opened his eyes again, Knight was already mid-strike.

Nate didn't dodge. Instead, he moved forward. Knight's fist came down, but before it could connect, Nate's own hand shot up, catching the blow. The entire arena seemed to freeze. Knight's eyes widened just slightly. Nate's grip tightened. For the first time, Knight felt resistance.

The force of Knight's punch pressed against Nate's palm, the impact rattling through his bones, but he didn't break. The muscles in his arm strained, his entire body screaming under the pressure, yet he stood firm. The glow beneath his skin pulsed brighter, steam curling from his back, his Heart Engine surging at a level he had never pushed before.

Knight's eyes flickered—just a fraction of a second. A mix of confusion and surprise. Then, just as quickly, it was gone, replaced by a sharp smirk.

Then, amusement returned, his smirk widening. "So that's what you've been hiding." His free hand shot forward like a bullet, aiming for Nate's ribs. This time, Nate was faster. He twisted at the last second, deflecting the strike with his forearm and countering with a brutal knee to Knight's gut. The impact echoed through the arena, sending a visible shockwave through Knight's torso.

Knight's fist drove into Nate's ribs like a wrecking ball, the force of it lifting him off his feet. He barely had time to brace before he hit the ground, sand exploding around him as he skidded across the arena floor. The world spun, his lungs refusing to take in air for a moment that felt far too long.

His ribs screamed in agony, and for a second, he thought something might have cracked. Maybe broken. But he pushed through it, forcing himself onto all fours. Every muscle ached, his body telling him to stay down, but staying down wasn't an option. Not against Knight.

The man stood over him, cracking his knuckles. "You don't know when to quit, do you?"

Nate spat a glob of blood into the sand and pushed himself up, swaying slightly but keeping his stance firm. He wasn't done. He couldn't be.

Knight exhaled through his nose, shaking his head. "Fine. Let's end this."

Knight charged, his foot slamming into the ground hard enough to leave a small crater. He swung another massive punch, but this time, Nate saw it coming. He ducked under the strike, stepping in and grabbing Knight's arm before twisting his hips and flipping him over his shoulder.

Knight crashed onto his back with enough force to send dust flying into the air, but he recovered fast. Too fast.

Before Nate could capitalize, Knight rolled with the impact and twisted, hooking his arm around Nate's neck and yanking him forward. They hit the ground in a tangled grapple, Knight's weight pinning Nate beneath him.

His opponent's sheer size made it almost impossible to maneuver. Knight's elbow came down, aiming for his jaw, but Nate barely shifted his head in time. The strike hit the sand beside him, and he used the opening to force his arm under Knight's, wrenching the larger man's limb into an unnatural angle.

Knight let out a sharp grunt but didn't let go. Instead, he shifted his weight and slammed his knee into Nate's stomach. The impact made his body seize, his breath catching in his throat.

He twisted desperately, using every ounce of his strength to shove Knight off, rolling free just as another strike came down where his head had been. His limbs ached, his lungs burned, but he pushed himself back to his feet.

Knight was already rising, dusting himself off like Nate's efforts were nothing but an inconvenience. His patience was running thin. "You're like a damn cockroach."

Nate didn't waste energy responding. He just raised his fists, steadying his stance.

Knight exhaled, stepping forward again. "I'll give you one last shot," he said. "Make it count."

Nate's grip tightened. He took a slow breath, feeling his Heart Engine ignite with everything he had left. The heat coursed through his veins nearly immobilizing him, his pulse hammering like a war drum. His skin glowed faintly, blood evaporating off his body, the air around him shimmering from the sheer heat radiating off of him. His muscles locked, every fiber of him ready to push beyond what should have been possible.

Knight's expression flickered—just for a second. He could feel the shift.

Then Nate attacked with speed Knight hadn't seen in a long time.

His first punch slammed into Knight's ribs with bone-crushing force. The armor-like plating cracked beneath his knuckles, but Nate didn't stop. He followed up with a left hook to the jaw, sending Knight stumbling.

Nate moved in, driving a knee into Knight's stomach before pivoting into a brutal elbow strike to the temple. Knight reeled, his balance faltering for the first time.

Nate gritted his teeth, planting his foot and unleashing a barrage of blows—faster, heavier, every strike backed by the full power of his boiling blood. A right hook crashed into Knight's face, followed by a gut punch that nearly lifted him off his feet. He staggered, but Nate wasn't finished.

He twisted his entire body into a savage roundhouse kick; the impact sending Knight spinning through the air before crashing onto his knees.

The crowd gasped, stunned silence settling over the arena.

Knight coughed, blood dripping from his mouth. His fingers dug into the sand, muscles trembling as he tried to push himself up. His eyes burned with fury, with refusal. He had never lost like this. No one had ever overpowered him. His body screamed at him to collapse, but his pride wouldn't let him.

With one final surge of strength, Nate leaped into the air, twisting at the peak of his jump. His entire body coiled like a spring, and then he brought his heel crashing down onto the back of Knight's neck.

The sickening snap echoed through the arena like a gunshot.

Knight collapsed, his massive body hitting the sand with a dull thud. He didn't move.

Nate stood over him, his chest heaving, steam still rising from his shoulders. His body wobbled, his vision darkening at the edges, but he forced himself to remain standing.

The stadium erupted. Some screamed in excitement, others in rage at the death of their champion.

The front row was chaos—some fans punched the air in victory, while others screamed at the arena floor, demanding a rematch, a redo, something to make this make sense. A few just stared, mouths hanging open, watching steam rise off the kid who had just killed a legend.

The announcer's voice boomed across the speakers, but Nate barely heard it.

Nate's muscles locked. His heart pounded like a war drum, beaten too hard, too fast, every thud threatening to burst through his ribs. His vision swam, his nerves screamed—his body wasn't just breaking down, it was actively shutting off. Nate's fingers twitched involuntarily. For the first time, he felt like he might actually tear himself apart.

He staggered, but he didn't fall.

Up in the VIP stands, the officials exchanged wary glances. The man in the military uniform leaned forward, studying the screen intently. "That kid just took down Knight. I want a full report on him immediately."

The older woman beside him pursed her lips. "He won't last much longer at that rate. If he doesn't collapse before the final round, he'll be dead before the night is over."

The Rogues were dead silent as they watched Nate's name flash as the victor.

The flickering TV screen showed Nate standing over Knight's body, steam still rising from his shoulders, blood evaporating from his skin.

Nat exhaled sharply, gripping the edge of the table. "He did it."

Morgan shook her head in disbelief. "I thought—he looked like he was about to drop."

Michael leaned forward, his expression hard. "Yeah. And now we have to get to him before he does."

Ava's eyes remained locked on the screen. "He's pushing himself too far."

Nat didn't hesitate. "We move tonight. Instead: There is no waiting. There is no second-guesses. We get him out."

Michael was already on his feet, grabbing his gear. "Twelve sharp."

"If he can hold out that long," Ava muttered, eyes still locked on the screen.

"He will," Nat said, voice like steel.

CHAPTER 28: UNFOLDED

Nate stood in the center of the arena, his body trembling, every muscle screaming in agony. His legs wobbled beneath him, the weight of exhaustion threatening to pull him to the ground. For a moment, he considered letting it happen—to just collapse next to Knight's lifeless body and let the pain take over. But somehow, through sheer force of will, he remained standing.

Nate let himself breathe, but even that felt like a mistake. His ribs felt like shattered glass shifting with every inhale. Nate's legs threatened to give out with each step. His head pounded, a constant thud, his body teetering on the edge of collapse.

His body was screaming at him, demanding him to rest, to just close his eyes for a second. But rest was death. And he wasn't ready to die.

He couldn't stop. Not now. But he wanted to. He had killed again and it sickened him that this was just for the government's sick entertainment.

The roar of the crowd faded into a dull hum as paramedics rushed onto the battlefield, their pristine uniforms stark against the bloodstained sand. They moved quickly, detaching Knight's detonation collar and hoisting his massive body onto a stretcher. It was the first time Nate had seen a body leave the arena intact. The murmurs in the stands reflected his own thoughts—why hadn't they detonated his collar like all the others?

Knight was dead. The fight was over. But the questions weren't.

Miles away, in their dimly lit hideout, the Rogues erupted in celebration.

Morgan let out a sharp exhale, slumping back in her chair. "Holy shit. He did it."

Michael shook his head, his voice laced with disbelief. "I thought—I don't even know what I thought. But if he can beat Knight, he can hold out until we get there."

Nat didn't waste a second before grabbing her gear. "We're not waiting around to find out. We move now."

Ava nodded, already securing her weapons. "If we don't get to Granger Heights before midnight, we're leaving his body behind instead of rescuing him."

Michael clenched his fists, his jaw tight. "Then let's move."

The Rogues moved swiftly, making their way through the darkened streets until they reached White Water Ports. Ryan activated his thermal vision, scanning the area. "S-six guards patrolling the docks. T-three more in the c-control room."

Nat's voice was sharp. "We take the ship quietly. No alarms, no bodies left behind."

They moved with precision, striking fast and clean. Within minutes, the small crew aboard the vessel had been subdued. No gunfire, no alarms—just a few unconscious bodies left behind as the ship quietly left port.

As the Rogues sailed toward Granger Heights, the tension on board was palpable. They were on the clock, and time was running out.

Back in the arena, the final fight of the day was about to begin.

A large, reinforced capsule rolled to the center of the battlefield, its metal exterior reflecting the arena lights. Standing across from it was Raphael, a mutant with the ability to secrete explosive sweat. He rolled his shoulders, flexing his fingers, already grinning like he'd won.

The audience stirred as the capsule doors slowly hissed open. From inside, a frail figure stepped forward—a malnourished young man with tan skin and long, unkempt hair. His thin frame and sunken features drew murmurs from the crowd.

"What's so special about this guy?" someone muttered.

Then the announcer's voice boomed across the speakers.

"Firestar!"

The moment his name was spoken, the murmurs shifted to recognition. The crowd wasn't cheering anymore. They understood now.

Firestar barely acknowledged Raphael. Instead, he lifted one hand, his fingers forming the shape of a gun.

Raphael smirked, stepping forward with a cocky strut. "Come on, man, at least—"

Before he could finish, Firestar flicked a piece of his fingernail. The sliver of keratin shot through the air, moving faster than the eye could track. Raphael's eyes widened ever so slightly as his life flashed before his eyes. The moment it made contact with Raphael's forehead—it exploded.

The blast sent a shockwave through the arena, a brilliant burst of color and blood painting the sand beneath them. When the smoke cleared, Raphael's body was gone.

The crowd sat in stunned silence.

Firestar didn't move. He didn't react. He simply turned, stepped back into his capsule, and disappeared behind the closing doors.

Nate sat in his cell later that night, his mind racing.

That fight had lasted less than a second. They kept Firestar in a capsule for a reason. The government didn't want him interacting with the other prisoners.

What else were they hiding? His thoughts shifted back to the detonation collars.

Every defeated contestant except Knight and Raphael had exploded. At first, he assumed Knight's past as a Super had earned him special treatment. But that didn't add up. The government didn't care about ex-Supers.

Which meant there had to be another reason. And then it hit him. What if the collars weren't always manually activated? What if they were triggered by heartbeats? The realization sent a shock through his system.

If the collars detonated when the wearer's heartbeat stopped, then what would happen if he could lower his heart rate to zero without dying? The thought was insane.

But insane was better than dead.

Dinner was quiet that night. The tension in the cafeteria was thick, the remaining prisoners either whispering about Firestar's display or eating in silence, lost in their own thoughts.

At a corner table, Nate sat with Echo and Manny, speaking in hushed tones.

"That's a cool idea and all," Echo muttered after Nate explained his theory, "but how the hell is that supposed to help the rest of us?"

"I have a plan," Nate said, his voice calm. "But I need absolute trust."

Manny exhaled sharply. "Bro, I don't even know what you just said about veins and heartbeats, but if it gets this damn collar off my neck, I'm in."

Echo tapped the metal band around his throat, considering. "We gonna look like freaks when you do it?"

"You already do," Manny muttered.

Echo smacked him upside the head. "Fine. We're in."

"I need to talk to a few more people first," Nate said, scanning the room.

His next stop was Lane. The mutant barely looked up as Nate slid into the seat across from him.

"So, I can either join your little escape squad, die in the Gauntlet, or become a government lapdog," Lane mused, shaking his head. "Can't believe I'm saying this to the likes of you, but my hands are tied." A smirk tugged at his lips. "Besides, killing some of these shitty guards sounds fun."

Nate nodded. One more on board.

He approached Iron's table next.

"I'm getting us out of here," Nate said simply.

Iron scoffed, barely looking up from his tray. "I don't need your help. I'm going to win this Gauntlet, and by tomorrow, everything will be back to normal."

Nate turned to leave, but Iron's voice stopped him. Softer this time. "What time is it?"

Nate didn't hesitate. "11:30."

Iron said nothing else. But he had planted a seed of doubt. By the time guards escorted Nate back to his cell, the pieces were falling into place.

The bruises were settling in. His ribs felt like shattered glass beneath his skin. His vision blurred every time he shifted positions. The fight had taken more out of him than he'd let on. His body was failing, and if he was going to make it through the escape, he needed to fix himself.

Slowly, Nate exhaled, closing his eyes and focusing inward.

He could feel it—his own veins, pulsing, moving, writhing beneath the surface of his skin like tangled wires. At first, it was just a dull awareness, like sensing a limb was asleep. But as he focused, he felt them shift. They weren't just carrying blood anymore; they were reacting. Instinctively, they started working.

The fractures in his ribs felt like molten iron inside his body, a deep, burning pressure that threatened to crush him from the inside out. But as he concentrated, his veins wrapped around the breaks, pressing them back into place like organic stitches.

The pain was unbearable.

Every second felt like being torn apart. Threads of veins reconnected, knitting together the shredded muscle and torn flesh. He could feel the damage inside him, every ruptured blood vessel, every micro-tear, every instance of internal bleeding pooling beneath his skin. His body wasn't just in pain—it was barely holding together and now it was fixing itself. Not fast, not perfect, but faster than it should.

His body screamed at him to stop, but he refused. His breathing was uneven. Sweat poured down his face. His hands trembled as he clenched his fists, forcing the process forward over the next several hours.

His body rejected the idea of healing so quickly. It fought him. Every adjustment was agony. His veins weren't meant to work like this, not naturally. He could feel them struggling, pulsing, burning, stretching beyond their limits. The pain wasn't just physical anymore—it was raw, deep, crawling into the very fabric of his being.

He suspected it wasn't true regeneration—at least, not like the stories of mutants who could grow back limbs or recover in minutes. This felt more like overclocking his biology. Like his veins, when consciously manipulated, could flood damaged areas with nutrients and oxygen, accelerating clotting, rebuilding tissue, and locking bones into place. But it came at a price. It burned energy fast, drained his body like a power surge through faulty wiring. The deeper he pushed it, the more it fought back.

But he endured it because he had no choice. The escape was coming and if he couldn't stand when the time came; it was over before it even started. It was almost time.

The heavy clank of steel doors shutting behind him echoed through Nate's cell, but his mind wasn't on the walls caging him in. He had a plan, a real one, and enough people willing to take the risk. That should have been enough to reassure him. But something in his gut told him things wouldn't go as smoothly as he wanted. Reptile had been watching him.

It wasn't overt, and it wasn't threatening, but there was an undeniable weight in his gaze whenever their paths crossed. Nate didn't know what the towering mutant wanted, and that uncertainty bothered him.

He leaned back against the cold concrete, staring at the ceiling, his body still aching from the fight with Knight. The bruises hadn't even begun to settle, and his muscles still felt torn from the inside out. If he had to fight again tomorrow, he wasn't sure how much he had left to give. The thought gnawed at him.

Would he even be able to hold out until the escape?

Footsteps broke the silence, measured and heavy. Nate sat up as his cell door slid open, revealing Reptile standing in the dim light of the hallway.

For a long moment, neither of them spoke. Then Reptile stepped inside, closing the door behind him.

"You've been busy," he muttered.

Nate crossed his arms. "You keeping tabs on me?"

Reptile let out something that wasn't quite a laugh but wasn't a full scoff, either. "It's hard not to when you're making moves loud enough for the entire prison to notice."

Nate didn't argue with that. Instead, he leaned forward slightly. "You here to stop me?"

Reptile exhaled sharply, shaking his head. "No. If I wanted to stop you, I would've done it already."

That made Nate pause. He studied the mutant carefully, trying to read whatever was hiding behind those reptilian eyes. "Then what do you want?"

Reptile was silent for a long time before finally speaking. "I need to know if this is real. If you actually have a shot at making it out of here. Because if you do, then I—" He stopped himself, his claws flexing at his sides. "I need a way out, too."

Nate narrowed his eyes. "You could've left anytime you wanted. You have more clearance than any of us. What's stopping you?"

Reptile's jaw tensed. "You think I'm here by choice?" He shook his head, his fists clenching. "I was a tool. A weapon they shaped from the moment I was born. You don't get to quit when you're in my position. You either do what they say or..." He exhaled sharply, his eyes darkening. "They make sure you can't do anything at all."

Nate observed him. "You talking about the collar?"

Reptile gave a bitter smirk. "I've worn this damn thing since I was a kid. They made me believe it was just for 'control,' but I know better now. I've seen what happens when someone in my position stops being useful." He gestured toward Nate's own collar. "We're not different. Not in their eyes."

For the first time, Nate saw something raw beneath the hardened exterior. Reptile wasn't just helping them out of convenience. He was desperate.

"I need to know that you're not just another idiot with a death wish," Reptile continued, his voice quieter this time. "If I back you up, I need to be sure it's not just going to get me killed."

Nate held his gaze. "You saw what I did to Knight."

Reptile smirked. "Yeah. And I also saw how close you were to dropping dead right after."

Nate exhaled slowly. "I'm not saying it's a perfect plan, but it's our best shot. I have people willing to fight for this. If you're in, we need you to do the same."

Reptile nodded, his expression unreadable. "Then I'm in."

He turned to leave, but paused at the doorway. "Eleven-thirty. That's when you're moving?"

Nate nodded. "I'll be there."

As Reptile disappeared down the hall, Nate finally let himself exhale. He had him, and it was really happening.

The next few hours crawled by, the tension thickening as prisoners whispered in hushed voices. There had been escape attempts before, all of them ending in blood and failure. Everyone knew what happened to the ones who tried to run.

No one expected this one to be different.

Nate sat in the cafeteria, his food untouched. Echo and Manny were talking quietly beside him, but he wasn't listening. His focus was on Lane, sitting a few tables away.

That was the wild card.

Lane wasn't reliable. He wasn't the type to put his neck on the line for someone else. If he decided to flip, everything was over before it started.

As if sensing Nate's thoughts, Lane glanced up and locked eyes with him. A slow smirk spread across his face. It wasn't reassuring.

Later that night, as Nate was being escorted back to his cell, Lane fell into step beside him.

"You're really banking on me, not stabbing you in the back, huh?" Lane muttered.

Nate didn't break stride. "You don't gain anything by selling us out."

Lane snorted. "Yeah, but watching this whole plan crumble could be pretty entertaining."

Nate stopped walking. The guards barely paid them any mind as long as they kept moving, so he turned, staring Lane down. "You can be a killer, you can be a bastard, but you don't get to be a coward."

Lane's smirk faltered just slightly.

Nate didn't blink. "If you're in, then be in. If you're out, walk away. But if you so much as think about screwing us over, I'll make sure you don't live long enough to regret it."

Lane was silent for a long moment, studying Nate like he was seeing him for the first time. Then, to Nate's surprise, he let out a sharp laugh.

"You're serious," Lane said, shaking his head. "Alright. Fine. I won't fuck with your little rebellion." He shot Nate a grin. "I'll even help. Just don't expect me to hold your hand if things go to hell."

Nate rolled his shoulders, the soreness creeping back into him. "Wouldn't dream of it."

As they reached their cells, they separated, and guards shoved Nate inside. He turned just as the guards locked the door, catching one last glimpse of Reptile further down the hall, standing motionless, waiting.

Nate exhaled, staring at the clock on the far wall.

His ribs still ached, but the sharp, stabbing pain had dulled. The wounds that should have taken weeks to heal had started sealing themselves—still tender, still incomplete, but workable. He could move, and that was enough.

11:28.

Two minutes.

This was it.

Either they were getting out of here tonight… or none of them were ever leaving at all

CHAPTER 29: WALL

As the night deepened and the time for the plan drew near, Nate felt a maelstrom of emotions twisting within him. The familiar shadows of fear and doubt lurked in the corners of his mind, but they were tempered by a fresh surge of excitement and a flickering ember of hope. This was it—the last night he would endure the suffocating grip of this hellish prison. No matter what happened next, he knew he would never see these walls again.

As 11:30 approached, Nate paced his narrow cell, his breaths measured and deliberate, grounding himself for the chaos to come. Right on cue, Reptile appeared outside the cell, his towering form a looming silhouette against the dim glow of the corridor lights. The cold, unblinking eye of the security camera remained fixed on Nate, a silent witness that streamed his every movement to the watchful eyes in the control room.

"You better be right about this, kid," Reptile murmured, his voice low and rough as it seeped through the reinforced door. The gravity in his tone reflected the gamble they were both taking.

Nate inhaled deeply, forcing his heartbeat to slow to a near-imperceptible crawl. The air in his lungs felt cold, heavy. He could almost hear the mechanical pulse of the collar as he fought against its restraints. His focus sharpened into a singular point, drawing all his strength into one decisive act. The collar's metallic clasp gave a soft, reluctant click before snapping open, clattering onto the thin mattress of his cot. The sound echoed through the small cell, the tangible proof of his defiance.

The door swung open, and Reptile stepped inside, his eyes reflecting a strange blend of disbelief and awe. He crouched down, bringing his imposing frame to Nate's level. "Do it," he whispered, a hint of desperation leaking into his gruff voice.

Nate extended his arm, veins slithering just beneath his skin, reaching out like living tendrils. They coiled around the collar's sensors, maneuvering with painstaking precision as he mimicked the stillness of death. The seconds dragged, each heartbeat a silent countdown until, finally, the device's light flickered and faded. Without ceremony, Nate ripped the collar off, letting it fall heavily to the floor. Reptile's hand instinctively went to his neck, his sharp teeth bared in a grateful snarl as he rasped, "Thank you."

There was no time for further words. Together, they surged into the dark hallways, their footsteps quick and deliberate. They knew the silence was temporary—the alarms would erupt soon, and the full force of Granger Heights would descend upon them. Their only chance lay in speed and coordination.

They navigated the labyrinthine passages, dispatching guards with ruthless efficiency. Reptile's sheer physical power rendered him a walking juggernaut, tearing through barriers and defenses alike. Nate's agility complemented this brute force, weaving through the fray, incapacitating guards with swift, calculated blows.

When they reached Iron's cell, the mutant sat on his cot, arms crossed, as though he had been expecting them. He met Nate's eyes with a sly grin. "We're really doing this, huh, kid?"

"As far as we can," Nate replied, his voice laced with a confidence that bordered on reckless. He repeated the process with Iron's collar, watching as the light died and the device snapped off. Iron stepped out, cracking his knuckles, ready to join the battle.

Methodically, they moved from cell to cell, freeing Echo, Manny, and Lane. The sense of camaraderie grew with each liberated ally, their shared desperation uniting them into a formidable force.

Lane smirked as his collar fell away, his eyes glinting with mischief. "If we really want a shot at getting out of here, we'll need that fire guy's power."

Nate nodded, turning to Echo, whose eyes were already closed in concentration. Echo's abilities swept through the building, mapping out the layout with eerie accuracy. "Second floor, left quadrant, above the lunchroom," he said, his tone surprisingly steady despite the gravity of their situation.

The group moved as one, their footsteps synchronized, their eyes scanning every shadow for threats. Nate directed them with an instinctive authority, signaling Lane to take point while Reptile covered the rear, his armored body ready to absorb any surprise assault. Iron acted as their battering ram, using his indomitable strength to clear obstructions, while Echo's sound waves preempted hidden dangers lurking around each corner.

They encountered their first major resistance near the security hub—a bottleneck manned by heavily armed guards. The corridor lit up with muzzle flashes as the guards unleashed a hail of bullets. Reptile moved forward, his body absorbing the rounds that would have cut down the others. Iron lunged forward, catching one of the guards by the helmet and slamming him into the reinforced glass of the observation deck.

Lane moved like a shadow, exploiting the chaos to slip behind enemy lines, his knife flashing in the dim light as he neutralized guards with swift, lethal strikes.

Nate ducked beneath a baton strike, delivering a punishing uppercut that shattered the guard's jaw. The sound of bone against bone resonated in the cramped space, a grim testament to the stakes they faced. Manny, despite his size, moved with surprising speed, his massive tongue snapping out to disarm opponents, turning their own weapons against them.

The battle was brutal, every step forward costing them precious time and energy. But with each victory, Nate's resolve hardened, his leadership emerging as a natural force that guided the team through the storm. He wasn't just fighting for himself anymore—he was fighting for all of them.

Finally, they reached the staircase leading to the second floor. Nate signaled for Echo to scan again, the sonic waves reverberating through the walls, pinpointing the guards' locations. They moved as a unit, flanking the next set of defenses, disarming reinforcements before they could mount a proper counterattack.

The approach to Fire's cell was a killing field—narrow, fortified, and guarded by automated turrets that hummed ominously overhead.

The moment they turned the last corner leading to Fire's cell, the air erupted with gunfire. Dozens of guards lined the narrow corridor, rifles aimed and ready, their muzzles flashing as the first shots rang out. The team barely had time to react.

Reptile charged headfirst into the barrage, his armored hide deflecting bullets as they ricocheted off his scales. Sparks erupted where rounds struck, but the sheer force of the gunfire slowed him slightly. He kept moving forward, his claws slicing through the first wave of guards, sending them crashing into the walls.

Iron followed closely behind, his fists raised like battering rams. A bullet grazed his shoulder, but he didn't flinch. Instead, he caught the nearest guard by the collar and slammed him into the reinforced glass of a security window, shattering it with a sickening crunch. Another soldier swung a baton at him, but Iron caught the weapon mid-swing, wrenching it from the man's grip before cracking it over his skull.

Echo and Manny stuck together, maneuvering through the chaos with practiced coordination. A guard aimed at Manny, but before he could pull the trigger, Echo was already there. With a sharp, concentrated scream, he shattered the man's eardrums, sending him crumpling to the floor in agony. Manny's massive tongue lashed out, coiling around two more guards before violently slamming them together, their helmets denting from the impact.

Lane was methodical, moving like a shadow through the corridor, his stolen weapons raised with a steady hand. He didn't waste bullets. Each shot was precise, a clean kill with no hesitation. His blade flickered in the dim light as he cut through the slower enemies, moving from one to the next without pause.

Nate moved fast, weaving between the chaos, taking out stragglers before they could regroup. A guard lunged at him with a stun baton, but Nate ducked, delivering a brutal strike to the ribs before following up with a sharp elbow to the back of the skull. The man dropped instantly. Another came at him, but Nate kicked off the wall, using the momentum to spin and drive his heel into the man's jaw, knocking him unconscious.

They didn't have time to clear out the rest. The hallway was still swarming with guards, and reinforcements were closing in fast. Nate knew they couldn't waste another second. Breaking away from the battle, he sprinted toward the security panel outside Fire's cell. His fingers fumbled with the stolen keycard, swiping it through the reader.

Red light. Access denied.

"Fucking hell!" He tried again, his breath coming fast and uneven. The battle behind him raged on, and he knew it wouldn't be long before the guards overwhelmed them.

"Move," Lane ordered, stepping beside him. Before Nate could question it, Lane raised his shotgun and fired point-blank into the panel. Sparks flew, and the door hissed open.

Inside the cell, Fire stood still, his presence eerily calm despite the chaos outside. He was thinner than expected, his tan skin stretched taut over wiry muscle, his long hair unkempt and wild. But his eyes were sharp, glowing faintly in the dim light.

Firestar's fingers twitched, and small sparks danced at his fingertips. His expression was unreadable.

"You're the HeartBeat guy, right?" Firestar's voice was cautious, but not afraid.

"Yes," Nate said quickly. "I'm here to get you out."

Fire raised his hand, shaping his fingers like a gun, aiming directly at Nate's forehead. His expression was unreadable. "Why should I believe you?"

Firestar's eyes narrowed. For a moment, he didn't move. There was something hard in his stare, something broken—like he had believed someone before and paid the price for it. Whatever the government had done to him, it had carved away more than just his weight and strength—it had chipped away at his trust. His hand didn't tremble, but the hesitation in his breath was enough to betray the war inside his head.

Nate didn't flinch. He pointed to his own bare neck, showing the raw, fresh marks. "Because I can get that collar off. Just like mine."

Firestar lifted his hand,—this time, aiming it past Nate, toward the guards outside.

He flicked his nail. A small explosion burst in the hallway, lighting up the cell for a fraction of a second. A warning shot. An assessment.

"Fine," Firestar muttered. "But if you're lying, I'll make sure you burn before they do."

Nate didn't falter. "Then let's go."

Fire hesitated, lowering his hand slightly. A flicker of something—trust, maybe—passed through his expression before he nodded. "Alright," he murmured. "I'm grateful… for you."

Nate wasted no time. His veins crawled out from under his skin, weaving into the sensors of Fire's collar, simulating a stopped pulse. The device gave a faint beep before unlocking. With a sharp yank, Nate ripped it off.

The second the collar hit the floor, the air shifted. Fire straightened, rolling his shoulders, his entire demeanor changing. His fingers twitched, and small sparks danced at his fingertips. He said nothing—he didn't need to.

They ran.

As they pushed toward the east side of the building, where the ship was supposed to be waiting, the alarms screamed louder. A series of explosions rocked the prison, shaking the walls, sending dust and debris raining from the ceiling.

"They're detonating all the remaining collars," Reptile growled. His slitted eyes flicked toward the ceiling, his expression grim. "They don't want us recruiting anyone else."

"Fucking hell," Iron muttered, spitting onto the floor. "Cowards."

"There aren't any more guards inside," Echo confirmed, his eyes briefly shutting as he scanned the area with sound waves. "They're all outside, waiting for us."

"Well, I guess we'll have to find them ourselves," Lane said, now fully armed with stolen gear, checking the magazine of his stolen rifle.

The group reached the eastern wall, the only thing standing between them and open ground. They had no time to find an exit. They would have to make one.

Reptile was the first to step forward. Without hesitation, he slammed his full weight into the weak point of the structure. The reinforced concrete cracked but didn't break.

Iron joined him, raising his fists and smashing them into the fractures. The wall groaned, cracks spider webbing outward.

Reptile slammed his full weight into the wall. But it barely budged.

Iron struck next, his fists cracking the concrete but not shattering it.

"It's too thick," Iron snarled. Sweat ran down his face. "We need more force."

The gunfire outside got louder. They were out of time.

Nate didn't think and moved. He threw himself at the wall alongside Reptile, his veins snaking out, digging into the cracks.

He forced his blood through them, expanding the fractures from the inside.

"ONE MORE!" Reptile roared.

Iron and Reptile slammed forward with everything they had. With one final, earth-shattering impact, the wall gave way. Chunks of concrete exploded outward, debris flying in all directions. The dust cloud billowed out, momentarily obscuring their view. Then, finally, they saw it.

The sky.

The moon hung high, silver light cutting through the dust as the fresh air hit them like a shock to the system.

For the first time in months, they had broken free. Nate gasped. He'd forgotten what fresh air smelled like.

But before any of them could move, before they could even breathe in the moment—

A hail of bullets rained down on them from all sides.

Muzzle flashes flickered in the darkness, elevated snipers positioned in hidden nests. Soldiers stationed behind armored vehicles lit up the area, their rifles blazing. They had been waiting.

The group dived for cover behind the wreckage of the wall, pressing themselves against the fallen slabs of concrete as rounds tore through the air. Fire rolled behind cover, his hands already heating up, preparing for retaliation.

But one of them didn't move fast enough.

Manny stood frozen, caught in the open, his massive frame riddled with bullet holes before he could even take cover.

Blood poured from his wounds, dark and thick, staining the dirt beneath him. His fingers twitched, reaching for something unseen. His legs slowly gave out underneath him.

He collapsed near the exit they had just created, slamming into the ground.

"MAN MAN!" Nate and Echo screamed in unison, their voices thick with horror.

Echo scrambled toward him, dropping to his knees, his hands shaking as they hovered over Manny's wounds, useless. "No, no, no—stay with me, bro! We're almost there, we're almost—"

Manny groaned, blood bubbling at his lips. His chest heaved unevenly. His voice was barely more than a whisper.

"Sorry, bros…" He forced a weak grin, even as his body trembled. "I'm not gonna make it out with y'all."

His fingers slipped from Echo's grip. His body stilled.

Echo's breath hitched. His whole body shook. He gritted his teeth so hard they almost cracked. He pressed his hands against Manny's chest, as if he could force him back to life.

"No. No, NO! NOT LIKE THIS!"

His scream ripped through the night—a sound so raw, so powerful, that the entire battlefield seemed to hold its breath.

The dirt trembled. The distant snipers hesitated, shifting in confusion.

Then came the second scream. Louder. Worse.

The ground beneath them rippled like the earth itself was flinching at Echo's agony.

Echo's breath hitched. He shook him again, harder. "No, come on, man, we're almost there!"

Reptile's eyes widened. "Shit."

He grabbed Echo, yanking him back just in time before a sniper round tore into the dirt where Echo had just been kneeling.

"He's gone!" Reptile roared. "MOVE!"

Echo's breath hitched, his muscles locked, but Nate saw it—the moment when the fight left him. His hands, still outstretched toward Manny, shook before curling into fists.

Nate clenched his fists, his pulse roaring in his ears. He watched as the light left Manny's eyes, but he had no time to mourn. If they didn't move now, Manny's sacrifice would mean nothing.

CHAPTER 30: BREAK OUT WAR

Echo's voice ripped through the chaos, raw and filled with anguish. "THOSE FUCKING ASSHOLES KILLED MAN MAN! He's Fucking Dead, Man!" His breathing was erratic, chest rising and falling with each ragged inhale, his hands shaking as they clenched into fists so tight his nails dug into his palms. His body trembled violently, veins bulging in his neck as he gasped between ragged breaths. "I'll Kill Every Last One Of Them!"

The group crouched behind the jagged remains of the wall, trapped between life and death, survival and slaughter. The air around them crackled with tension, the relentless hail of bullets smashing into the rubble above their heads like a violent drumbeat. Stone and dust rained down on them, mixing with the acrid stench of gunpowder and blood, coating their skin in a fine layer of grime. Each impact shook the fractured wall, sending tremors through their bones, each second stretching into a suffocating eternity.

No one moved.

Every instinct screamed at them to run, to fight back, but the sheer overwhelming force of the gunfire pinned them in place. They knew that if they lifted their heads or shifted in the wrong way, the gunfire would tear them apart.

Then it stopped. The sudden absence of sound was almost deafening. The gunfire that had ruled the night vanished, leaving only the ringing in their ears and the slow, unsettling crunch of boots on gravel. Their breath hitched—no one dared to move, the quiet more terrifying than the gunfire itself.

The group exchanged tense glances, their bodies still coiled, ready for the next onslaught. Then, cutting through the eerie silence, a voice rang out—booming, authoritative, and laced with contempt.

"Muttborn filth."

Slowly, they risked a glance over the rubble, and their stomachs dropped.

Standing at the forefront of a small army was none other than Lariks Reach, warden of Granger Heights. The sight of him alone was enough to make the air feel heavier. He wasn't just a man—he was an executioner, a symbol of absolute authority. His uniform was pristine, untouched by the battle unfolding around him, and the golden insignia on his chest gleamed under the harsh floodlights that bathed the battlefield.

Behind him, hundreds of soldiers stood in rigid formation, their weapons trained and fingers poised over triggers. A wall of firepower, each rifle a promise of death. The deep growl of idling tanks rumbled through the ground, their massive cannons aimed directly at the escapees, while snipers perched in the towering nests that lined the concrete perimeter, scopes gleaming like the cold, unblinking eyes of executioners and the wall.

The wall stood behind them, an unbreakable, monolithic barrier, towering high above everything, thick enough to withstand an airstrike, stretching into the night like a merciless sentinel. There was no going back.

Lariks took a step forward, his presence alone suffocating, his polished boots crunching against the gravel as he lifted his revolver, casually resting the sleek barrel against his shoulder. His face, twisted with smug arrogance, scanned the group like a wolf surveying cornered prey.

"You have one chance," he said, his voice carrying across the battlefield with an almost casual cruelty. "Surrender now. Return to your cells, and you will live to fight another day. Step forward, kneel, and accept your new collars, or I will erase you from this world."

The group didn't move.

His smirk faded slightly, replaced by a flicker of irritation. "I'll give you until the count of ten."

A hush fell over the battlefield. The soldiers around him shifted, their fingers tensing over their triggers.

"Ten... nine... eight... seven..."

Nate's breath felt like fire in his chest. Every second felt like a countdown to their execution. His pulse pounded in his ears as his body coiled like a spring, ready to move.

"...six... five..."

Then the sky erupted.

The battlefield ceased to be night. Light swallowed the world in an instant, a burning gold-white inferno that stretched across the sky like the heavens had cracked open. Shadows stretched long, then disappeared entirely as the air itself warped from the heat. Then—BOOM. The atmosphere detonated. A streak of fire ripped through the night, faster than anything human, leaving trails of embers spiraling in its wake.

Nate's eyes widened, realization dawning. "It's Firestar," he muttered, his voice barely above a whisper. "He's giving us a chance. Let's move!"

Above them, Firestar soared like a burning comet, his entire body wreathed in flames, casting an eerie glow over the battlefield. Every soldier's aim snapped to him. Desperate, they fired wildly, tracer rounds tearing through the night, but he was too fast, too high.

Lariks' expression shifted from arrogant confidence to sheer panic. His lips parted, and for the first time since the battle began, his voice cracked.

"Men—MOVE BACK!" He shouted with desperation, his fear undermining his usually commanding tone.

Firestar hovered above them, the fire eating at his body, glowing veins pulsing beneath his skin. His eyes, hollow and burning, swept across the battlefield like an executioner picking names from a list. Then he whispered—the words hitting like a death sentence. "You all made this hell. Now, burn in it."

His entire body ignited, flames curling over his skin like living tendrils. The glow intensified as his form cracked apart, his very being fracturing into raw energy. His body itself became a weapon. Then he let go.

The sky exploded.

A storm of destruction rained down upon the battlefield.

Fireworks shot from every inch of his body, streaking toward the ground like a meteor shower of death. Hundreds of blazing projectiles tore through the ranks of soldiers, their vibrant trails turning the night into a hellish kaleidoscope of color.

The first impact struck the leftmost tank, obliterating it in a fiery shockwave that sent its charred remains flying into nearby infantry. The second missile ripped through a squad of soldiers, their bodies engulfed in a swirling inferno before they even had time to scream.

The battlefield descended into pure chaos.

Lariks barely managed to stumble backward, shielding his face from the heat as his soldiers screamed, scattering in all directions. Explosions tore through the lines, reducing the once-disciplined army to chaos and breaking their formations in a blinding blaze that consumed tanks, men, and weapons.

"NOW!" Nate roared.

The group sprang into action.

They erupted from behind the rubble, racing through the storm of fire and death. Explosions erupted around them, sending waves of heat and shrapnel slicing through the battlefield.

One of the tanks' cannons swung toward them, its massive barrel locking onto their position. The operator inside, frantic and desperate, lined up the shot.

But Nate was already moving.

His blood surged, his veins burning with adrenaline. His vision narrowed as his muscles coiled like steel cables. In a single, explosive movement, he launched himself toward the tank, his body moving faster than his pain.

His heel smashed into the cannon, bending the thick metal like wet paper. The operator's eyes widened in sheer horror, his finger jerking against the trigger in blind panic.

The shot fired—straight into the crushed barrel.

The resulting explosion tore through the tank from the inside out, its remains bursting apart in a firestorm of molten steel.

Shrapnel tore through nearby soldiers, their armor useless against the heatwave that followed. More fireworks streaked overhead, their vibrant, deadly light reflecting in Nate's bloodstained eyes.

Reptile roared as he tore into another tank, his massive claws ripping through its reinforced armor like it was nothing. His scaled fists crushed the exposed internals of the vehicle, ripping metal apart in a frenzy of destruction. Soldiers scrambled away, some raising their weapons in desperation, but Reptile was already moving.

Grabbing the remains of the tank with monstrous strength, he hoisted it off the ground, swinging the wreckage like a wrecking ball. The crushed metal slammed into a cluster of soldiers, flattening bodies, shattering bones, and turning the battlefield into a blood-slicked graveyard. Without hesitation, he leaped into the fray, his monstrous form barreling through enemy lines, his claws slicing through armor, weapons, and flesh alike. Soldiers screamed as he ripped them apart, one after another, unstoppable in his rampage.

On the right flank, Echo took in a deep breath, planting his feet firmly as the chaos swirled around him. His chest expanded, his lungs filling with raw power, and then he unleashed everything he had.

The sound wave erupted from his throat like an explosion, a shockwave of pure force so powerful that the very air seemed to bend around it. The sonic blast ripped through the enemy ranks, throwing soldiers into the air like rag dolls. Helmets shattered, armor cracked, and eardrums burst, blood spraying from the ears and noses of every soldier caught in the blast.

Some tried to flee, but Echo's scream continued, growing louder, pressing down on them with relentless pressure. Vehicles trembled, glass shattered, and some of the weaker men collapsed outright, their brains unable to withstand the force.

Meanwhile, Lane moved through the battlefield like a specter. Unlike the others, he didn't charge. He didn't need to.

Every soldier who looked at him sealed their own fate.

He left his stolen helmet off, ensuring that any man who dared meet his gaze was consumed by horror. Those unfortunate enough to lock eyes with him froze in place, their weapons falling from their hands as their worst nightmares shattered their minds.

Some screamed, others begged unseen horrors for mercy, their bodies convulsing as they collapsed to their knees, sobbing uncontrollably.

Lane moved without hesitation, without remorse. A blade slid across a throat. A rifle shot found a skull. His movements were silent, efficient, and merciless. Dozens fell before him, helpless prisoners of their own terror.

Across the battlefield, Lariks stumbled back, eyes darting wildly as the forces he had so confidently commanded were being wiped out before his very eyes. He breathed heavily, his once-pristine uniform now stained with dust, sweat, and the blood of his own men.

With trembling hands, he raised his custom revolver and aimed it at Reptile, his voice shaking with rage.

"What are you doing helping scum like this, Reptile?" he spat, squeezing the trigger.

The gunshot cracked through the night, a bullet slamming into Reptile's back. The mutant staggered forward slightly, a deep, ragged growl rumbling in his chest.

Then he turned slowly, eyes locking onto Lariks. The bullet wound barely seemed to phase him. If anything, it only pissed him off. His tail whipped through the air, his clawed fists curling, his muscles tensing.

"Killing scum like you," he growled.

Before Lariks could react, Reptile lunged.

The warden barely had time to lift his gun before Reptile's massive fist crashed into his chest, caving in his ribcage with a sickening crunch. Lariks' eyes bulged, his mouth opening and closing like a fish gasping for air, blood bubbling up from his lips.

Then, with a final, bone-shattering blow, Reptile's claws sliced clean through Lariks' neck.

The warden's head was torn from his shoulders, his lifeless body collapsing into the dirt.

But the battle wasn't over yet.

Nate and Iron stood back-to-back, their movements a brutal, seamless dance of destruction.

Nate darted between enemies, dodging bullets by inches, moving so fast that gunmen barely had time to adjust before he was on top of them. He grabbed a soldier by the wrist, twisting it until bones snapped, then turned and slammed his knee into another's face, crushing their skull. Each hit fueled by his immense rage over his fallen friend.

When the gunfire became too overwhelming, he grabbed fallen soldiers as makeshift shields, buying himself precious seconds before cutting down the next wave. Bullets ripped through his stolen cover, grazing his arms and legs, but he didn't stop.

Escape was so close. He couldn't stop now.

Beside him, Iron moved with brutal precision. His body shimmered, his metallic armor shifting and reforming to block incoming bullets. But even he wasn't untouchable. A few rounds tore through weak points in his armor, drawing deep cuts along his ribs and shoulders.

Undeterred, he charged forward, his fists like wrecking balls. Helmets caved under the sheer force of his blows, skulls shattering beneath his relentless onslaught.

Then, from above, a sniper's bullet sliced past Nate's cheek, cutting a thin, stinging line of blood.

He barely registered the pain as he shouted, "Reptile, the nests!"

Reptile snarled and leaped, his powerful legs launching him toward the towering walls. He scaled the stone like a lizard, his claws digging deep, moving with terrifying speed.

The snipers barely had time to register his presence before he ripped them from their perches, hurling them into adjacent nests.

Bodies crashed against the stone, spines snapping, limbs twisting unnaturally. The watchtowers became graveyards in seconds.

Despite everything, the enemy's numbers didn't seem to dwindle. More soldiers poured in from the prison gates, the endless tide of reinforcements turning the battle into an uphill war.

Nate panted, his arms trembling from exhaustion, his body screaming in protest. They couldn't keep this up. Then, the fireworks stopped.

Nate barely had time to glance up before he saw Firestar plummeting toward the battlefield.

His body burned brighter than the sun, his form warping under the sheer heat of his own power.

A massive firework surrounded him, crackling with an energy so intense that the entire battlefield seemed to glow under its radiance.

The soldiers hesitated, watching in horror. With a final, defiant scream, Firestar launched himself at the wall. The impact shattered the reinforced concrete. The ground trembled as massive chunks of the wall collapsed, crushing entire sections of the army. A deafening detonation of fire and raw energy. The explosion ripped through the air. When the smoke cleared, a massive hole stood where the wall had been.

The path to freedom was open. Nate's heart pounded in his chest, the roaring in his ears drowning out the chaos. "GO THROUGH IT!" he shouted, his voice cutting through the battlefield.

The group ran as one.

Gunfire whizzed past them, bullets grazing their skin as they navigated the rubble. The night screamed in bullets, in dying men, in the echo of the world they were leaving behind. They didn't look back.

Reptile grabbed Echo by the collar, dragging him along, even as he fought against the weight of grief and exhaustion. Iron shielded the weak, blocking rounds with his shifting armor, his movements slowing, but never stopping.

Lane didn't hesitate. Didn't falter. He executed every man who aimed a gun at them, every enemy that stood in their way.

As they passed through the breach, the frosty night air hit them, a chilling contrast to the fire and blood behind them.

Then, beyond the ruins of the battlefield, the ocean stretched before them. But they didn't stop. They couldn't.

CHAPTER 31: SEMI-FREE

The group pushed forward, their bodies aching, battered, and drained, but they had no choice except to keep moving. They gasped for each breath, every muscle screamed in pain, but adrenaline pushed them toward the dark horizon where freedom waited. Echo and Lane lingered at the back, covering their retreat with relentless firepower. Echo let out a burst of sound so powerful that it sent sand and debris flying, forcing any lingering shooters to scramble for cover, while Lane, calm and efficient, lined up his shots and dropped anyone who dared come too close.

The roar of the ocean grew louder as the water came into view. The waves churned under the moonlight, and just off the shore, a small vessel maneuvered toward them. Its lights flickered in the dark, a beacon in the chaos.

"That must be them. Let's go, guys!" Nate shouted, pushing himself forward.

The boat cut through the waves, closing the gap between them with urgency. As it approached, Nate recognized the figures aboard, and despite everything—the exhaustion, the injuries, the sheer madness of the last few hours—a grin broke across his face. He barely had time to process it, but relief and gratitude surged through him in a wave so strong it nearly knocked him off his feet. The Rogues had come for them.

One by one, they scrambled up onto the deck, hands grabbing onto whatever they could to pull themselves aboard. Some collapsed immediately, their bodies giving in now that survival was no longer in question.

Morgan and Ava were there in an instant, grabbing Nate, gripping him so tightly he thought they might never let go.

Morgan's tears soaked into his torn shirt as she clung to him. "You stupid bastard," she sobbed between ragged breaths, smacking his shoulder. "Do you have any idea how much I wanted to kill you myself?!"

Nate let out a weak chuckle. "Sorry to disappoint."

Ava's hug came just as fiercely. "Never do that again, you hear me?" She pulled back, scanning him, making sure he was real. "You always gotta make shit difficult, don't you?"

Nate muttered, managing a small smirk. "You know me."

Michael stood nearby, arms crossed, his usual hardened stare cracking just slightly. "You're just full of surprises, huh, lil bro?" His voice held steady, but his eyes shone with something that almost resembled pride.

Nate's smirk faded, his exhaustion catching up to him. "We need to move. Now."

"Already on it!" Nat shouted, throwing herself toward the controls. "Ryan, HIT IT!"

The engine roared to life; the boat lurching forward as it tore through the waves. For a split second, Nate allowed himself to breathe. Then the night exploded with blinding spotlights.

Helicopter rotors sliced through the air, the deep hum of warships deploying filled the distance. The sirens from the prison howled like a dying beast, sending out one last cry for blood. Nate's stomach dropped.

Blood Curdle   277

They weren't free yet.

Before anyone could react, Reptile stood and moved toward the edge of the boat. Without a word, without hesitation, he leaped overboard.

Echo spun around, fury flashing across his face. "That big bitch is just leaving us now? After all that?! You gotta be kidding me!"

"Hold up, Ech!" Nate snapped, keeping his eyes on the water.

A heartbeat later, the entire boat lurched forward with monstrous force. Everyone staggered, gripping onto whatever they could as the vessel practically skipped across the water. The engine screamed, the hull creaked, but they surged ahead faster than ever.

Nate gritted his teeth as realization dawned. "He's pushing us."

Beneath the waves, Reptile's massive form moved with terrifying power, propelling the boat forward with inhuman strength. It wasn't just speed—it was desperation, determination, the final push they needed to outrun the fleet hunting them down.

Gunfire erupted. Bullets ripped through the air, tearing past the boat, splintering wood. The sound of the helicopters grew deafening, their machine guns spitting fire into the water.

"KEEP YOUR HEADS DOWN!" Nat shouted, her hands gripping the wheel like a vise as she zigzagged through the waves.

Lane dropped to one knee, rifle steady. His eyes narrowed as he exhaled slowly, adjusting for the distance, for the rocking boat, for the speed of the rotors. He squeezed the trigger and the bullet slid almost seamlessly through the barrel and the air towards the rotors.

The tail of a helicopter burst apart, the aircraft twisting violently before spiraling into the ocean. A massive plume of fire and smoke erupted where it hit, sending shockwaves through the water.

Echo pressed his hands against the deck, his chest rising with deep, controlled breaths. Then, he unleashed a scream so raw, so devastating, the very air trembled. The force tore through the night, slamming into another helicopter with the force of a missile.

The rotors sputtered, the aircraft buckled, and in an instant, it lost control, crashing into the ocean.

The pursuing warships didn't let up. Their spotlights cut through the darkness, locking onto the escaping vessel.

Nate's fists clenched. If they didn't do something now, the next few minutes could turn into their grave. As if in response to his thoughts, the ocean itself seemed to shift beneath them.

The boat rocked as Reptile pulled himself up to the side, his scaled body dripping wet, his chest heaving with exhaustion. His slitted eyes locked onto the largest warship, and without a word, he dove back in.

Seconds later, the ship lurched violently to the side. The warship, massive even against the waves, trembled under his assault.

A deep, guttural groan of twisting metal filled the air as Reptile tore into the hull, ripping at it from below. Water rushed in, the ship tilting sharply, its spotlight cutting a jagged beam across the waves as it struggled to stay afloat. They were actually gaining distance.

Finally, the island's faint glow faded into the night. The gunfire grew distant. The horizon swallowed the searchlights. They had made it.

A heavy, almost surreal silence settled over the boat as they drifted into the open sea. The tension hadn't left completely, but the reality was beginning to sink in. They were no longer prisoners. They were free.

For the first time, Nate felt the weight of Granger Heights started to lift from his shoulders. The group gathered on the deck, passing around a flask of water, each sip feeling like a sacred moment.

Nat leaned back, staring at the stars. "You know," she said with a small chuckle, "I didn't think we'd make it."

Iron wiped the blood off his knuckles with the back of his arm. "Barely."

Echo, still catching his breath, lifted the flask. "To Manny. He'd want us to laugh, not cry."

The words hit hard.

Nate took the flask gripping it tightly before tipping it slightly. "To Manny."

The others followed, each murmuring the name of their fallen friend, their hands gripping the flask like a last tribute. No one said more. They didn't need to.

The boat rocked gently, the sound of the waves the only thing filling the quiet.

Nate leaned against the railing, staring out at the horizon. The ocean stretched endlessly before them, its calm surface a stark contrast to the chaos they had left behind.

Morgan stepped beside him, her voice soft. "You did it."

Nate shook his head, his throat tight. "Manny's gone and we lost too many."

Morgan's grip on his arm tightened. "You gave us a chance. That's more than any of us had before."

His eyes remained fixed on the horizon. The battle was over, but the war wasn't.

"It's not over," Nate muttered. "They'll come for us. For all of us."

Morgan nodded. "Then we'll be ready."

Toward the front, Iron was shirtless and slumped against a crate while Ryan patched up the bullet wound in his shoulder. Echo gritted his teeth as Natalie tied off a makeshift bandage around his leg. Neither complained—they just breathed through it, as if pain was routine by now.

The group slowly gathered near the back of the boat, bruised and battered, but finally together. Michael passed around a thermal blanket someone had scavenged, and Ava leaned against the side railing, eyes closed. For a few minutes, no one spoke. The hum of the ocean and the gentle lapping of the waves gave them something they hadn't felt in a long time—peace.

Nate sat down beside the others, shoulder to shoulder with Morgan. Even Lane, off to the side cleaning his rifle, seemed less like a threat and more like a worn-out soldier. Nat adjusted the course and leaned back against the wheel, her eyes flicking from star to star in the open sky.

Nate stayed silent, staring at the horizon, the weight of everything pressing down on him relieving for a moment. The world was quiet. Too quiet.

Before he could recoup, Nat's voice cut through the stillness.

"Nate... what happened to Xavier?"

His entire body became rigid.

His mind, exhausted yet still haunted, reeled as a flood of memories slammed into him at once.

Nate didn't answer right away. His eyes drifted toward the water—dark, endless, and unknowable. He closed his eyes. For a moment, everything was quiet again. Then he opened them. The weight was back.

Meanwhile inside State 1, President Noland sits in his office, the sterile white walls and the immaculate furnishings do little to mask the chaos behind closed doors. A dozen advisors scrambled between desks, their hushed voices filled with panic as they relayed information through secured lines. Noland stood at the center of it all, his jaw tight, fingers pressed into the edge of his desk as he listened to the latest report. The breakout was already spreading through the media, whispers of rebellion slipping through the cracks before they could even attempt to control the narrative.

His patience snapped. "Get Apollo on the phone immediately," he barked, his voice slicing through the frantic energy in the room. The nearest aide nodded quickly, dialing before handing him the receiver. The phone rang several times before a smooth, confident voice answered.

"Yes, President Noland?" Apollo's tone was calm, but there was an unmistakable hunger beneath it, like a predator who had just scented its prey.

Garratt Oubre

Noland didn't waste time. "We have a situation. Several highly dangerous criminal mutants, including The Reptile, have broken out of Granger Heights." His words were clipped, controlled, but there was an undeniable edge of frustration.

There was a pause on the other end, then a low chuckle. "I'm on it, Mr. President."

The call cut off abruptly. Noland exhaled sharply, tossing the phone onto his desk as he turned to his staff. "Lock down every border. I want satellite surveillance over the entire coast and an emergency broadcast prepared within the hour."

"Yessir." The staff all said in unison.

President Noland's hand clenched into a fist as he gave his last order "And get me a meeting with Grayson as soon as possible."

Meanwhile, Apollo stood in the Pinnacles' high-tech headquarters in State 2, the dim light of multiple holo-screens illuminating his chiseled features. His fingers tightened around the phone until it cracked, the pieces scattering to the floor as a grin tugged at his lips. His piercing golden eyes glowed faintly as he reached for the emergency signal, his thumb hovering over the activation pad.

The Pinnacles had been itching for real action. Granger Heights had been their playground, a constant supply of entertainment as they watched mutants fight for their lives. But now? Now the game had changed.

With a flick of his wrist, he activated the emergency beacon, a sharp, high-pitched frequency blaring through the base's corridors. The Pinnacles would answer the call, as they always did.

Apollo cracked his knuckles. "This'll be fun."

Deep in State 5, in a mobile base disguised within an abandoned building, Yvi leaned against a console, arms crossed over her chest. The dim glow from multiple monitors cast sharp shadows across her sharp features, her short black hair barely brushing against her pale skin. Every screen displayed different feeds—news reports, satellite footage, and the last recorded moments of the Gauntlet.

She turned toward Alex, who stood motionless, his cybernetic body tense as he stared at the flickering images. His body was an unsettling blend of flesh and machinery, thick plates of armor fused into his frame like a permanent exoskeleton. A reinforced mask hid his face, but she still felt his unease.

"Alex," Yvi said, her voice softer than usual. "Are you okay? You've been off since you watched the Gauntlet last night."

There was a long pause before he finally responded, his voice distorted by the synthetic enhancements in his throat. "I just have a bad feeling about all this."

Yvi frowned, her gaze shifting to the images on the screen. Nate's face was frozen mid-fight, his body battered but still standing. Firestar's final explosion flickered on another feed, the aftermath too chaotic to process all at once.

She sighed. "It's a mess. But if you think something worse is coming, we should be ready."

Alex didn't respond, but his fingers flexed slightly, the servos in his mechanical limbs whirring as if preparing for war.

Far to the north, under the cover of darkness and ice, Xavier moved with purpose through the desolate outskirts of Ledge Town. The air was thick with smoke from distant factory chimneys, the glow of industry casting eerie shadows across the crumbling buildings that lined the streets.

Obsidian Point loomed in the distance, its towering walls stretching into the night sky. Unlike Granger Heights, which thrived on its sickening broadcasts and high-profile spectacles, Obsidian Point was a ghost. No cameras, no entertainment—just the brutal, unrelenting punishment of those deemed too dangerous to be seen by the public.

Xavier's footfalls were silent as he approached, his body shifting subtly as layers of dense bone armor grew along his arms and shoulders. His fangs, sharper than before, peeked out from his lips as his jaw clenched. His expression was unreadable, but the gleam in his eyes spoke of something dark—something that had been brewing for a long time.

He wasn't here to be caged. He was here to crack the walls of Obsidian Point open. And he wasn't planning to leave alone.

Special thanks to all beta readers.

Jayde Brignac

Jeremy Brignac

Angela Milem

Dustin Milem

Kenneth Oubre

Brianna Oubre

Andre Chapoy

Jason Quinteros

James McGowan

Camilla Huffman

Written and edited by. Garratt Oubre

Cover art by. John Bhenzon

Support Blood Curdle's Development On
Patreon: https://www.patreon.com/Bloodcurdle

Art by. Garratt Oubre
Blood Curdle Will Return